Nerdplay

Annabel Chase

Red Palm Press LLC

Chapter One

Cricket

To the uninitiated, my office looks like it's been ransacked by a classroom of unruly kindergartners stuck indoors on a rainy day. Anyone who's been around me long enough, however, knows this is all part of my organizational process.

Spread papers around floor.

Group them by categories only I would understand.

Find a place to store them until the papers turn yellow with age.

I'm terrified of throwing anything away in case some governmental entity or business decides to harass me for proof of something or other and I can't provide it. Some people have nightmares about monsters or a violent death. The majority of my nightmares involve bureaucracy. Another one involves a talking Elmo doll and a blowtorch, but I keep that one close to the vest.

A voice interrupts my thoughts. "Funny. This is exactly how I left you last year."

I spin around on my backside to greet my visitor. "You made it."

Gloria Landry is the tallest short person I've ever met. If police were taking witness statements about her, people would describe the stout five-foot-two woman as an Amazon on cocaine.

"Sorry I'm late. My mother—"

I wave her off. "You don't need to explain. You're here now." I hop to my feet and give her a warm hug. "I've missed you."

"Missed you too, Cricket."

Gloria is fifty-two, single, and always arrives at camp a couple days before I open for the season. She cleans in exchange for free room and board; otherwise, she couldn't afford to come. The rest of the year, Gloria cares for her elderly mother, a task that is physically, emotionally, and financially draining for her. She lives for these two weeks at camp, a fact that makes me simultaneously happy and sad.

"Seriously, though. Still with the papers?" Gloria shakes her head in dismay. "You know you can scan them into your computer and toss the copies, right?"

"Where's the fun in that? Then I can't play The Floor Is Lava with all my essential paperwork."

"I wouldn't call any of that essential."

I swipe a sheet of paper off the floor. "Are you telling me that the property tax bill in my grandfather's name from 1988 isn't a critical document? Sheesh. And you call yourself a friend."

"When you hold on to things that aren't important, it becomes harder to identify the things that are."

I suck in a breath. "Why, Gloria Landry. You've missed your true calling as a fortune cookie writer."

"I've missed all my callings." She shrugs. "But at least I get to be here for the next two weeks and forget my real life."

I hug her again. "This is your real life, too. Where's Buffy?"

"Hold me a little tighter and you'll figure it out."

I let go and look down at her front pocket. "Snoozing away?"

"The car ride knocked her out. She travels like an infant."

Buffy is Gloria's 70-gram emotional support sugar glider. The animal is her constant companion, except when said companion panics, flies away, and needs to be tracked down by yours truly. It happens at least once every summer. Sometimes twice. It seems Buffy could do with her own emotional support animal.

"Are the cabins unlocked? I can get started." Gloria is a whirling dervish with a mop. The cabins are spotless in the same amount of time it would take me to fill a bucket with water. I'm not exactly a sloth, but Gloria treats each cleaning opportunity as an outlet for the feelings she represses fifty weeks of the year.

"I haven't had lunch yet. Are you hungry? We can eat together first." I know Gloria, and there's no way she stopped to eat on the drive here from Harrisburg. Anything that would delay her arrival is a hard pass.

"Is the kitchen stocked?"

I crack a smile. "Delivery came this morning." I loop my arm through hers. "Chocolate chip brownie from Sweetie's?"

"Not this year. My doctor suggested I cut back on saturated fats. Gotta get the bad cholesterol under control." She pats her soft middle. "This is what happens when you pass fifty. You'll see." She looks me up and down. "What am I saying? Even in the glory days of my youth, I wasn't built like you."

Gloria and I scrounge around the compact cafeteria kitchen and take our findings to a picnic table by the lake, where we catch up with our mouths full and marvel at our pristine surroundings. Lake Willa is the centerpiece of the property. Pops named it after his devoted wife, my sweet grandmother. Theirs was the kind of marriage that people don't write stories about because there's no conflict—loving, long, and lasting. The odds of getting as lucky as them... Well, if I had those kinds of odds, I'd drive straight to Atlantic City.

"How many campers this year?" Gloria asks.

"Similar to last year. Thirty."

I glimpse my house through the trees. It's log-cabin style, built by my grandparents during the first year of their marriage and where they lived until their respective deaths. Every moment of happiness I experienced in my childhood happened either in that house or right here at camp.

Gloria cuts through the calm with a question that causes nausea to ripple through me. "I hate to ask, but inquiring minds need to know. Is the Prick coming this year?"

There's only one name we skirt in favor of pronouns or disparaging nicknames. "Oddly enough, he registered again, but I highly doubt we'll see him."

"Two years in a row. So strange. Why spend the money to register if you have no intention of showing up?"

"No clue." I have zero interest in talking about him, not now and not ever. I want to enjoy camp like I used to before that lying, cowardly troglodyte tarnished my favorite place on Earth.

Gloria pokes around her salad bowl like she's hunting and gathering the actual food. "Maybe his girlfriend kicked him to the curb."

"Even if she did, it wouldn't matter. Can we please change the subject?" I hope I don't sound too snippy. Gloria was my rock during that awful experience; she doesn't deserve to draw my ire. That honor belongs to one person only.

"I'm sorry. I shouldn't have brought him up."

I turn my face toward the sun and close my eyes. "It'll be so great to see everyone again."

"I know. This place feels more like home than my actual home." There's a brief pause and then, "How are finances?"

Once again, her question drags me back to reality, kicking and screaming. "The camp will survive the year." Barely.

"Any ideas on how to turn that around?"

"Not yet. Word seems to have gotten out because I've been beating back a property developer with a stick. He's like a shark that smells blood in the water."

Camp Abernathy has been on this land since my grandfather first acquired it in 1967. The property then passed to my father, whose early demise meant it passed to me sooner than expected. I've been the sole owner and operator for the past five years, as well as the creator of Comic-Camp, the two-week adults-only camp that begins in T-minus two days. You'd think I'd be ready to welcome the campers, but I'm not that organized. Every year I'm reminded how much work is involved for very little financial reward. If only I could survive on good vibes, I'd be set for life.

Gloria reaches across the table to grip my arm. "You wouldn't actually sell, would you?"

"You know me better than that." I wrench myself free and polish off my last sandwich square, washing it down with a refillable bottle of water. "This camp is about building community, not my bank account."

"And that's why we love you, but you need to stay afloat. I'm sure you have bills to pay."

She has no idea. Every year the bills get higher and my bank balance gets lower. Very soon my inheritance will be gone. I'll cross the bridge over those troubled waters when I get to it.

Gloria rises to her feet. "I'll get started on the cleaning now."

"I can help you after I tidy up the paperwork."

Gloria snorts. "In other words, I'm on my own."

"If I could afford to hire someone, I would."

"And if I could afford to pay you for my spot, I would. We both do what we can. I wish you'd ask some of the other regulars for help. They'd do it in a heartbeat."

"Adam already works as a counselor for the kids' camp. I can't ask for more favors."

"It isn't a favor when he gets his registration covered in return. Besides, they love this place as much as you. We all do. If they thought for one second that the camp was in jeopardy, they'd volunteer as tributes."

I squirm uncomfortably on the bench. "I can manage on my own."

"Just because you can doesn't mean you should." She pats my shoulder as she passes by. "I'll handle the cleaning. You handle the rest, as usual, Boss Lady."

"Thanks, Gloria. You're the best."

I remain seated at the picnic table for a few more minutes, soaking up the midday sun. The lake glistens like starlight and a comfortable shudder ripples through my body. This camp is my happy place, the physical manifestation of my soul, and there's nothing on earth a property developer could do to convince me to sell.

CHARLIE

I watch as Matt Lyman shoots the foam ball from behind his desk. The ball swishes through the basket attached to the back of his office door. He slides open the desk drawer and produces another ball.

"Your turn," he says.

"No thanks."

His grin is designed to taunt. "Afraid of a little competition?"

"More afraid of Joel opening the door and me hitting him smack in the face."

"Dude, you need to lighten up." He squeezes the green ball. "It's foam." He shoots again and scores.

I toss a file on his desk. "I didn't come to play. Joel asked me to bring you this."

"Is that the Dungiven file? Sweet." He flips open the file. "You don't mind, do you, buddy? You've got LandStar. Now I've got Dungiven. Seems fair."

"I don't mind."

We both know that's a lie. I mind very much. After all, I'm the one who cultivated the relationship with Dungiven's CEO, and now my boss has handed that client on a silver platter to my only real competition for partnership. Melvin, O'Reilly, and Gaines is a medium-sized law firm. The upside is my ability to move up the ranks faster than at a large firm. The downside is that the department can only choose one of us to make partner this year. You'd think I would relish the Gladiator-style experience of pitting associates against each other and turning colleagues into competitors. After all, it's the capitalist way. But something about it doesn't sit right with me. Maybe because, for the first time in my life, I might actually lose.

Matt seems to read my mind. "What's the matter, buddy? Worried you won't clinch the contract for Land-Star?" He practically salivates at the prospect. Matt's out for the same amount of blood, whether it's a business deal or a 'friendly' game of hoops.

"I'll have the contract wrapped up in a pretty bow soon enough. I'm driving out there tomorrow."

"Hey, at least you get to bill travel time. That's at least four hours without any real work." Matt grins like his entire goal in life is receiving money for the least amount of effort. If you didn't know any better, you'd think he was lazy, but I know it's all part of his act. Matt Lyman is fiercely competitive. He wants people to believe his achievements are effortless. If he weren't so annoying, I'd find him a fascinating character study.

My assistant and I have crafted lighthearted psychological profiles of most people in our department. Jeannie is much more skilled at this than I am. She can read people faster than it takes me to process their names. I once told her she should've been a lawyer, but she said she can't stand the bullshit that comes with the job. According to her, it's much easier to be the administrative assistant in the shadows whose name half the lawyers only remember when they want something, and even then, they sometimes get it wrong. Bert in litigation calls her Jane, no matter how many times he's been corrected. I'd blame a faulty memory, but I'm fairly certain the guy has never called his wife by his mistress's name, or he'd be divorced by now.

Jeannie waves frantically as I return to my office from Matt's. I swerve to the right to check in.

"Joel came by your office," she says in a hushed tone.

I stifle a groan. Joel Niven is the head of my department and my direct boss. He likes to press people's buttons and watch how they respond. He once ordered octopus in a seafood restaurant because he knew another partner had a moral objection to it. When he refused to change his order, she left the restaurant, leaving him with the new client she'd painstakingly pursued for a year. His take was that commitment to the client should trump everything else, including the plight of any marine life. *How intelligent can they really be if they end up on a plate in Center City?* I believe was his exact quote.

"Joel said he'll pop back later this afternoon."

That buys me a little time. The phone rings and Jeannie effortlessly switches to her professional voice. "Charlie Thorpe's office. Who may I say is calling?" Her expression shifts as she puts the caller on hold. "Your father is on the line. Should I tell him you're in a meeting?"

"How does he sound?"

"Like he has a silver spoon stuck up his ass."

I heave a sigh. This day is already ruined. What's one more challenging personality?

"I'll take it at my desk. Thanks." I give myself a quick pep talk before I enter my office and pick up the phone. "Hi, Dad."

"Charles. Your mother asked me to call. She wants to make sure you save the date on your calendar for our fortieth wedding anniversary. We're hosting a party at the house."

Forty years of wedded ... whatever toxic relationship they called a marriage. Congrats, I guess.

"August first. It's already on the schedule."

"I hope we can announce your new title by then."

Ah. Now I understand the real reason for the phone call. "Why?"

The question is unnecessary. I already know why. They intend to show us off to their guests. Michael and Elizabeth are easy. My siblings give my parents something new to boast about every month. I, on the other hand, have only one card to play. It isn't enough to make partner. The more important part is to become the youngest partner in the firm's hundred-year history. Bragging rights are everything to my parents. They view Keeping Up With the Joneses as necessary to survival as oxygen or water. Their three children serve as their primary weapons in the battle of proving their social superiority.

"We have announcements about your brother and sister. We wouldn't want to leave out our firstborn son."

You pathetic loser, he forgot to add. "If I hear anything before then, I'll be sure to let you know."

"I'm sure you'll come through for us."

"I'll do my best. Talk to you later." I hang up, feeling worse than I did before the call. I could be President of the United States, and my father would still want a list of my recent achievements to send in a press release to the people on their social register.

The LandStar file sits open on my desk. According to the multiple less-than-subtle hints dropped by Joel and a couple other partners, this deal is all that stands between me and partnership. The rumor mill says that Matt is all flash and no substance, and they would much rather promote me, but they need me to prove I can hold my own at the big kids' table, which is why they gave me LandStar. The company's owner, James Riggieri, is a bully and a tyrant, which happen to be personality traits I am intimately familiar with. You give me lemons, I've got your lemonade ready.

The train ride home is more crowded than usual today and reeks of piss and pot. I only drive to work on the days I have a client meeting outside the city. Public transportation and recycling are the extent of my commitment to the climate change crisis; not because I don't care but because I don't have time to think about it.

My house is outside Center City in a town on the Main Line. I was perfectly happy living in an apartment in Old City, but my parents thought it was beneath me (read: beneath *them*) as a thirty-five-year-old lawyer to rent an apartment, so they persuaded me to buy a house in the 'burbs in preparation for the life they envisioned for me. According to their unofficial chart of milestones, I should have a devoted wife and 2.5 kids by now.

My younger brother Michael is married, and his wife Kayla is pregnant with their first. He's also a highly regarded surgeon, which my parents remind me at every opportunity. My sister Elizabeth isn't married, but she's in a serious relationship with another professional golfer. My parents don't mind as much that she isn't married because a husband and children would interfere with her golf tournaments. They could care less about the money; it's all about collecting those shiny trophies.

I see my neighbor across the street clutching a pile of mail, but he ducks inside before I can lift my arm in greeting. Strange that my instinct is to wave when I've barely exchanged more than ten words with anyone on my street. For the most part, they park their cars in their massive garages and enter their houses from there. We all have lawn services and gardeners, so even in the nice weather, there's no reason to linger outside. Those who don't have a home gym have a club membership elsewhere.

People in the city talk about the epidemic of loneliness, but I think it's far worse in the suburbs where you indulge in the misguided belief that you *ought* to be interacting with your neighbors. In the city, there's no such expectation.

I enter the house and immediately check the fridge for leftovers. Then I remember that I attended a client dinner last night. No such luck. I'm mildly disappointed. I don't mind cooking, but I'm tired. My workload has been piling up, which puts my job at eighty percent of my day, with the remaining twenty percent divided between sleeping and eating. Not much of a life, but I know some people have it far worse for far less money, so I can't complain.

I give my set of weights a passing glance. *Not today, Satan.* At this point in my life, exercise is a necessary evil. I wish I enjoyed it, but I'd much rather play a game of 21 with some of the guys and get in a workout that way. Not many opportunities for shooting hoops these days, though. Not many friends either. The ones I had got tired of me canceling plans because of work and eventually stopped texting.

I plug in the camp's address and check the travel time. Ninety minutes without traffic. I mentally add an extra ten minutes for rush hour if I hope to get to the Poconos by midmorning tomorrow.

At 10 p.m., my phone rings on my nightstand and I recognize Riggieri's personal number. I immediately hit the accept button. "Charlie Thorpe speaking."

"Charles, it's James Riggieri. I understand you're driving out to the Poconos tomorrow."

"Yes, sir. I thought a face-to-face meeting would be

better." I learned from a young age that it's much harder to say no to someone when they're standing in front of you.

"She doesn't know you're coming, does she? She'll only lock the door and pretend not to be home."

I can't help but smile at that. Her tactic sounds eerily similar to mine when unwanted company darkens my doorstep.

"I haven't given her a heads up."

"Good. I don't need to remind you how badly I want this deal, Charles."

"I'm aware, sir, and I have every intention of making it happen." For both of us.

"Call me afterward with a full report."

"Yes, sir. I will."

He hangs up. I leave my phone face up and the ringer on in case he calls again, which has been known to happen. I stare at the whirring ceiling fan for another hour and try to visualize my success. It's a practice that's served me well over the years. I picture myself placing a contract with two signatures in Joel's hand. He slaps me on the back, congratulating me.

I'm pretty sure I'm smiling when I fall asleep.

Chapter Two

Cricket

"Cricket, I need your help!"

I pause my pretense of filing and look up at Gloria. "Buffy?"

She nods. "I had the windows open to air out the cabin. She heard a bird squawk, and it scared her."

"On that basis, you'd think she'd stay inside."

"She has more drops in the cute bucket than the smart bucket."

I push away from my desk and stand, happy to have an excuse to go outside and stretch my legs. "I'll take the trees near the parking lot. You take the copse."

Gloria sets a blueberry on my desk. "Incentive." She disappears before I manage to reach the door.

I head outside with the lure, scanning the tree line for a sugar-glider shaped outline. As I reach the parking lot, I notice an unfamiliar car rolling to a stop. An Audi coupe.

The driver's door opens and out steps a tall man, maybe six-four, in a very nice suit. At least I assume it's very nice, based on the price of his car. He's conventionally handsome, if you're into that sort of thing, which I am not. Give me

Kylo Ren's sexy awkwardness over pretty blond boy Luke Skywalker any day of the week. He looks like the professional guy they send to serve divorce papers, yet also good-looking enough to be the stripper version.

Wait. Do people hire strippers to impersonate service processors?

I push my glasses to the bridge of my nose. "Hey, do you see a bat? Not the kind you swing, unless you're abusive, in which case, you should be barred from adopting an animal, or quite frankly, from breathing."

Versatile Handsome Man glances skyward. "Aren't bats nocturnal?"

Smart, hot, and driving a car with all four of its hubcaps? Clearly, he's a jerk. The universe wouldn't bestow too many blessings on one person, unless that person is Pedro Pascal.

"She's nocturnal, normally, but Buffy's not a bat. She's a sugar glider. I assumed you wouldn't know what that is, so I thought it was easier to call her a bat." I look up. "No offense, Buffy, wherever you are! I know the difference!"

His eyebrows pinch together, like he's trying to decide if he should continue to converse with this deranged individual.

"If you're here for camp, you're early, but you should know we're not a business-attire establishment. We're not even business casual. We are full-on casual." I snap the elastic waistband of my terry cloth shorts.

His gaze lowers to my abdomen, and I suddenly feel self-conscious, which is strange because I haven't experienced self-consciousness since the onset of puberty.

In my peripheral vision, I catch a blur of movement as Buffy swoops down to land on the overdressed visitor's shoulder. To his credit, he remains as still as a statue, which tracks because he looks like he's been chiseled from stone; I'm talking the fancy granite you choose for your kitchen countertops when you have an unlimited budget, not that I would know. My countertops are laminate.

"Congratulations, you found Buffy, or more accurately, Buffy found you."

He doesn't seem as pleased by the development as I am, possibly because of the trail of excrement that now streaks his suit jacket. I quickly remove Buffy from his shoulder before he offers to send me his dry-cleaning bill.

He stares at me with a dazed and confused look on his face, as though this is his first time being christened by a gliding possum, which it probably is. I mean, what are the odds?

He finally recovers his voice. "Are you Courtney Abernathy?"

"I am."

"Charles Thorpe, from Melvin, O'Reilly, and Gaines LLP." He hands me a business card.

I glance at the card before tucking it in my back pocket. "How can I help you, Charles Owen Frederick Thorpe the Fourth, Esquire?" What a mouthful. His parents must be Very Self-Important People.

"I'm here on behalf of our client, LandStar."

He has to be kidding me. "You work for James Riggieri?"

"I do."

Buffy seems skittish, so I switch her to the deep nether regions of my shorts pocket. "And your client James Riggieri asked you to pay me a visit?"

"He did."

"Riddle me this, Mr. Esquire. Why would Riggieri send

his lawyer when I've shot down all his previous proposals? It's not like there are documents to sign."

"He decided to try another angle."

"What's the angle?" I point to his shirt. "Does he think that tie might bore me into submission?"

He glances down. "What's wrong with my tie?"

"Nothing. You look like a Brooks Brother."

"That's a perfectly acceptable store."

"Sure, if your favorite color is neutral. Tell your client what I've already told him—I'm not interested in selling." I turn around and start back toward the ring of cabins where my office is located. Today is busy enough without needing to entertain another pointless offer from LandStar.

I'm not entirely surprised to hear the pitter-patter of size 11 Guccis scurrying to catch up with me. Like his client, I get the distinct impression that Charles Peter Parker Henry VIII isn't well acquainted with the word 'no.'

"Here, take a look at the contract and tell me how we can do better," he says, falling in step beside me. He thrusts a document at me, and I push it away.

"Why bother? I don't speak legalese."

He exhales his frustration. "Aren't you at least interested to hear the latest offer?"

"I don't care if it's a trillion dollars. The answer is an unequivocal no." I stop outside my office door. I don't want his presence to contaminate my personal space.

"Look, we both know your camp is bleeding money. Unless you have deeper pockets than your well-loved T-shirt suggests, I highly recommend you consider my client's generous offer."

I look down at my blue T-shirt with 'Nerdy By Nature' written across the chest in a stylish script. He's right—it *is* well loved and there's nothing wrong with that. Not everybody can identify a luxury brand at thirty yards. Not everybody *wants* to either.

"Tell your generous client that this area doesn't need mega mansions or upscale condos for rich weekenders."

"Don't be silly. Rich weekenders go to the nice parts of the Jersey shore. This would be for upper middle-class weekenders and summer homeowners."

I raise my eyebrows. "There are nice parts of the Jersey shore?"

That smart remark results in a smile that owes a heavy debt to a skilled orthodontist. His teeth probably cost more than my truck.

"I take it you're a big fan of deforestation, Mr. Gucci."

"I wouldn't describe myself as a fan, and my name is Charlie Thorpe."

"When you actively support a cause, you're a fan."

"Deforestation can sometimes be a byproduct of real estate development, that's true."

I spread my arms wide. "Look around. This land is mainly forest. I doubt your client intends to squeeze his luxury buildings between the pine trees."

"Be straight with me, Miss Abernathy. Is your resistance due to a legitimate reason or are you just plain stubborn?"

"Can't it be both?" I tap the door with my knuckles. "This camp belonged to my grandparents. It has sentimental value."

"When do the kids arrive?"

"Not for another two-and-a-half weeks."

He flashes a grin. "Perfect. Plenty of time for us to discuss the future of the camp."

"I said the kids arrive in two-and-a-half weeks. The adults arrive tomorrow."

He blinks twice. "Adults? Like the counselors?"

"No, the adult campers. The first two weeks of the season are devoted to the adult version of Comic-Camp, before the kids arrive." I enjoy watching his reaction. It isn't often I get to see one anymore. The locals know me and the camp.

The information works its way from his brain to his lips. "Nerd camp for grown-ups?"

I cluck my tongue. "And here I thought you were a top-shelf lawyer. Shouldn't you have done your research before driving all the way up here? What was the drive from Philly —two hours?"

"Thereabouts." He surveys the background. "What does that entail? Science labs?"

"Not that kind of nerd. We're more of the pop-culture variety. Activities designed for people with common interests. Comic-Camp gives them a sense of belonging that they don't necessarily get in their daily lives. Two weeks of sword fights, zombie battles, tabletop games…" I wave a hand at the campground. "All set in peaceful tranquility."

His gaze shifts to the lake. "Nothing about that sounds peaceful."

"I'm talking about inner peace."

"And your grandparents were the first ones to let their freak flag fly?"

"No. It was a regular summer camp for kids back then. I added the adult portion five years ago, but I grew up here." I look around at the thriving landscape. "I have memories of every tree branch. Every stone."

"I'm sure my client won't object if you stuff a few rocks in your pockets on the way out."

I want to wipe the smug look off his chiseled face. Seriously, did he source those cheekbones straight from an underground quarry in Italy? His stone-cold features suit him.

"It isn't only the setting. It's the experience. The same campers come back season after season. It's a home away from home for many of them. One place they know they'll be among like-minded people."

"Sounds like law school."

I raise a skeptical eyebrow. "Oh? Do they have combat archery in law school?"

"The law used to offer trial by combat. Does that count?" He snort-laughs and it annoys me that the sound does nothing to detract from his good looks. Life is so unfair.

"Unless you're here to register for camp, you're a trespasser. I'm friends with the chief of police and trust me when I say he'll have no problem escorting you from the premises on my say so."

The look on his face says he doesn't doubt it. "Well, you have my contact information. If you change your mind..."

I fold my arms. "I won't."

He seems uncertain what to do next, which I have to admit, I kind of enjoy. "Bye now," I say with a friendly wave. Okay, friendly is a stretch. More like mocking.

"It was a pleasure to meet you, Miss Abernathy."

"You're a terrible liar, which I would think is a job requirement for you. Maybe you ought to consider another line of work."

A shadow passes over the slab of marble. I might've missed it if I wasn't gazing so intently at his face.

Wait. Not gazing. Looking. Because that's what people do during a conversation, unless you're one of my neurodivergent campers who struggles with eye contact.

"Have a good day." Charles turns on his heel and strides

toward the dirt parking lot. I'm surprised his Audi didn't reverse in horror at the lack of blacktop.

"May the Force be with you," I call after him. There's no way a jerk like him would get a *Star Wars* reference.

I spin toward my office and nearly collide with Gloria. "Sorry about that," I say.

"It's okay. Who was that man?"

"A lawyer."

Her eyes widen. "Are you in trouble?"

I plaster on a smile to ease her anxiety. "No, not at all. Nothing to worry about."

"Oh, good. Do you have Buffy?"

I pat the pocket of my shorts. "She's safe and sound."

"I hope she didn't cause any trouble."

I scoop the animal out of my pocket and transfer her to Gloria. "On the contrary, her timing was impeccable. She gave our visitor a little gift."

Gloria glances past me to where the Audi had been parked. "Was that the man who wants to buy the camp?"

I sigh. Can't get anything past Gloria. "He works for the man who's trying unsuccessfully to buy the land. LandStar doesn't care about the camp."

Gloria smiles her appreciation. "I'm glad to hear you say that. I can't live without this place. It's my oasis."

I give her shoulder a gentle squeeze. "I know. It's mine, too."

In truth, the money would be helpful. My personal bank balance is so low that instead of a number, my statement yields a voice note from Whoopi Goldberg that says, "You in danger, girl." But there's no way I'm selling this land. Pops would roll over in his grave if he had one. Fine, his cremains would circle his hourglass like a drain. My family left me a legacy, and I fully intend to honor it.

"Most of the cabins are done. I'm going to break for lunch," Gloria says.

"Thanks. I'll eat with you, if you don't mind."

Gloria lights up. "Picnic table?"

"I'll meet you there in five." I duck into my office to grab my water bottle and the peanut butter and jam sandwich I'd stuck in the mini fridge.

I join Gloria at the picnic table that's closest to the lake. She's already tucked into her salad.

"It's a beautiful day," she says.

It is. And this view never ceases to amaze me. It changes by the hour as well as by the weather. Sometimes it's moody and gray. Other times, with beams of sunlight bouncing off the water's surface, it's downright magical. I wouldn't trade it for anything in the world.

"If they're going to send someone else to plead Land-Star's case, at least they sent a good-looking one this time. Maybe if you keep saying no, they'll get progressively hotter."

I laugh. "I think they might've peaked with Mr. Marble." I swill my cold water. "How's your mom?"

Gloria's face crumples. "Her memory is rapidly declining. To be honest, I feel guilty for coming this year. What if she doesn't remember me by the time I get back?"

"Gloria, you deserve to have a life of your own. Your mom would want that for you, too." Like me, Gloria is an only child with only child problems. There are no other family members to pitch in, and she can't afford full-time care. She saves what she can to pay the home aides for the two weeks she spends at camp, which is why I'm willing to barter with her. I won't deprive a woman of her only joy in life.

"I know." Gloria closes her eyes to bask in the sun's warm glow. "I'm so happy to be back, you have no idea. This year was harder."

"I'm sorry. I don't know how you do it."

She opens her eyes and focuses on her salad. "Buffy helps." She tugs a lettuce leaf from her container and holds it over her pocket. The sugar glider's head sticks out to accept the offering.

"Any dates to speak of?" I ask.

Gloria blows a raspberry. "Please. You know I gave up on relationships years ago. It's too challenging with Mom. At least you don't have to worry about that." She winces. "Sorry, that was thoughtless of me."

"It's okay, and you're right. The definite upside to being an orphan is there's no risk of aging parents to care for." My mom died first—cancer when I was sixteen. That's when my father began his downward spiral. I had a good relationship with my mom, but Dad and I didn't tend to see eye-to-eye, which only worsened after my mom's death. He was so different from his father. Sometimes it's hard to believe one was raised by the other. Pops would be mortified to learn about his son's years of gambling and general irresponsibility. It was a miracle the camp managed to stay afloat. If my father hadn't suffered a heart attack and died five years ago, it probably wouldn't have.

Gloria offers an encouraging smile. "This will be the best year yet, you'll see."

I choose to believe her.

CHARLIE

My fingers clench the steering wheel as I drive south along the Blue Route toward Center City. I crank up the volume on Mozart's "Sonata for Two Pianos." My brother, the venerated surgeon, told me that classical music is a good way to reduce stress, so I immediately went home that night and created a playlist on Spotify. I only listen to it when I feel the need—and I definitely feel the need after my encounter with Miss Batshit Crazy.

Riggieri didn't warn me that she was feisty and slightly off her rocker, only that she'd turned down his previous offer. Based on her response, it sounds like our client dangled more than one carrot. I wish I'd had all the information before I drove all the way there. In this traffic, I was in danger of missing a three o'clock meeting.

My phone bleeps and the screen on the dashboard lights up with the one person I'm not in the mood to hear from—Matt Lyman. Still, I answer. I'm a glutton for punishment.

"Hey, buddy," His voice is as slick as the oil he uses in his hair. "How'd your meeting go?"

I opt for the bald-faced lie. "Great. I think I made progress."

"Then I guess we both had good days."

I force a cheerful tone. "Congrats to both of us," I say, tightening my grip on the wheel. If his deal goes through and mine doesn't, I can kiss that partnership goodbye, as well as any future family gatherings. Christmas, it was nice knowing you.

"Well, you know, there are a couple rounds of negotiations to plow through, but I feel confident," Matt says.

Confident isn't the word I'd use. Arrogance is Matt's whole personality. It irks me to no end. My younger brother is a medical wiz, and my younger sister is already a golf pro at the tender age of twenty-three, but neither one of them acts like Matt. He's a legend in his own mind.

"Glad to hear it," I lie. "I'll see you at the office."

"You should get here before Ashley leaves. She's wearing that tight black top with the deep V."

"I'll do my best." I hang up before he can get into detail about his assistant's anatomy. If I were Ashley, I would've filed a complaint with HR long ago. Matt swears up and down she basks in the attention, but I have my doubts. A mere conversation with him makes me want to take a hot shower and scrub myself clean.

The clock inches closer to three, so I call Jeannie to warn her I might be late.

"Then put the pedal to the metal," she says. "Abby and David are showing up for it."

Terrific. Two senior partners in my department. Two senior partners with voting power. Tardiness is not an option.

"Thanks for the intel."

I hit the gas and go. I'm shocked I don't pass any cops. The parking gods have also smiled upon me. I snag a spot on the street right outside the building and hurry inside.

"Afternoon, Charlie," the security guard greets me.

"Hey, Gus. How's it going?"

"Can't complain. You working late again tonight?"

"You know me. It's my home away from home." I press the elevator button and wait.

"You should join a club. Try to get yourself out of the office more."

"I like the office. I'm comfortable here."

"Then maybe you should try being uncomfortable for a change. My grandma used to say that the only true growth is through discomfort."

The elevator doors open. "Sounds like a wise woman."

"She was. Have a good afternoon, Charlie."

"You, too." I hit the button for the fifteenth floor. If I can make it to the conference room without being seen like a true corporate ninja, maybe I can make it to the meeting on time.

The doors open and Joel stands there like Satan greeting me at the gates of Hell. So much for my stealth skills.

"Hey, Charlie. I was wondering if we'd see you today. How'd it go in the Poconos?"

I step out of the elevator. "It was a start."

"A start? Our client isn't going to be satisfied with that." He claps me on the shoulder. "You're our closer, Charlie, or you were. Don't tell me you've lost your golden touch."

"No, sir. I think I might've caught her at a bad time. There was a missing bat ... or something."

"Hey, that sounds promising."

"Sir?"

"Maybe there'll be a rabies outbreak. The camp is forced to shut down. Our client picks up the land even cheaper."

"Promising, right," I say, noncommittal. I don't see how a rabies outbreak is a win for anybody, but I don't argue.

26

"We might be able to exploit that. I've got a meeting out of the office, but we should talk later. Explore the options."

"I'll be here."

Joel aims his famous finger gun at me and makes a clicking sound as he swaps places with me in the elevator. "And that's why we love you, Charlie boy."

Love isn't the word I'd use.

Jeannie is at my desk, holding a stack of files. "Hey, you're back. David asked me to leave these for you." She sets them on the corner of my desk. "How was your meeting?" Her gaze immediately snags on my jacket. "What happened to your suit?"

"I got shit on." I remove the jacket and attempt to hang it on the hook on the back of the door, but Jeannie swipes it from me.

"I'll take care of it."

"You don't have to do that. I'll drop it at the cleaners after work."

"Not with your hours, you won't. No dry cleaner is open twenty-four hours, Charlie." She levels me with a flat, unimpressed stare. While Joel and the other partners laud me for my commitment to the firm, Jeannie thinks I'm wasting my prime on a partner that can't love me back, or something along those lines.

"Thanks. Tell them not to touch it. It's from a sugar glider. I have no idea if those things carry any diseases."

She scrunches her nose as she examines the stain. "I'll be sure to mention it. Can I get you anything to eat?"

"No, thanks. I'll eat after the meeting."

"Door open or closed?"

"Closed, please."

She smiles. "Meeting starts in three minutes."

"I know."

She closes the door, taking the besmirched jacket with her. My phone lights up with a call from LandStar. Shit.

I inhale sharply and pick up the phone. "Hello, Mr. Riggieri."

"Charles. I hope you have good news for me."

"She hasn't agreed to the sale yet, sir, but she will."

"What makes you so sure?"

"Because this deal is my assignment, and I haven't once failed to get the job done."

There's a pause and then, "That's what Joel said, which is why I expected better news."

I want to remind him that I'm a lawyer, not a magician, but I know the joke won't go over well. Instead I say, "Remind me, Mr. Riggieri. How many times have you made an offer on the property so far?"

His harrumph could give Scrooge a run for his coveted money. "How should I know? Every time I think about what a gold mine that moron is sitting on, it sticks in my craw."

The blatant disrespect aside, Courtney Abernathy seemed like the opposite of a moron. "Well, the property has been in her family for generations. It holds sentimental value."

"Like I said—the girl's an idiot, which she's proven about five times over by now."

Five times sounds like harassment to me, but I bite my tongue. I'm already on thin ice with this client and the firm has made it very clear how important LandStar's business is to them. Riggieri has threatened to walk if we can't land this deal for him. We lose LandStar and I lose the partnership.

No pressure.

"I expect another update by Friday," he continues, "and it better involve good news. Monitor everybody. Snap a photo of some kid rinsing off paintbrushes in the camp creek so we can finagle a CERCLA lien against the property. Whatever it takes."

"On it, sir. We'll speak again soon." I hang up before he can blather on. I wish Riggieri were a rare breed, but sadly, he's interchangeable with many of the firm's clients who seem to think the world should bow at their feet. Money brings out the worst in certain kinds of people.

I arrive at the meeting with thirty seconds to spare. As much as I try to focus on the agenda, my mind keeps returning to the Poconos. Specifically, to the unexpected powerhouse named Courtney Abernathy. The camp wasn't at all what I expected. *She* wasn't at all what I expected. It isn't every day I try to negotiate with someone in short-shorts and a Nerdy By Nature T-shirt. The image of her long, toned legs flashes in my mind. There was absolutely nothing nerdy about those.

It takes me another five minutes to immerse myself in the discussion. The fact that it involves a private equity fund doesn't help. The most entertaining aspect involves watching lawyers climb over each other to appear smarter and more important than they actually are. The only requirement from me was to show up, which I did. Another whoosh in the basket. Take that, Matt.

When I return to my office, Joel is seated in my chair with his legs propped up on my desk. He hasn't bothered to move any of the paperwork out from underneath his dirty albeit expensive shoes.

"Hey, Joel."

He smiles but doesn't move. "I spoke to Riggieri. He's foaming at the mouth about this camp. Says if we can't convince her to sign a contract, then he wants us to find another way."

I don't follow. "Another way?"

"Leverage, Thorpe. He wants us to find leverage. Anything we can use to force her hand or take the land outright."

"I ran a title search and checked with—"

Joel holds up a hand. "All the official methods have been exhausted. It's up to you to think outside the box. You can do that, can't you?"

"Of course," I say without hesitation.

"You know Lyman also has his eye on the partnership seat."

"I'm well aware."

"Between you and me, I'd prefer to have you seated next to me at the table. My wife likes your company. Says you're polite and not a raging narcissist."

"That's ... nice to hear." Joel's wife also likes to mention swinging in my presence, but I decide to keep that nugget to myself. I wouldn't get involved with a married woman, and I certainly wouldn't get involved with one who bears an uncanny resemblance to my great-aunt Kathleen.

Joel slots his hands together and slides them behind his head. "Talk to me, Thorpe. How can we toss this trophy at Riggieri's feet?" His gaze had a predatory sheen to it, like a lion dreaming of what he might do to a gazelle.

"Find leverage, like you said."

"What are you thinking? A private investigator?"

My mouth decides to run faster than my brain. "Better than a P.I. Me."

He swings his legs off the desk and straightens. "What do you mean?"

"The next two weeks of camp are for adults. I register as an attendee. Sneak around the campground. Find a smoking gun and shoot."

His smile broadens. "I like the way you think, Thorpe. Dig up some dirt. Maybe a couple skeletons."

"It's a two-week program. That gives me plenty of time to find what we need."

His excitement fades. "She's already met you though. Think she'll let you register?"

"I'll do what I do best." I flash a smile. The one that gets me a table at a fully booked restaurant or a date with a beautiful woman who refuses to give my friends the time of day. "Persuade her." There's no way I can register online. The second Courtney sees my name on the registration form, she'll no doubt reject it. My chances are much better if I'm already standing in front of her with a packed bag.

Joel slaps his hands on the desk and stands. "I'll divide up your current caseload so this can be your sole focus. You've got two weeks. Make this happen and the partnership is yours. I don't care what Lyman brings to the table. LandStar is our top priority."

"I won't let you down."

The moment he leaves, I start to hyperventilate. I pull the knot from my tie and unbutton my collar to get some relief.

What was I thinking? I won't last two weeks in a place like that. I'll simply have to find what I need as quickly as possible and jet. No time for s'mores, or whatever they do when they're trying to recapture the glory of their misspent youth.

Jeannie bolts into my office and shuts the door behind her. "Did I hear you volunteer to attend summer camp for the next two weeks?"

"You heard correctly, which means you were eavesdropping right outside the door."

She doesn't look the least bit apologetic. "Are you sure you can do this?"

I chuckle. "I'm pretty sure I can handle canoeing on a lake, Jeannie."

"I'm not talking about the activities. I'm talking about slithering around the camp like a traitorous snake."

"LandStar is one of our most important clients."

"Yes, yes, and if you get them what they want, you get to be partner. I heard Joel." She rolls her eyes. "It's impossible *not* to hear him. He has the confident voice of a mediocre white man."

"A promotion is good, Jeannie. It's what we want."

"As much as I appreciate that you said 'we,' you know perfectly well they won't promote me with you. You'll share Cindy with Joel, and I'll get some green-eared junior associate who doesn't know how to wipe his nose without being handed a tissue."

She's right, at least about not promoting Jeannie with me. "You know I'll go to bat for you."

She offers an indulgent smile that would seem condescending on anyone else. "You're a good guy, Charlie. Better than this firm deserves. I wish you could see that."

"This is Melvin, O'Reilly, and Gaines. There's no better firm in the city." I nod at the files on my desk. "Can you please make sure these files get to where they need to go? Joel said he'll divvy up the work while I'm gone, but you know how easily distracted he gets."

"I'll take care of it, Charlie. You don't need to worry about a thing while you're gone." Is it my imagination or does she sound almost sad about it?

"Thanks, Jeannie. You're the best."

"That's why they pay me an insufficient amount to compensate me for the amount of bullshit I put up with."

She starts to sort through the files. "Keep me updated. I want to hear all the camp gossip. Doesn't matter that they're strangers. I'm invested."

"I'll do what I can to keep you entertained." I wait until she leaves to let the reality of my situation sink in. A single thought plays on a loop in my head—what have I gotten myself into?

Chapter Three

Cricket

No matter how many times I've gone through it, the first day of camp is always a whirlwind. With my owner and operator hat on, I barely have time to enjoy the reunions with everyone. I spend most of the day in crisis management mode and cleaning up the paperwork in my office that I never got around to organizing. And by 'cleaning up,' I mean stuffed into the bottom drawer in the filing cabinet and promptly forgotten.

As always, Adam was the first to arrive, wearing his customary glossy black helmet, sweeping cape, and chest panel—it's as if the Sith Lord himself decided to take a break from the empire and see all that camp life had to offer. His beloved canine companion was by his side, a Yorkshire terrier named Chewy. The five-pound dog is every bit as anxious as Buffy, which is why Adam insists on bringing him every year. He tried a kennel once and Chewy left with two weeks of nervous diarrhea and an intense fear of ducks. Fortunately, there are no ducks on our lake.

As twilight descends upon the camp, thirty campers gather around the firepit to toast marshmallows and catch up. This is my happy place, seated on a stump beside a glowing fire with my favorite people in the whole world. I wait all year for this moment, and I fully intend to suck the marrow out of it.

We kick off the first evening of camp as we always do, with each person sharing the high and low of their year since the last time we were all together. No one's suffered too horribly, I'm pleased to hear. Although we have a group chat that runs throughout the year, introverts aren't the best about sharing what's really going on in our lives—the feed is mostly memes and TV or movie recommendations—so these two weeks are the best shot we have for real communication.

"What about you, Cricket?" Laura asks. The petite white-haired dog groomer is one of the OGs of Comic-Camp, having attended every year for the past five years.

"No highs or lows to speak of," I reply. I slice my hand through the air. "One long straight line."

Angela's look is disapproving. "You haven't used any of the apps I recommended, have you?"

"I live in the Poconos. How many eligible men do you think there are within range of my house?" Everyone at camp has at least one area of expertise. Sixty-year-old Angela's are older men and Prohibition cocktails.

"You won't learn the answer to that by spending every night at home with fictional men," Angela says.

"Why not? Fictional men are the best. They appear when you summon them and they never, ever disappoint you."

"Well, they disappoint you partway through the story," Stefan corrects me, "but then they more than make up for it by the end."

"See? Stefan gets it," I say. I love rewatching my

favorite fictional heroes because I know what to expect, and therefore I am never upset or distressed. Without fail, Aragorn will always ascend the throne as the King of Gondor and marry Arwen. The Avengers and their allies will always defeat Thanos at the pivotal moment. If the story doesn't have a happy ending, I have no desire to invest. As far as I'm concerned, the real world is one long dark night of the soul, except the bright spot that includes these two weeks.

"Stefan also dresses as a Viking," Angela says, quickly followed by an apologetic look. "No judgment, darling."

"Are you sure?" Gloria asks. "That sounded dangerously close to judgment."

"All I'm saying is that Stefan lives his life as a fictional man," Angela replies. "Obviously he's going to agree with Cricket's take."

Stefan adjusts his horned helmet. "Vikings are historical, not fictional."

I adore that Stefan unabashedly and unapologetically takes up space in a healthy way. He fully owns his Scandinavian corner.

"Your headgear is fictional, bro," Bradley says. "Vikings didn't actually wear them."

Stefan heaves a sigh. "It's a visual shorthand. I don't have the right hair or beard, and I can't carry around swords or spears, so the helmet is the easiest and fastest way to telegraph my identity to others."

"I think you look great," I tell him.

Bradley spears another marshmallow. "Dudes, I don't know how you and Adam don't sweat to death in those helmets." In black jeans, work boots, and a Metallica T-shirt, Bradley doesn't necessarily seem like the kind of man who would support helmet-wearing adults, but he's proven himself to be one of the most open-minded and open-hearted people I've ever met.

Adam produces a small portable fan. "This helps."

"What's the matter?" Laura asks.

I swivel on the stump to look behind me. "Who, me?"

"Yes you. Your body is tenser than a Schnauzer on the grooming table."

I stab a marshmallow with my stick and hold it close to the flames. "It's nothing."

"She had an unwelcome visit from a lawyer," Gloria interjects.

Angela's ears perk up. "What's the problem? Is the camp in trouble?"

"No problem," I insist. "There's a property developer who seems to feel entitled to my land simply because he wants it."

"Typical man."

Angela would know. She's been married to about half a dozen of them.

"Present company excepted, of course," Gloria adds with a sharp look at Angela.

"None of the men here are typical," Angela says. "This is an adult camp for self-proclaimed nerds."

"My granddad's a pretty typical nerd."

We laugh at Olivia, Ben's eleven-year-old granddaughter. Technically the rules don't allow anyone under eighteen to attend Comic-Camp, but I gave Ben special dispensation this year to include her due to unforeseen family circumstances.

"Speaking of typical nerds, I'm happy to see you added robo races to the schedule this year," says Ben, our resident wise man.

"It was a special request." I catch Bradley's eye across

the firepit and smile. The electrician lobbied hard for the addition after inheriting a collection of robot toys from his late uncle. I got the distinct impression he doesn't have anybody near home who would share his enthusiasm, which I completely relate to. I know people who live in the area, but there isn't a single one of them I would call a friend.

A sense of calm washes over me as I gaze around the campfire. There isn't anything I wouldn't do for my campers. They deserve these two weeks of freedom to be themselves. To cosplay without fear of snickers behind their backs. To fight zombies on a battlefield. To play a tabletop game until the sun goes down with no regard for meals or responsibilities.

I'm excited for camp to get started, although I know from experience these two weeks will fly by in a heartbeat. I already dread that final afternoon.

By the time I roll into my cabin for sleep, I'm bone-tired, but it's a good tired. I'm reunited with my people, and all is right with the world.

All except the nagging feeling that the lawyer's visit won't be the last word from LandStar.

CHARLIE

I choose my wardrobe carefully. If I want Miss Nerdy By Nature to believe my intentions are pure, I need to play the part. I unearth a Race to Mordor T-shirt that was gifted to me by my law school roommate, who clearly didn't know me very well despite sharing cramped quarters for three years. I also pack a pair of dress shoes and zip a suit into a fabric travel bag for any urgent meetings that spring up, which happens all too often in the legal world. Someone else's lack of planning becomes my emergency with alarming frequency.

I poke through my drawers and closet for anything else pop-culture related that I could fold into my suitcase.

No, wait. Would a *Star Wars* devotee arrive wheeling a RIMOWA suitcase? I think not. I pull an old duffel bag from the bottom of my closet and repack.

It won't be easy to win over Courtney Abernathy, but I never met a challenge I couldn't overcome and this nerddom will be no exception.

The drive is an hour and fifty minutes today. On the highway, I play Chopin as I bob and weave through long lines of semi-trailers.

"Elizabeth calling," my car says.

I accept my little sister's call. "Where are you today? Palm Beach?"

"Your house."

"What are you doing at my house?"

"I need a place to crash. Do you mind?"

In other words, she doesn't want our parents to know she's in town. "Be my guest. I'm gone for the next two weeks though."

"I'm sorry, what's this? Has the worker bee finally flown away from the hive for a well-deserved vacay?"

"Not exactly. It's a work thing."

Her sigh tickles my speakers. "I should've known."

"Is Bruno with you?" I ask.

"No, that's kind of why I'm here. I'm avoiding him."

"Because?"

"Because he's annoying, and I can't tell him that without it becoming a whole deal."

"I can see your conundrum."

"I don't want Mom and Dad to know we're on the rocks. They were hoping for an engagement to announce at their anniversary party and if it doesn't happen, I'll be their big disappointment."

"You and I both know that role is reserved for yours truly."

"Bullshit, big brother. You're the golden boy. Knowing you, you'll be announcing your sole ownership of the firm by the time August rolls around."

I laugh. "You only say that because you haven't met the partners at my firm."

"Are any of them single?" She pauses. "Never mind. I see how much you work."

I wince. "Ouch."

"No offense," she tacks on. "You know I love you, but I wouldn't dream of setting you up with any of my friends."

"I'm starting to rethink this whole letting-you-stay-in-my-house thing."

"Face it, Charlie. You're married to your job. Who takes two weeks away from the office and spends them at a work event? I hope it's at least somewhere close to a beach."

I glimpse the mountains in the distance. "Not quite. Listen, I'm almost there. I should go so I don't miss my exit. Don't eat all my pickles."

"What?" She feigns a poor connection with a hissing sound. "What's that? You want me to eat all your gourmet pickles? If you insist."

She hangs up before I can object.

I don't relish the idea of Lizzie in my space while I'm

gone, but at least I know my kitchen will be spotless when I get home. My sister is the queen of ordering out.

I take the turn toward Lake Willa and inhale an anxious breath. Courtney Abernathy was feistier than my usual business associates. More attractive too. Then again, most of my work interactions involve balding men over forty, so a beautiful woman in her thirties is a nice change of pace.

Did my stream of consciousness upgrade her from attractive to beautiful? I slam the door shut on that line of thinking. *Not helpful, Charlie.*

Today the parking lot is packed with a variety of vehicles—mostly older sedans, jeeps, and a couple trucks. I slide my Audi between a pickup truck and a VW Beetle, grab my duffel bag from the passenger seat, and follow the painted wooden signs that direct campers to Courtney's office.

There's no line outside her door, which I guess is no surprise given that camp officially started already.

I enjoy her look of surprise when she looks up and registers my presence. "You again."

I flash the smile I reserve for new clients. "Me again, but I'm not here to get you to sign anything."

She looks dubious. "No?"

"You said I could stay if I registered as a camper." I spread my arms wide. "So here I am."

"*You* want to attend camp?"

"Is that a problem?"

"Shouldn't you be playing sportsball somewhere?"

"I gave up sportsball a long time ago." I try to maintain a casual air. "I liked your description of this place—a home away from home. A place to belong. I'd like to have that experience."

As soon as the words leave my mouth, I realize there's a kernel of truth in them. Some people would cite my office as my home away from home. While there's a certain comfort in that space, it's more about safety than acceptance. As long as I'm at my desk in my ergonomic chair with my view of the city, I'm somebody. My job is the equivalent of a statement piece—and when I can add 'youngest partner in the firm's history,' even better.

She seems to read my mind. "You don't have that feeling when you're lording over the plebes in the city from the top floor of your fancy skyscraper?"

"Mine's the fifteenth floor."

She winces. "Oomph. How many more ambulances do you need to catch to reach the penthouse?"

"That's not the kind of law I practice."

She cracks a smile. "I know, but I don't have any ready insults for a corporate lawyer."

"While I'm here, try to think of me as Charlie Thorpe." I gesture to my T-shirt. "See? No boring tie."

"Got it." She seems unimpressed by my *Lord of the Rings*-inspired attire. Hmm. I figured this one would be a winner.

"Does that mean I can stay?" I hear the hopeful tone in my voice, and it takes me by surprise. I think a small part of me wants her to refuse, but if she refuses, then I can kiss partnership goodbye.

Interesting.

"What makes you think I have availability? For all you know, there's a waitlist."

"Is there?" I've seen enough documentation to know it's unlikely.

"No. There is one cabin open. Technically someone registered for it, but he was a no-show last year, and I imagine he will be again this year." She hesitates. "Are you sure you want to do this? There's not a ball to be seen. I assume that's what you're into."

"Until I wasn't."

She shoots me a questioning look. "You look like you're active."

I can't tell whether that's a compliment. "I run, play basketball and golf, lift weights—the usual."

"Those things aren't usual here. There's no gym either, if that matters to you, although I can recommend a sturdy branch for pull-ups if you don't want to skip that part of your routine."

I decide to humor her. "I'd love to see it."

She seems to be waging an internal debate. "Inclusiveness *is* our motto."

"I thought your motto was 'let your geek flag fly?'"

Courtney cocks her head, assessing me. "You seem like you could use a little help with that." She opens the drawer and slaps a key on the desk. "Welcome to camp, Chucky."

"It's Charles, or Charlie. Nobody calls me Chucky." Unless you're a grade-A douche like Matt, who sometimes uses the nickname in an attempt to belittle me while appearing friendly.

"No one ever calls you Chucky, like the murderous doll?"

"Nope." A tiny white lie never hurt anybody.

"Huh."

"Why? Do I remind you of a murderous doll?"

"Must be the hair."

I automatically smooth the top of my head. "Do your frames always match your outfit?"

She pinches the arm of her glasses. "I consider them part of the ensemble. If only you could see the red, white, and blue frames I wear on Flag Day. They're shaped like stars."

I try to picture someone like Courtney working in my office, but the image refuses to come. Most likely she'd be summoned to HR on her first day and told to ditch the funwear. I remember the day Rob Fuentes showed up with an earring and they gave him an ultimatum—lose the earring or lose the job. He quit. I thought it was a foolish decision given the amount of his student loans, but I gave him mad props for his commitment to his principles.

"Do I get a welcome tour?" The more I learn about the camp, the faster I can find my leverage and return to my comfortable life. Her office is the obvious starting point, but she seems like the type to have boxes of paperwork stuffed in the loft of a barn.

"Absolutely. Sorry, I should've offered. It's been a few years since we've had a new camper. Everybody this year is a repeater, except one." She smiles. "And now two."

"Lucky me."

I locate my cabin with the help of an impressive map that looks like it belongs in a fantasy novel. With a pitched roof, ruddy walls, and small, sparing windows, mine seems identical to the other residential cabins.

I toss my belongings on the bed and meet Courtney back at her office for the tour, where she hands me a printed schedule.

"It's on the members-only page of the website, but as I mentioned, the connection is unreliable so it's best to keep this with you. We'll start there." She points to the nearest building, which resembles the other cabins, except for the sign on the door that reads 'Danger Zone.'

Inside is a selection of tables—I spot an assortment of Legos on one, a chess set on the second, and basic science equipment on the third. At present there's only one person occupying the space, a girl who looks far too young to be attending an 18+ retreat.

"Charlie, meet Olivia."

The girl pulls her face away from the microscope. "I'm going to bring back dinosaurs like *Jurassic Park*, and this campground is the perfect place to experiment."

"Because it's isolated?" I ask.

"And plenty of food. Dinosaurs eat *a lot.*"

I shoot a nervous glance at Cricket. "She means the cafeteria, right?"

"Officially, yes," Olivia says, as she shakes her head no.

I strain to listen. "Do I hear music?"

Olivia holds up her phone. "I play the theme song on a continuous loop for inspiration."

"Good luck, Liv. Let us know when we should prepare for the raptors." Courtney eases us out and closes the door.

"Should we be worried about that?" I ask, as we walk to the neighboring building.

"Relax. It's a kid's microscope and a petri dish full of seeds and liquid soap. The only thing she's liable to develop with that is a rash."

"I thought these two weeks are adults only."

"They are, but there are exceptions to every rule." She pauses. "Like someone who turns up with a duffel bag and entitlement issues and asks to register at the last minute."

"Hey, you told me it was okay."

"I know what I said."

Next is the cabin designated for board games. There's already a group gathered around a table, including a white-bearded older man who bears a striking resemblance to every wizard I've ever seen in a movie. Generic Wizard turns over the hourglass.

"Hey, isn't the sand in those things usually white?" I ask.

Courtney casts an idle glance at the hourglass. "Usually."

"Then what happened with this one?"

"That isn't sand."

"It's her grandfather," the wizard says.

"Ben!"

I jump back. Everybody laughs, and I relax. "Oh, I get it. Another prank. I thought we were all done with those."

"No, it isn't a prank," Ben tells me. "Those are her grandfather's ashes. He spread himself a little thin if you ask me, but that was his dying wish. Even wrote it in his will."

I look at Courtney for confirmation, and she nods. "Pops loved his family. Game nights were some of his most precious memories. He didn't want to be left out after he died."

I pick up the hourglass and examine its contents. "And your family was okay with his request? Just because someone makes a request in their will doesn't mean you're legally obligated to honor it."

"I know," Courtney says. "I liked the idea. It was vintage Pops." She plucks the hourglass from my hand and sets it on the table. "And now I get to think of him fondly every time I'm playing a game I enjoy. It's a win-win."

I don't know how I feel about it, but I decide to roll with it. "Playing a game with a dead man is definitely a new experience for me."

"I imagine you'll be having a lot of those experiences the next two weeks, old sport."

We rise from her grandfather's ashes and move on to a cabin crammed with people in costumes seated around a table.

"Dungeons & Dragons," she explains. "Everyone, this is Chucky."

"Charlie," I say, a little loudly given the quiet of the room. And now I sound aggressive. Great.

A few players grunt in response, but they barely look up from their tabletop game.

"What's with the pointy ears?" I ask, gesturing to one of the women.

"They're elf ears," Courtney explains like it's the most natural thing in the world, which it seems to be here.

The elf turns to glare at us.

"They're in character," she whispers. "We should leave them to it." She closes the door behind us. "I refuse to be the reason somebody gets scorched by a dragon horde. I'll never hear the end of it."

"I don't understand. I thought camp was supposed to be toasting marshmallows and learning how to pitch a tent."

"I told you this camp is special."

"And you get enough campers who enjoy this sort of thing?"

"I hit max capacity every year."

"But not this year or I wouldn't be here."

She shrugs. "Like I said, I had a no-show and gave you his cabin."

"Lucky me."

"I bet you say that a lot."

I review the sheet. "What's a fan fiction meetup?"

"There's a group that gets together to co-write a story during the two weeks they're here. If you're interested, you should let them know. They've already chosen this year's concept."

"Which is?"

"Sherlock meets *Supernatural*."

"A spooky mystery, like *Scooby-Doo*?" I'm embarrassed that my frame of reference is a children's cartoon, but it's all I've got.

"*Supernatural* as in the TV show."

"I'm not familiar with it."

"That's okay. There's something here for everyone, even you, Charles M. Schulz the Third. I promise." She counts on her fingers. "Lego club, book club, chess, amigurumi, painting—but only for tabletop figurines."

"What's amigurumi?"

"You should show up and find out. It's on the schedule." Her smile reminds me of my sister Elizabeth's, like she's hiding a mischievous secret that she can't wait for me to discover.

"I'll add it to my calendar." I make a show of tapping my phone screen and typing.

"You might want to write it down with an old-fashioned pen and paper. Phone service here can be as unreliable as the Internet."

"How do you live?" I ask. It comes out more judgmental than I intend, but seriously. I couldn't function without basic infrastructure.

"It's easy when everything I want is right here." She beams at the campground. "Especially these next couple weeks."

We saunter past the residential cabins to the lake's edge. "This is nice."

She breathes in the fresh air. "It sure is. Lake Willa is the jewel in the camp crown."

"Is the water safe to swim in?"

"Absolutely. We have canoes and kayaks too. There was a pontoon boat, but it broke down two years ago."

"Couldn't be fixed?"

Hesitation flickers across her features. "No," she says flatly.

"My file said this is a family business."

"It is. I happen to be the only family member left."

She says it so casually, like I asked for directions to the nearest store.

"I'm sorry," I tell her.

"That's life, right? You gain people, you lose people."

In a twisted way, I envy her. I'm not saying I wish I was the last family member standing; I'm not a monster. There is, however, a certain freedom that comes without their circulation in your orbit. No pigeonhole. No expectations. I'm thirty-five, yet my parents still have a way of making me feel five years old. It seems like I've spent my entire life trying to jam my square shape into their round hole. It's exhausting at times.

Okay, all the time.

"I take it your nuclear family is alive and kicking," she says.

Definitely alive and most definitely kicking. "What makes you assume I come from a nuclear family?"

She gives me A Look. "Your name is Charles Manson Laughton the Third. Your people stay married come hell or high water."

"I guess that's true. My parents are celebrating their fortieth anniversary in August."

"See? And your siblings? Let me guess—a brother and a sister, right?"

I blanch. "Did you look me up online?"

She laughs. "With the wonky Internet service here? No, sir. You give off a strong upper-middle-class suburban vibe."

There's no point in being offended when she's right. "I have a brother and a sister. You may have heard of her. Elizabeth Thorpe." I wait for the usual light of recognition, but it doesn't come. "She's a professional golfer."

"Oh, I wouldn't know. I don't follow any sports."

"None at all?"

"I mean, I know who the Eagles are, and that the correct response to any fan is, 'Go Birds,' but I haven't seen a game, and I couldn't name a single player if my life depended on it."

I gape at her. "I haven't met anyone this side of Harrisburg who hasn't watched at least one Eagles game."

"Sorry. Not my thing. Now if you ask me to name all the songs from the musical episode of *Buffy the Vampire Slayer*, that I can do."

"Huh," I say, because I'm too dumbfounded to come up with anything else. I knew she was different from the people I usually mix with, but this is next level. "Is that where the sugar glider got her name?"

She nods. "Gloria is a big fan. She rewatches her favorite episodes whenever she's in a funk. What's your comfort TV show?"

Her questions stump me. "I don't watch much television."

"Not even a legal drama?"

"The last thing I'd watch would be a legal drama." I already bring my work home with me every night, no need to treat it as entertainment too. "I've seen a few seasons of *Survivor*." My father liked to watch it, presumably to guess the winner in advance and win the family pool, although I've always had a strong suspicion he was making mental notes in the event of a shipwreck or a nuclear war. If there's one thing my father is dead set on, it's winning, whether it's at poker or life itself.

"Good," she says. "Now I know who to come to when we run out of food."

"That happens?"

She laughs. It's low and throaty, like she's been a chain-smoker since birth, and it doesn't match the rest of her. "Don't worry, Chucky. You'll have more hotdogs than your system can handle these next two weeks. I recommend experimenting with different condiments."

I hear a collection of shouts from the adjacent area. "What's happening over there?"

She checks her phone. "Robo races. Want to see?"

"Sure." I'm not sure the excitement involved warrants the level of noise I'm hearing.

"No betting allowed, if that's what you're thinking."

I straighten. "Do I strike you as a gambler?"

"Not with a collar as starched as yours. Good point."

As we crest a hill, I see the source of the excitement. As promised, small robot toys have been placed in a straight line. Their owners stand behind them holding remote controls.

"Pick your favorite," Courtney says. "My metaphorical money's on number four."

"They all look the same."

The older woman in front of us turns around with a harsh glare. "Then you need your eyes checked."

"I guess she has a favorite, too," I mumble.

Someone blows a whistle and the toys are off! Their mechanical legs move so fast they become blurred. People clap and cheer and chant their favorite robot's name. I pick out Astro and Brutus among them.

"Is this a daily event?" I ask.

"No, twice this week and twice next. If you offer the same activity every day, campers get bored."

"Really? I do the same thing every day."

She gazes at me, unblinking, but says nothing.

"Is the new guy going to join in?" the older woman asks. She's attractive, maybe sixty, showing off toned arms and a face that has seen more than its fair share of sun.

"Which one would you like to race?" Courtney asks.

I hesitate before selecting the white T-Rex, prompting a smile from my escort. "I totally called it," she says. "I bet you were a dinosaur fanatic as a kid. You should be helping Olivia. You probably had all the species memorized once upon a time."

"As a matter of fact, I did." I sound as surprised as I feel. I'd forgotten about my dinosaur phase until now. I tore through every book in the local library, as well as the school library, until my parents cut off what they deemed an unhealthy obsession. If I was going to have an intense interest in a subject, it had to have the potential to either make me wealthy or make them look good. A career as a paleontologist would do neither.

"If you want to go back to the Danger Zone, I'm sure Olivia wouldn't mind adding a fellow scientist to the team," Courtney says.

"Not right now, thanks." I can't afford to get too caught up in the camp activities. There's only one reason I'm here, and unlike this robot race, everything is riding on my ability to claim victory.

Chapter Four

Cricket

The lawyer is going to be the bane of my existence these next two weeks. I thought sticking close to him would be a good idea, but I'm not so sure I can handle two weeks of forced proximity with Charles Darwin Dickens IV. It's like having a Ken doll amidst a dream house full of Weird Barbies; he doesn't fit our aesthetic.

When he takes a break from activities to check email from his evil lair—I mean cabin—I seize the opportunity to complain to my friends, who are currently gathered at the lakeside picnic area for a snack break.

"Why did you even tell him about the available cabin?" Gloria asks, once I've word vomited my frustration.

I hate to admit my answer out loud. "Because deep down I wanted to stick it to the Prick. If he actually dares to show his face again, I can refund his money and send him packing."

Gloria presses her lips together. "I can see why that would be satisfying."

"And when he doesn't show up, I get a little extra money. A win-win."

"Except now you've let another fox in the henhouse," Laura points out.

Ben strokes his white beard in solemn contemplation. "There is that."

"I, for one, am glad he's joined us," says Angela. "New blood is reinvigorating for all of us."

I peer at Angela. "It's because you think he's hot, isn't it?"

"Honey, his hotness isn't up for debate. Your new friend has elevated this camp from nerdo to nitro."

I bristle. "He isn't my friend."

"He's a rebel spy," Adam chimes in.

Gloria frowns at the dark warlord. "Wait, aren't we the rebels?"

Adam thumps his chest panel. "With one notable exception."

"Gloria's right," Ben says. "Charlie is a lawyer who works for the emperor, and he's clearly infiltrated our ship in an attempt to gain intel to crush the rebellion."

I sort of hate that they're giving a voice to my suspicions. I would love to be wrong. I want to believe he was so enamored by his visit that he immediately decided to spend two weeks in blissful tranquility.

My next T-shirt purchase should read 'Naive by Nature.'

"Well, you agreed to let him stay," Laura says. "You didn't agree to make his experience a pleasant one."

"You should sign him up for cosplay and have him wear Princess Leia's gold bikini," Bradley suggests.

"Pretty sure that's where he'd draw the line." Although the image I've conjured in my mind is hilarious perfection.

"Don't be so sure about that," Laura says. "If he needs this deal badly enough that he's agreed to stay here for two weeks, there's no telling what he might do. Test the limits and find out."

I laugh. "Your heart is as black as your eyeliner, Laura."

Stefan lifts his head to regard us. "We come here to escape the bullies in our lives. It wouldn't be fair to behave that way to someone else, regardless of their ill intentions."

Angela tugs the horn of his helmet. "Hmm. This man may resemble a Viking, but he sure doesn't sound like one."

Laura shrugs. "It would only be a bit of fun before we send him back to the Death Star."

"What kind of fun?" Stefan asks, uncertain.

Angela's mouth curves in self-satisfaction. "I can think of an idea or two." She flicks her slender fingers. "Benjamin, be a dear and fetch my scarves from my cabin."

"There'll be no bondage at camp." I place a hand on Ben's shoulder to keep him rooted in place.

"What about good old-fashioned pranks like when I was a boy?" Ben offers. "We can short his sheets."

Angela perks up. "Steal his towel when he's in the shower."

"Disembowelment," Olivia adds with an air of excitement.

Multiple heads jerk toward her.

"What?" she replies with a casual shrug. "I watch nature shows. The animal kingdom is brutal."

It sure is.

"I'll put plastic wrap on his toilet," Bradley volunteers. "I brought plenty with me."

I dare not ask why.

"And I can pay him a visit in the middle of the night," Angela says.

Adam shivers. "That would scare me senseless."

Based on the predatory gleam in Angela's eye, I think 'scare' is the wrong verb for that sentence.

"I wouldn't advise that," I tell her. "The guy seems pretty fit. Wouldn't surprise me if he knows how to throw a punch."

Angela touches her taut cheek. "Hmm. This facelift was too expensive to risk injury. I'd need at least one more husband before I could replace it."

"We should view this as an opportunity," Stefan insists. "If we can make him see the camp through our eyes, maybe he'll see the value in it and persuade his client to walk away."

The rest of us burst into laughter.

"He's a lawyer," Bradley reminds him. "The only thing he'll see value in is the land we're standing on."

"Fine," Stefan relents, "but whatever we do, it has to be lighthearted. Nothing mean-spirited. If we wouldn't laugh if someone did it to us, then we shouldn't do it to him."

"That seems fair," Ben says.

I look around at the group and realize there isn't a cruel bone in any of their bodies, although the jury's out on Olivia.

"So, we're all in agreement on Operation Revenge of the Nerds?" I ask. I relax when every hand goes up. This is why I love camp. For two weeks of the year, I get to feel safe and secure, like nothing can hurt me. It's reassuring to have that feeling back again.

I knock on the door to the interloper's cabin. As annoying as it is, I recognize the need to observe him closely and track his movements. If he's truly up to something, I'd like to be able to catch him in the act.

"Be right there," Charlie calls. The door opens and the first thing I see is a bare chest. A very nice, firm bare chest.

"I came by to see how you're settling in and to give you the full activities list so you can plan your schedule." I hand him a sheet of paper, making sure to avoid ogling his chest, which results in me awkwardly making direct eye contact instead. Honestly, the chest would've been better.

"Um, thanks." He glances at the sheet. "Wow. So many activities."

"See anything that speaks to you? If not, the cafeteria is open if you're more interested in a nipple right now." It takes a beat for me to process what I said, and I quickly try to course correct. "A nibble. A bite to eat."

"I'm always hungry," his full lips reply, and my stomach betrays me by dipping like I'm on the downslope of a roller coaster.

I somehow manage to maintain my composure. "We serve three meals a day, but the cafeteria is always open for snacks. We try to keep food contained to one building to avoid any wildlife issues, which means no food in your cabin. Did you have a chance to read through the rules and regulations?"

"First thing I did when I got here." He flashes a charming smile. "Lawyer habit."

"If you have any questions, you can text me. My number is at the top of the paper, although it's usually better to track me down."

"Because of the unreliable phone service," he says.

"You're a quick learner."

He studies the schedule. "I can't tell you what half these things are."

"Ring toss starts in five minutes. You game?"

He limbers up his wrist, which draws my attention to the sinewy muscles of his arm. "If you don't mind losing."

I snort-laugh. "Because you're a professional ring toss player on the side?"

"Because I was a baseball player. And my brother's a surgeon and my sister's a professional golfer."

"What does that have to do with it?"

"We Thorpes have excellent hand-eye coordination. It's encoded in our DNA."

"Consider me warned." I've played ring toss every summer for the past thirty years. Mr. Genetic Lottery has nothing on me.

"I'll grab a snack from the cafeteria and meet you ... where?"

"Near the area marked Grassy Knoll. There's a map in your welcome packet that you might want to reference."

He dips to the right and plucks another sheet of paper from his bed. "You mean this one?" He moves closer to me, holding the map. "Can you show me? I don't see it." His forearm skims mine, and it feels like a thousand butterflies break free from the prison that is my stomach.

I jerk my arm away and point to the spot on the map. "There." The word comes out garbled, but Charlie doesn't seem to notice.

"Thanks, I'll see you in a few minutes."

I turn my head before he can see the drool gathering at the corner of my mouth. *Calm down, hormones. You act like you haven't seen a handsome man's bare body before.* Granted, it's been a couple years, and the previous body did not compare to this one.

I clamp a hand over my mouth. Am I objectifying someone? Mortified, I hurry to catch up with the others at ring toss before Charlie arrives.

"Where's the spy?" Bradley asks, craning his neck to see past me. "It probably isn't safe to let him wander around the campground alone."

"Relax, he's getting a snack. Infiltration makes a man hungry."

Bradley clucks his tongue. "He *claims* he's getting a snack. What if he's planting false evidence?"

"Evidence of what? The camp is actually a meth lab? Give the police procedurals a rest, Bradley."

Angela shushes us. "Here he comes."

I turn to see Charlie crest the hill. "Everyone, this is Charlie. Charlie, this is everyone." I wave a hand airily.

The greetings are chock full of friendly enthusiasm.

"Mind if I join the game?" he asks.

"Step right up," Ben says. "The more the merrier."

Charlie ambles closer. "What kind of ring toss is this?"

I hold up a gold circlet. "This is the One Ring."

"Yes, I can see that."

His blank expression suggests otherwise. "The One Ring to Rule Them All."

Realization settles in. "Oh, I get it." He motions to the target. "And that's the mountain."

"Mordor."

"Right. Mordor."

"Like it says on your T-shirt," I point out, grateful that he's once again fully clothed.

He looks down as though he's forgotten what he's wearing.

"You need to throw the ring around Mordor," I explain. "The team with the most ringers wins."

"Technically, shouldn't I be tossing the ring *into* Mordor?"

I slap a ring in his hand. "Take off your lawyer hat for a minute. It won't hurt, I promise."

He mimes hat removal. We divide into teams. The Hobbits versus the Elves. I'm a Hobbit and Charlie is an Elf.

I quickly learn he wasn't kidding about his innate abilities. He lands every ring he tosses.

"He's a ringer," someone shouts.

Still, his team loses when Angela tosses her ring past Mordor. It rolls across the grass and lands in a firepit. I expect sour grapes from Charlie, but he's a surprisingly good sport and tells us "good game." I wonder if it's part of the ruse or if he genuinely doesn't mind. I hate that I can't tell when a man is faking feelings. I ought to be an expert by now.

I consider the earlier suggestion to test the limits of Charlie's commitment to LandStar. Suddenly it seems like the best idea I've ever heard.

"You know what, Charlie? You should sign up for Hero 101."

"Why that one?"

"Because deep down all men long to be heroes. Here's your big chance to act out the fantasy."

Charlie seems to mull it over. "Okay. Count me in."

"Wow. I didn't think it would that easy to convince you."

"I already have the hair," he says, dragging a hand through dark blond locks. "Might as well go all in."

"Already have the ego, too," I mutter.

Charlie pulls out the schedule. "Where's Hero 101? I don't see it."

I tap the paper. "The area between the lake and the arts and crafts cabin. I'll walk with you."

"You don't have to babysit me. I'm sure I can find it."

"And miss out on the pleasure of your company? What kind of hostess would I be?"

Although we smile at each other, the tension between us is palpable and it isn't the good kind. It's the kind that says, 'I don't trust you and you don't trust me, but let's pretend otherwise.'

"What's up with the guy in the Darth Vader costume?" he asks, as we stride across the campground.

I hold up a finger. "While Adam may technically be dressed as a certain famous Sith Lord, he likes to refer to himself as the Original Shadow Daddy."

Charlie shoots me a quizzical look. "Why?"

"Legal reasons."

"I mean why Original Shadow Daddy? What does that even mean?"

I pat his arm. "Oh, you sweet summer child. It's nice to know we have something to teach an educated man like you."

The group is already assembled by the time we reach the area. It's many of the same campers from ring toss with the addition of Hunter and John. Hunter is easy to identify because he wears a camouflage pattern every single day. Different outfits. Always traditional camo. John, on the other hand, is hard to identify unless you know him. He has that kind of thin, pale appearance that makes you think he might have the ability to walk through walls.

"We need three judges," I announce.

"We already have two of them," Hunter replies, motioning between he and Bradley.

Angela raises her hand and wiggles her fingers. "Consider me the Russian judge. Anything less than absolute ten out of ten perfection and it's a five from me."

Charlie visibly shudders. "She and my father would get along famously."

I clap my hands. "Participating heroes, take your places."

Charlie shifts from foot to foot. "What's the first test?"

My smile is sticky sweet. "Take your spot and find out, hero." I point to a sturdy oak tree.

"Those broad shoulders would make Captain America weep," Angela murmurs.

As much as I want to, I can't argue with her. His shoulders nearly span the breadth of the huge trunk. He looks— dare I say it—hot. I immediately repent by mentally referring to him as Charles Xavier, except it occurs to me that I also find Charles Xavier dangerously attractive. Abort mental mission! Abort!

A few other campers line up as well, including Olivia. I toss a questioning glance at Ben, who simply nods.

"A key characteristic of a hero is the ability to withstand level-ten damage." Stefan turns to Gloria. "Release the hounds."

The 'hounds' are tennis balls. Gloria switches on the machine and balls start flying, mainly at Charlie. They pelt his limbs, and one narrowly misses his groin.

"Thank goodness," Angela breathes.

Finally, he jumps aside and lets the remaining balls hit the tree. "Heroes have to demonstrate agility, too, right?"

Angela fans herself with a large leaf. "On a scale of Chris Hemsworth to Chris Pratt, that was a Chris Pine."

"What about Chris Evans?" Charlie asks, seemingly ready to plead his case. The lawyer in him is stronger than the Force.

"Not even close, my dude," Stefan says. "You don't have America's ass."

"He *is* America's ass," I say under my breath.

Olivia waves her hands from her place in front of a tree. "Can we do it again? Nothing hit me."

"You bruise too easily," Ben tells her gently. "I can't send you home looking like a plum."

Her face crumples.

"You can do the next one," I say. "It involves balance."

She perks up. "Oh, I'm good at that. I did gymnastics until last year."

"How about you, Charlie?" I ask. "Any gymnastics in your illustrious background?"

"No, but I dated a gymnast. Does that count?"

Angela pins him with a come-hither stare. "But could she suck her own toes?"

"Gross," Olivia says. "Who would want to do that?"

"No one," Ben answers quickly. "Absolutely no one."

Over the next half hour, the heroes perform feats of balance and strength. At one point, I realize I'm ogling Charlie's biceps as they strain under the weight of the tree branch. Those muscles deserve a little hero worship, no doubt about it, but I'm not the one willing to play acolyte. Olivia then complains she's being treated like a child until she's given the chance to lift the same branch as Charlie. After that, she's more than happy to partake in the kid version.

I notice Angela inching closer to the dock. The next thing I know, she flips over a kayak and pushes it into the water. "Hurry! There's a kitten on top of an overturned kayak in the water. What do you do?"

"Why would a kitten be on a kayak?" he asks.

"It's roleplaying. That means roll with it!" Angela shoos

him forward. "This Russian judge wants to see him shirtless."

But Charlie doesn't do her the favor of ripping off his shirt. The only articles he's willing to remove are his socks and shoes, which he sets carefully on the grass away from the water's edge.

"What are you doing?" Hunter yells. "That kitten is drowning, man."

Charlie turns to address him. "My shoes are Gucci. I can't get them wet. They'll be ruined."

A collective groan follows his declaration.

"Give him an F!" John shouts. I swear it's the loudest declaration he's ever made.

"Touch grass," Olivia adds with disdain.

"We don't really assign grades for performance, you know that," I say.

"Sex with you must be very lackluster," Angela replies. "If you don't give feedback, how will they ever improve?"

My cheeks burn and I pray Charlie didn't hear her comment.

"What's that about lackluster sex?" he asks.

Terrific. Now I want to melt into a puddle and evaporate into the earth. "Just rescue the kitten on the kayak, hero."

Charlie wiggles his toes as he wades into the water. "I can't remember the last time I walked outside in bare feet. This actually feels good."

"What about the beach?" I ask.

"I have water shoes."

"Well, at least you know he wears condoms," Angela murmurs.

Heat flames my face. I swear the woman is trying to set me on fire.

Charlie retrieves the kayak and pulls it to shore, although now his clothes are soaking wet, offering another glimpse of his enviable physique. I try to focus on his bare feet. There's nothing sexy about those, except—

Dammit. Even his feet look good. On what bizarre planet do a man's feet trigger such a positive physiological response? I must be ovulating. That's the only explanation.

My phone pings and I'm grateful to realize it's dinnertime. Time flies when you're practicing saving the world.

Olivia objects. "We haven't done the hero pose yet," she insists.

Charlie's face is completely blank. "What's the hero pose?"

"Like you jumped from a helicopter and landed in the middle of a group of bad guys." She drops to a crouched position, one hand on the ground, one leg splayed and the other knee bent. Slowly, her head tilts up so that she's gazing menacingly at the bad guys as she blows a loose strand of hair out of her eye.

Charlie elbows me. "She's looking at me. Am I the baddie?" he whispers.

"I think we both know the answer to that."

Olivia remains fixed in her position. "Quick! I need a snappy one-liner. I'm still perfecting mine."

Angela shakes her wrists in excitement. "Ooh, how about 'look what the cat dragged in?'"

Olivia's head droops. "That only works if the bad guy is saying it."

"I've got one," Stefan interjects. "Looks like I got the drop on you, boys."

"Good enough," Olivia says. "Looks like I got the drop on you." She pulls herself to a standing position and bows with a flourish. "Your turn, Charlie."

He jogs in place for a second, then closes his eyes and blows out a breath.

"I've never seen Spider-Man do that," I say.

"Leave him alone," Olivia says. "Can't you see he's getting in the zone?"

Charlie shoots me a triumphant smile that makes me want to drop kick him into the lake. He pretends to jump from a great height, then copies Olivia's landing.

"I need a quick line too," he says. "I was so determined to stick the landing, I forgot to think of one."

"Sorry," Stefan replies. "I gave Olivia my best one."

Charlie looks up at us. "Can you hurry? I'm getting a leg cramp."

"We deduct points for cramps," I tell him. "Heroes don't get those. They ingest the requisite amount of potassium."

He glares at me, then says in his best hero voice, "Thought I'd drop in for a chat, fellas."

"Why are the bad guys always *guys*?" Olivia asks, bristling with irritation. "Girls can be bad, too. We're equal opportunity evildoers."

Charlie stands upright and stretches his hamstring. "Thought I'd drop in for a chat, villainous ladies. Better?"

Olivia grins at him. "Better."

How about that? Charlie's actually being a good sport. Probably a legal tactic to throw me off his shady scent. Then again, all his interactions with Olivia have been positive so far. He seems like a natural with kids. I bet he'd make a great dad.

Ugh. My ovaries have entered the chat.

I quickly shut them out of the conversation and return to reality.

Charlie's hands are on his hips. "What else do heroes do? Is there a cat that needs saving from a tree?"

"Those are emergency rescue workers," Gloria says.

"I know, but aren't they heroes too?"

"Darn right they are," John agrees.

"Last year we filmed training montages," Bradley reminds me.

Ben smiles. "Yes, we did. I added the Rocky theme song to mine."

Charlie appears uneasy. "I'm not up for a video."

I sense his tension and decide to poke. "Why not? Afraid it'll make the rounds at the office?"

"The Internet is forever," he says.

"I didn't post mine anywhere," Ben objects. "It was for my own enjoyment."

Charlie chuckles. "You've never helped a client recover a sex tape and it shows."

"You've actually done that?" I ask in a low voice.

"It isn't my specialty, but when you have an important client, and that important client has a daughter..." He shrugs. "I was glad I could help."

"But you said the Internet is forever. How did you help?"

"We were able to recover the video before the ex-boyfriend managed to do anything with it."

Angela edges closer to him. "And might you have a copy of said video?"

Ben clears his throat. "We have a minor present."

"A minor who's worked up an appetite," Olivia adds. "Can we eat now?"

I gesture to the main area. "The cafeteria is open. First come, first served."

Charlie taps the brim of Adam's mask. "Don't you get hot in there, buddy?"

"Sweltering, but some of us must suffer for our art."

"Make sure you stay hydrated. It'd be too easy to pass out in this heat."

"I have electrolyte powder packets in my cabin, but I appreciate your concern."

"Just looking out for the little folks." He stops to give me a pointed look. "Like a hero would do."

Either Charlie's a great actor, or he actually had fun today. Is it wrong to hope it's the latter?

He falls in step beside me as we follow the hungry mob.

"How'd I do?" Charlie asks.

"You can tie me up anytime," Angela interrupts as she passes us.

"I believe the hero does the untying," Charlie corrects her.

She keeps walking without turning around. "I said what I said."

"Is she always like that?" Charlie asks.

"Yep."

Charlie sniffs the air as we enter the building. "Do I smell hot dogs?"

"You do, indeed. It's a camp staple."

"As it should be." He peels his T-shirt away from his chest. "I should change my damp clothes first."

"Probably a good idea."

"Save your hero a seat?"

"I would use the term loosely. Superman wouldn't dream of stopping to take off his boots before entering the water."

He holds up the loafers. "That's because Superman doesn't pay Gucci prices. I'll meet you inside." He veers off toward his cabin, and I linger outside the cafeteria to make sure he doesn't double back toward my office. I have no idea what he thinks he might find there, but it's the only place I can think he'd want to snoop other than my house, which would be too difficult to manage. It isn't far, but it's far enough that he'd have a hard time explaining his absence.

I fill my plate with a hotdog slathered in mustard, corn on the cob that will undoubtedly get caught between my teeth, and a small salad drenched in a packet of bleu cheese dressing.

"We're living the dream," Gloria says as she bites into her hotdog.

Charlie sets his tray down beside mine. "You saved me a seat."

"You told me to."

"I know, but I didn't expect you to actually do it." His plate has two hotdogs, two cobs of corn, and a pile of salad without dressing. "My compliments to the chef."

I gesture toward the kitchen. "Bernie takes care of the food. She's a treasure. She's been working here since my grandparents owned the place."

"How old is she?" Charlie asks.

I spear lettuce onto my fork. "Nobody knows."

"And nobody here is gauche enough to ask a woman her age," Angela says pointedly.

A mischievous twinkle forms in Gloria's eye. "We are, however, gauche enough to share that Angela is on the hunt for a fourth husband."

"Some people collect Pokémon trading cards. Angela collects husbands," I add.

Angela guffaws. "Think of them more as replacements for ones that are broken or lost."

"Have you identified any potential replacements?" Charlie asks.

Angela glances casually around the room. "Herb is currently at the top of my list."

Charlie cranes his neck. "Which one is Herb?"

"The man in the Hawaiian shirt."

Charlie pulls a face. "That guy? Seriously?"

Angela takes a dainty sip of her water. "Why not? I prefer men the way I prefer my snatch—bald and stuffed with sausage."

Charlie nearly chokes on his water. He sputters droplets all over the table.

"You don't strike me as a prude, Charles," she says.

"I'm not. I wasn't expecting that answer. You do you, Angela, or I guess you do him. I think it's great." His eyes shift to me as he tries to telegraph his shock.

"Ooh. I see an opening." Angela rises to her feet. "I'll catch up with you later." She's drawn to Herb like a heat-seeking missile, or like she has a glass of tonic water and he's a bottle of gin.

"I didn't understand why a woman like Angela would come to a place like this until now. Camp is the ideal hunting ground for her."

"It's best not to date other campers," I say.

"Oh? Why is that?"

"Because it ruins the vibe for everybody when the relationship inevitably ends." I gnaw on the corncob and push the intrusive thoughts from my mind. This is my happy place, and I refuse to give it up, not for the Prick, not for LandStar.

Not for anybody.

CHARLIE

Man, I really wanted to nail that hero activity, if only to show Courtney that I don't need lessons on heroism. I'm perfectly capable of putting others' needs ahead of my own. Stupid expensive shoes.

I remove the shoes in question and jump in the shower. I should've done this straight after my unexpected dip in the lake, but I didn't want to miss the conversation in the cafeteria. Sometimes people let details drop that could be useful in my 'investigation.' Thankfully I only have one message from work and it's from Jeannie asking me to send pics. Unlike everyone else at my office, she means actual pretty pictures of the lakeside setting and not evidence to use against Courtney and the camp.

This isn't a vacation though. My entire future is riding on what I accomplish here these next two weeks.

I check the schedule for the evening's activities. S'mores at the main firepit are happening in ten minutes. Everybody loves s'mores. It could be the ideal opportunity to sneak into the office and search for information. While everybody else is busy getting their fingers sticky, I'll be using mine.

Despite the late hour, there are remnants of daylight, so I forgo the flashlight I packed and saunter toward the office trying to appear casual. As I round the corner of a cabin, I spot Courtney outside the office door, chatting to a couple campers I haven't met yet.

I'll have to try the office another time. It won't be easy. There always seems to be someone lurking in the area.

Courtney is too popular with her campers. They aren't content with her joining in their fun and games; they want to be around her twenty-four seven, which makes my job more difficult. Maybe I should schedule an ice cream truck. There'd be a line a mile long and nobody would venture far with a melting ice cream cone. That would give me plenty of time to root through the files.

Could I expense an ice cream truck? At this point, I'm fairly confident my client will pay for an entire ice cream company if it means getting his grubby hands on the land. I have to admit, I'm beginning to admire her moxie. Nobody says no to James Riggieri. Even the partners at the law firm are loath to tell him he can't do something, which is how I ended up with this assignment in the first place. If it goes to shit, they can point the finger at the senior associate, nothing to do with them. If I fail, I'll be out of a partnership *and* a job. Not loving those stakes.

Suddenly Courtney's moxie seems less admirable and more frustrating. It would be bad enough to lose out on the partnership, but to lose my job...

I've never been fired before. I can only imagine how that would go over at my parents' anniversary party in August. Knowing my parents, they'd disinvite me to avoid the shame of their less-than-superhuman eldest child. I suspect that's part of the reason they're riding me so hard about this promotion. They don't want it for me; they simply want to brag to their friends about yet another Thorpe accomplishment. So far, I'm the dud. If they can claim the youngest partner in my firm's history, then they'll feel like they haven't failed as parents.

"Hey, the melting marshmallows are over yonder," Courtney says when she spots me. The other two campers make themselves scarce at the mention of marshmallows.

I freeze like a deer in headlights. "Me?"

She strolls toward me. "Not a s'mores fan?"

"I'm not a dessert person in general."

"Wow. That's a tragedy of epic proportions. What kind of monster doesn't like dessert?"

"I thought this is supposed to be a judgment-free zone."

"Not when it comes to your lack of a sweet tooth. We are all free to judge the shit out of you for that." She glances toward the orange glow in the distance. "You said you play baseball. How's your throwing arm?"

"I said I *played* baseball, past tense."

A tiny wrinkle appears between her eyes. "How past?"

"High school."

"What position?"

"Pitcher."

"But you didn't play in college?"

"No."

"Why not?"

"Because I wanted to focus on my studies." I don't offer the real reason—that my parents tried to make baseball my entire identity. They hired pitching coaches and talked nonstop about college scholarships. Once that happened, the joy was gone. I played my first year in college out of guilt and then feigned an injury so I could make a graceful exit. To this day, my parents mention my dislocated shoulder on occasion in the same tone people use to discuss a cancer diagnosis.

"Your studies? Ha! Maybe you belong here after all."

I don't belong here. I belong in a cushy office with a view of the city. I belong somewhere with air conditioning and no insects.

"Why did you ask about my arm?"

"Come and see." She links her arm through mine and guides me to a barn across the property.

"I didn't realize you had animals."

"Not that kind of barn." She opens the door and ushers me inside.

I stop short at the entrance. There are enclosures set up for a variety of activities, each one involving a target. Courtney picks up an axe from a nearby bucket. "Stall Five."

I grab another axe and saunter to the fifth stall. I look at the target and do a double take. "Hey, that's my picture."

"Huh. How did that get there?" She hefts an axe and throws it with vigor. The blade lodges sideways across my neck.

"You must get a lot of practice."

"You'd be surprised what I can do under pressure."

"Same." I fling my axe at the target and hit myself directly in the middle of my face. "A little on the nose, but I'll take it."

"Hardy har. You're here for one day and already you're cracking puns. What's next, a Chewbacca suit?"

"I draw the line at masks."

"What do you mean? You wear one every day."

I hear the shuffling of feet and notice the older woman, Angela, enter the barn. She's tall and thin with the kind of sinewy arms that suggest regular workouts. Impressive at her age.

"Hi Angela," Courtney says.

She takes in the sight of us, a gleam forming in her narrow eyes. "Am I interrupting something?"

"Not at all," Courtney says quickly. "Join us."

"I brought my own blindfold. I hope you don't mind." She dangles a pale pink eye mask.

"Is she drunk?" I whisper.

Courtney ignores me. "Those are for pin the tail on the donkey."

Angela's delicately drawn eyebrows pinch together. "Oh no, dear. I've sworn off Democrats."

"You've changed parties?"

"Only when they switch to a cash bar, like this one." She waves an airy hand around the barn.

"We don't have a cash bar, Angela."

"Oh, delightful because I didn't bring any with me."

"Because this is a barn, not a bar, and we don't serve alcohol," Courtney continues.

Angela points at my photo. "Who would choose to malign such a gorgeous face? At least besmirch someone who's already unattractive."

"Because ugly people deserve an axe to the face?" Courtney asks.

Angela doesn't seem to hear her. "I'm surprised you didn't put up a picture of what's-his-name."

Courtney doesn't shoot daggers with her eyes, she hurls axes. "You know the rules, Angela."

The older woman dawdles toward a bucket. Courtney sighs as Angela reaches for an axe.

"Should I intervene?" I ask in a low voice.

"I'll handle it." Courtney leaves the stall to deal with Angela. "I take it things didn't go as planned with Herb."

"He says he's in the market for a younger woman. For the love of Yul Brynner, has he seen his reflection in the mirror? I've seen moons with fewer craters."

"I'm sorry, but it's for the best. Camp should be romance free."

"Romance has nothing to do with it, darling."

Courtney gently removes the axe from the older

woman's grip. "Why don't you go back to your room and put on a nice charcoal mask before bed?"

"Yes," Angela murmurs, more to herself. "My skin does feel a little on the dry side. Thank you, Cricket." She staggers out of the barn and my axe-throwing companion returns to the stall.

"You're good at that," I say.

She casts me a sidelong glance. "Is this flattery or a genuine compliment?"

"Does it matter?"

"Always. I'll take authenticity any day of the week."

"You should tell that to your buddy in the retro sci-fi warlord suit."

"That *is* authentic."

I laugh. "How is walking around in the costume of a fictional character authentic?"

"Because it's a character that truly resonates with him."

"So Adam's an evil overlord at heart?"

"He's telling us he's complex and morally gray. It's a form of self-expression."

I'm still smiling. "Like those people who dress up in animal costumes to have sex with each other?"

"They're called furries and, yes, that's also a form of self-expression. You're welcome to take the chipmunk suit this week. Our regular Simon couldn't make it."

I can't tell if she's joking. "And what do you wear?"

"Can't tell you or it ruins the mystery. Half the fun is not knowing who's behind the mask."

"So much for authenticity," I say.

She narrows her eyes and hurls the axe at the target. The blade hits my picture right between the eyes. I'm glad she's not shooting an apple off my head.

"Nice game," I say. "Do I get to put your picture up next time?"

"Good luck finding one."

"Everybody has at least one public photo online. You'd have to be either a spy or a ghost to avoid it."

She collects the axes. "I fall more into the ghost category."

I'm unclear how to interpret that. I walk to the target and rip down my picture. "You'll need to try harder if you think a stunt like this will be enough to make me leave."

She bares her teeth. "Consider the gauntlet thrown."

My gaze drifts to the shredded picture. Pretty sure it already was.

We part ways and I bypass the firepit to get an early night. Garbled singing drifts to my ears as I slip inside my cabin. I have no idea what song it's meant to be, but they seem to be enjoying themselves. I wonder whether Courtney joined them after the barn.

Her commitment to the camp is admirable. I didn't know people could even have such strong emotions about their livelihoods. Jobs were the means to an end. An income. A status symbol. Her passion for this camp is next level. It makes me feel … envious.

I fold down the sheet and climb into bed in my boxer briefs. It's much too hot for a sheet or anything else. I have to hunt down a smoking gun before I sweat to death.

An image of her knowing eyes flashes in my mind. She's made it clear she's suspicious of me and who can blame her? She's right. I'm the enemy to every single camper here.

Who cares if they have to find a new gathering place next year? It isn't the worst outcome in the world. It might even be good for some of them to break out of their protective shells. They probably don't interact with other humans the other fifty weeks of the year. Time to mix things up.

I clasp my hands behind my head and exhale.

Fuck me. I do care. I wish I was more like Matt, who would've dug up whatever intel he needed to seal the deal and screeched away in his Cybertruck by now.

I stare at the wood-beamed ceiling, thinking. Maybe there's no intel to be found. Maybe even if someone as ruthless as Matt were here, he'd be unable to unearth a single item to be used as leverage. I could spend the rest of camp holed up in her office reviewing documents and not find a shred of evidence to help my client.

In that case, I might as well enjoy myself a little while I keep my eyes and ears open, right? It's such a rare opportunity to shed my suit and soak up the sun while the mosquitoes soak up my blood. I'll have to ask to borrow bug spray. I didn't show up as prepared as I thought.

Not for any of this, and definitely not for Courtney Abernathy.

Chapter Five

Cricket

I skip sunrise yoga this morning. In my defense, there's a distinct absence of an actual sunrise. Instead, there's a light mist and thick fog that roll off the lake. Although it's atmospheric, it isn't what I'd call a mood lifter. It's perfect for the zombie apocalypse later though. It's always nice when Mother Nature cooperates with the activities schedule.

It rained overnight, which means the grass will be too wet and slippery for a couple of the planned activities, so I make sure to modify the schedule before the first block begins. As I pass the arts and crafts cabin, I notice a light on and make a quick detour. There's nothing on the schedule this early.

I open the door, not sure what to expect. Esther and Wendy, our two oldest campers, are seated side by side at the table with a basket between them. Crochet materials are spread across the surface. The moment I enter, they both drop their hands below the table... Well, a couple beats later because their reaction time isn't what it used to be.

"Good morning, ladies. What are we working on so early?"

"There's no amigurumi on the schedule today," Esther explains. "We thought we'd work on a project before the figurine painting starts."

"What are you making?"

The older women exchange looks. Slowly, they raise their hands to show me.

"I can't tell what they are."

"That's because it's been a while since you've seen one," Esther says, promoting a snicker from Wendy.

I approach the table for a closer look. "Is that a ... plushie penis?"

Esther holds up the craft for closer inspection. "It's my new side hustle. I've been crafting penises and other naughty products for my Etsy store. Bridal parties go nuts for them."

I examine the plushie. For a penis, it's kind of cute. "You're using crochet stitches."

Esther nods. "That's why I've enlisted Wendy's help. She's a wiz when it comes to crochet."

"Esther had a large order come in right before she left."

"I didn't want to cancel on you or them," Esther continues. "You know how much I love this camp, but I also don't want to let down my customer."

"Plus her rating will go down and it'll be bad for business," Wendy adds. "Reviews can be brutal."

"How many more do you need to make?"

The women exchange another look. "Fifty," Esther admits.

"Fifty? That's one big bridal party."

"It's for the bridal shower. The maid of honor wants to include them in the gift bags."

"I hope you get them finished so you have time to enjoy the rest of camp."

"We will," Esther says. "Even if I have to double my arthritis medication."

"Please don't do that."

I exit the cabin and make a mental note to keep Olivia away from any amigurumi sessions. I can just picture the back-to-school essay highlighting what she did over the summer break.

After posting the revised schedule in the discord group as well as a physical copy on my office door, I head to the cafeteria for breakfast. Bernie is setting out a bowl of bananas as I arrive.

"Everything going okay?" I ask.

"The strawberries are turning already, so I'll have to buy more for this week unless you want me to skip them."

There's no question that I have to skip them. The budget is too tight this year. "How are the blueberries?"

"Ripe and ready."

"Okay. We'll stick with what we have for this week. Thanks."

I take a banana and a small yogurt container and join a group in progress, where I'm greeted with a chorus of 'good morning.' I notice Charlie sandwiched between Angela and Stefan.

"How does this compare to your usual five-star accommodations, counselor?"

"I miss my morning cappuccino, but otherwise not too bad. It isn't every day I wake up to the sound of ... nothing."

"That's my favorite part," Adam says. His mask is off as he nibbles on a banana.

I rip off the lid of my yogurt, triggering Chewy's senses. The Yorkie's head pops up and he scents the air.

"Do you mind?" Adam asks.

He knows I don't. We've been doing this for years. He dips his spoon into my yogurt and offers it to Chewy. The dog's little tongue makes short work of the yogurt.

"The rest is mine," I tell Chewy. The dog settles back down on his companion's lap.

"Well, I woke up to the sound of Hunter singing in the shower," Angela says. "His cabin must be next to mine."

Charlie's brow creases. "He doesn't strike me as the kind of guy who sings at all, let alone in the shower."

"Everybody sings in the shower here. It's basically a competition to see who sounds the best," Angela says with a wink at me.

"The acoustics are amazing," Adam agrees, catching on to the ruse.

"What's your go-to song?" Charlie asks.

Angela is the first to volunteer. "Mine is 'Juicy.'"

Of course it is.

"What's yours?" I ask Charlie.

"I don't sing in the shower."

"Why not?"

"Because I'm not much of a singer."

"Not even when you're alone in your douchemobile?"

"I tend to play classical music."

"That's the beauty of the cabin shower," Stefan says. "Everybody sounds like Adele."

"You should try it next time," Angela tells him. "Maybe you'll surprise yourself with how good you sound."

Leave it to Angela to know how to appeal to a man's ego.

"Maybe." Charlie offers a dimpled smile that casts a spell on my uterus. Where in his perfect bone structure has he been hiding those dimples? I quickly dismiss the thought. Charles Thorpe is the enemy. The Nazgul to my Frodo.

"You all seem to know each other so well. I'd like to hear more camp stories," the Nazgul says. "The more embarrassing the better."

"We don't share embarrassing stories about each other," I say in my warning tone.

Angela chortles. "Are you serious? That's all we talk about—that and when Cricket will finally ditch the vibrator and start dating again."

Heat flames my cheeks. "We definitely don't talk about that."

"Sorry, dear. I meant we as in us." Angela gestures to everyone else.

"I would rather you didn't speculate about my romantic life."

"Or lack thereof. Darling, you wasted the best years of your body on a man who didn't deserve you."

"I'm only thirty-two," I object.

"Fine. You have another two years." She looks me up and down. "Maybe one, depending on your daily squats routine."

"Am I supposed to have a daily routine that involves squats?"

"Definitely only one year left. You need to spend less time focused on our activities and more time focused on your own."

"I do sunrise yoga. That's basically daily squats for the soul."

"It isn't your soul that will attract a man."

"It will if it's the right one," I insist.

"I agree with Cricket," Adam chimes in. "It's the inside

that matters. If they're only interested in the outside, then they're not a match."

Stefan pounds his morning milk like it's a tankard of ale. "I'd like my outsides to match my insides. Then I'll worry about finding a love match."

"What do you mean?" Charlie asks.

"I can't expect to form an authentic connection with someone else when I don't have one with myself."

"No, I mean how do your outsides not match your insides?"

"I have the heart and soul of a Viking," Stefan says. "I'd like to embody one more completely."

"You wear a horned helmet," Charlie says. "How much more like a Viking can you look? Chainmail?"

"Most Vikings didn't wear chainmail," Stefan replies. "Too expensive. Technically they didn't wear these helmets either, but most people don't know that. That's why I wear it, so people can identify who I am without me having to explain."

"Although to be fair, people demand an explanation like they're entitled to it," Adam says. "Believe me, I get it."

"I thought you were content with your appearance," I tell Stefan.

"Oh, I am, but with a few tweaks I could fully inhabit my ideal self."

"Oh honey, we could all use a few tweaks," Angela interjects. "That's human nature."

"I've been carting around a pair of custom boots that I haven't even worn," he says.

"Why not?" I ask.

"Because I don't think I'd do them justice like this. I need to be the whole package."

An idea occurs to me, and I send a quick text to Laura at the other table.

Angela stretches her arms above her head. "Speaking of tweaks, I need to go back to my cabin to finish my skincare regime before the fan fiction club meetup."

"I didn't know you were joining them this year," I say.

"Apparently they'd like someone with experience to write the steamy parts." Angela rises from the table. "Not all heroes wear capes. Ta-ta for now."

Laura nearly topples over Angela in her rush to get to our table. "What's the grooming emergency? Is it Chewy?"

Hearing his name, the Yorkie releases a yip from under the table.

I point to Stefan. "This man needs your professional help."

Laura frowns. "This man is not a canine."

"I can bark if it helps," Stefan offers.

"Can you style him so he looks more like a Viking?" I ask.

"Don't wash it or cut it for a month," Charlie says. "Problem solved."

Laura scrutinizes Stefan's head. "No, no. I'm seeing it. Sort of a punk rock meets the devil." She touches a strand of Stefan's light brown hair. "I can work with this."

Optimism sparks in Stefan's eyes. "Even if you mess it up, I won't care. I'll be grateful you were willing to try."

Laura pats his shoulder. "Come on, Stefan Eriksson. Let's see what we can do."

Adam pins her with a hopeful look. "Can Chewy and I watch? We love a good transformation story."

"As long as there's no side commentary," Laura tells him. "It's a good thing I packed my electric razor."

Charlie slides down to my end of the bench. "Looks like it's just us."

I swallow another spoonful of yogurt. Before I can respond, Olivia appears out of nowhere, tapping my arm incessantly. "Cricket, can I feed Buffy today?"

"I think I saw your name on the list for tomorrow morning."

She looks mildly put out. "Can't I have a turn today?"

"You'll have to ask Gloria. She's in charge of Buffy's schedule."

Olivia continues to stand in front of me in awkward silence, as though conjuring another reason to continue the conversation. I suspect she's missing her parents. I know how she feels. My family has been gone for years, and I still have moments where I miss them so much, my whole body aches with it.

"Or why don't I ask Gloria if you can do it now?"

Olivia's smile is triumphant. "Good idea."

I send a text to Gloria and receive an immediate response. "Gloria says to meet her at her cabin in the next two minutes and you can have a turn."

Olivia doesn't say a word. She spins on her heels and flees the cafeteria without a backward glance.

Charlie chuckles. "She seemed very appreciative of your efforts."

"She's eleven. Forgetting manners due to genuine excitement is a rite of passage." Olivia needs a spark of joy wherever she can find it right now. If I can facilitate that in any way, I'm happy to do so.

"You're much softer than my parents."

"Much younger too." As much as my hormones urge me to stay here with the anatomically correct Ken doll, my brain knows better. He isn't interested in me; he's interested in my land. His plan is to fake it 'til he makes it.

Not on my watch.

"I'll see you later, Charlie." I stand up abruptly and take my banana to go.

Camp is running smoothly today, thank goodness. There are always hiccups like the unexpectedly moldy strawberries and changing the schedule due to weather, but as long as there's nothing too costly or upsetting, I'm happy.

After one round of check-ins, I duck into my office to take care of a few administrative tasks. They're my least favorite part of the job. I'm not the most organized person in the world and I lose focus when there are too many details, but I can't afford to hire anyone. I already barter with Gloria for cleaning and Adam for counselor duties when the kids arrive following adult camp. The other counselors are college students who volunteer.

An hour flies past, and I'm distracted by the sound of footsteps passing back and forth in front of the office door.

"Olivia, is that you?"

The footsteps grind to a halt and the door creaks open. The first thing I see are a pair of Gucci loafers, followed by Charlie's sheepish face.

"Can I help you?"

"I wasn't sure if you were here."

"You could've knocked." But that would've no doubt thwarted his plan of sneaking inside.

"I didn't want to interrupt you."

"And yet you have." I set down my pen. "What's up?"

He slides into the office and perches on the edge of my desk. "Why this camp?"

I lean against my chair, clasping my hands in my lap. This ought to be good. "You've been loitering outside my office with *that* question?"

"I'm curious."

"I told you. It's a family business."

"I know, but you're young. You could've sold it. Hell, you could sell it right now. Why take it on all by yourself?"

"Because camp is the highlight of the year for many of them. And people need this; they need joy in their lives. They need silliness and *fun*."

"I'm not talking about the camp itself. The theme. Why niche down to nerds only?"

His question surprises me. "Isn't it obvious?"

"Not to me." He flashes a smile. "Explain it to me like I'm a pinheaded jock."

"We need a safe space to be ourselves. You heard Stefan this morning. Where else can someone express a sentiment like that and not expect people to judge him for it? We all need a place to be our most authentic selves."

"Shouldn't that be our homes?"

"Sure, when we're by ourselves, that might be true—unless you're Gloria, who looks after her ailing mother. Or Ben, who spends most of his time at home with family members who don't share his interests."

"Or someone like you, who lives alone in an isolated area."

A lump gathers in my throat. "See? You get the picture."

"What's it like here outside of the summer season?"

"Not gonna lie, winters can be brutal, but I wouldn't trade this place for anything."

His blue-green eyes twinkle. "Not even for a generous sum of money?"

"If you're here to tempt me with a wad of cash, don't bother."

He returns to his feet. "You're right. Money does crazy things to people anyway. You don't want that."

"Money doesn't do anything except amplify who they really are. If you ever want to truly know someone, give them a million dollars and watch how they behave."

A smile ghosts over his lips. "I'm trying to give you more than a million dollars, but you won't take it."

"Ah, but what you see is what you get with me. No need to throw money at me to extract that golden nugget."

"I'm beginning to see that." He drags a hand through his hair. "I can't pretend to get the whole Viking thing with Stefan, but I can see it's a big deal to him."

"Why do you need to understand it? You have empathy, don't you?"

"Do I? I'm a lawyer, don't forget."

"Trust me, I haven't forgotten." Not for one second. "I think Monopoly is today's board game. If you hurry, you can join the game before it starts. Hunter is fairly strict when it comes to latecomers."

Charlie takes the hint. "Thanks. I'll check it out."

My body remains tense until the door closes, blocking any further view of him. Whenever he's in my orbit, I develop an acute case of brain fog. His presence seems to muddy the waters of the mind I'd made up about him. I was sure he was here to snoop, yet his questions were insightful and even his comment about Stefan seemed to come from a genuine place. He may be here for the wrong reasons, but he doesn't seem like a terrible person, only a misguided one.

My phone pings with a reminder that it's snack time. I wander down to the picnic area to join the campers. There's already a lively group present. The enthusiastic chatter warms my heart. The group chat is no match for the energy when we're all in person together.

Charlie sits among the campers, which means he didn't take my suggestion to join the Monopoly game. No surprise. He's here for the wrong reasons and we all know it.

He waves when he spots me and slides over, motioning for me to sit next to him. I scan the seating area for another available spot, but there isn't one. Reluctantly, I join Charlie on the bench.

"Granola bar?" he asks, holding out a chocolate-chip-flavored one.

"Sure."

As I unwrap the bar, Laura appears at the edge of the picnic area, clapping her hands. "Listen up, everybody. It's time for the big reveal. We need an appropriate soundtrack."

Music begins to play from someone's phone, and I immediately recognize the beginning of Led Zeppelin's "Immigrant Song." It's perfect.

A sturdy figure cuts through the shadows. He doesn't simply stride toward us, he struts.

Valhalla, he's coming.

When Stefan steps fully into view, Laura's handiwork is evident. The horned helmet is gone. His beard has been trimmed into a V. He does a slow-motion twirl, showing off the shaved back of his head. Laura left more hair on top, along with longer bangs. His oversized T-shirt and cargo shorts have been swapped for a natural linen tunic and baggy trousers. The flip-flops are now brown boots made of leather and bone. Stefan has finally made those boots proud.

Thunderous applause follows his dramatic entrance. Stefan's smile melts my icy heart into a puddle. I didn't realize we had a watered-down version of the Viking until this moment. With these few extra touches, he's now Stefan in his purest form.

"Wow," Charlie whispers. "It's like a light went on. He's a whole different person."

"No, he's the whole *right* person. Now he feels more like his true self."

"Incredible what a simple haircut can do." Charlie seems enamored of Stefan's transformation, and I think I like him a little bit more than I did earlier.

"Where's the helmet?" Gloria asks.

He spreads his arms wide. "Now that I'm the whole package, I don't need the helmet."

I cut through the onlookers to hug Stefan. "Congratulations. You look amazing."

"I feel amazing."

Angela squeezes next to us. "You won't stop wearing the helmet for good, though, will you?"

"I'll wear it on occasion. I like it, even if it isn't historically accurate."

Old habits die hard.

"Dare I ask what kind of bone they used on your boot buttons?" Ben asks.

Stefan lifts a foot. "Antlers."

Ben looks visibly relieved. I'm not sure what he thought they were, nor am I asking.

"I think you look really cool," Olivia tells him.

Stefan bows. "Thank you, young lady. I pledge not to pillage your village."

"Ooh, all it takes is one compliment and we can save our cabin from a raid?" Gloria gives him the once-over. "In that case, I like your trousers. They remind me of those parachute pants that were popular in the Eighties."

"Thank you."

Stefan is high on life right now and I'm here for it. "You did a great job, Laura."

She's beaming as brightly as Stefan. "It feels good to do good," she responds and starts to cry, which triggers tears from Stefan. Before I know it, half the campers are wiping the moisture from their eyes.

I return to the bench where Charlie is still seated. "Same as working at a law firm, isn't it?"

He grunts. "Yes, exactly the same. Tissue boxes are one of our biggest expenses."

"Seriously, though, has anyone ever cried at your office?"

"Only tears of terror."

"Have you ever cried at work?"

"No, but I haven't cried since I was a kid."

"Really? Not even at the movies?"

He casts me a sidelong glance. "Which movies do you think I've watched that would trigger that kind of response?"

"No idea. I always seem to cry during a movie. There's something about sitting in the dark and becoming invested in someone else's story that makes me emotional."

"Then maybe turn the light on the next time you watch."

"There's nothing wrong with letting the tears flow," I say, although admittedly I got tired of seeing my red-rimmed eyes in the mirror in the aftermath of my breakup with the Prick. I try to put a positive spin on them, though. Those tears were necessary to clear the toxins from my system.

"I'd like to hear you say that to my father."

"I'd be happy to." I pull out my phone. "What's his number?"

Charlie shakes his head. "Trust me. You do not want that experience."

"Fine, but you do want the experience of movie night. We have one coming up, but I think people would object if we leave the light on. Kind of ruins the cinematic ambience."

"When's movie night?"

"Tonight at six. You should really pay attention to the schedule."

"Save me a seat?"

"If it means I get a front-row seat to watch you cry, then hell yes."

"Sorry. This face is a marble mask."

Sadly, I didn't disagree.

Chapter Six

CHARLIE

The afternoon kicks off with zombie apocalypse training. I have no idea what this entails, but I'm curious to find out. I haven't seen *The Walking Dead, Zombieland* or any of the other undead-related entertainment they mentioned, so I'm starting at a disadvantage.

"Bradley, Hunter, and Fiona have volunteered to be the zombies," Courtney announces.

"Are we sure about this? Hunter sometimes takes his role a little too seriously," Gloria says under her breath.

Hunter is the heavyset guy dressed from head to toe in camouflage and a jaw that sharks would envy. I make a mental note to avoid him. If his bite breaks the flesh, there isn't a hospital nearby for treatment.

"It's fine," Bradley says. "This is basically tag with zombies."

"It's much more involved than tag," Hunter interjects. "It's the apocalypse. You need to think like a prepper *and* a military operative."

"I can do neither of those." I do, however, have experience as a winner. I hope that's enough to sustain me during these imminent dark times. "Is there a time-out signal?"

Hunter pins me with a pitying look. "This is the apocalypse, my friend. The only time out is permanent."

Got it. No breaks for the weary. "I'll soldier on then."

"No firearms, Hunter," Courtney says. "You know the rules."

Hunter kicks the dirt in protest. "What if I roleplay a human instead?"

"Still no."

Firearms aside, I'm concerned that he would refer to his status as a human as roleplaying.

Courtney hands out three walkie talkies. "These are your only form of communication. No phones."

Gloria snags the first one. Olivia and Adam swipe the other two.

"You need to survive until you hear the whistle blow a second time. If you're alive by then, congratulations, you're a winner."

Hunter points at his eyes with two fingers and then at me.

"Stick with me," Olivia advises with a solemn gaze.

There's no need to convince me. I'd bet good money on this kid's survival.

"You get a five-minute lead," Courtney says, followed by an ear-splitting whistle that signals the start of the game.

People scatter in multiple directions. Everybody seems to have a plan of action except me. Olivia grabs my arm and tugs me in her direction. Ben is shockingly spry for an older guy. He makes it to a small bridge that spans the width of a creek.

"Can the zombies swim?" I ask.

"Good question." Ben rubs his beard.

Olivia presses the button on the walkie-talkie. "This is Olivia's Team requesting information."

"Go ahead, Olivia's Team." Gloria's voice is interrupted by static.

"Can zombies swim?"

Adam's voice breaks through. "Affirmative."

That rules out an aquatic escape route.

"Zombie Hunter spotted by the cafeteria," Adam reports in a panic.

"That's confusing," Ben says. "Makes him sound like someone who hunts zombies."

"What's your position, Team Gloria?" Olivia asks.

There's no answer from Gloria, only static.

Olivia's eyes widen. "Comms are down!"

"No communication is a problem," Ben says.

Not for me. I view this as an ideal opportunity to do some sleuthing. I break away from the group. "I'll do recon. See if I can spot any zombies in our area."

Ben places a hand on my shoulder, holding me in place. "We should stay together. There's safety in numbers."

Olivia pushes her grandfather's hand aside. "If the hero wants to sacrifice himself, who are we to stand in a hero's way? We'll hide near this bridge. Report back as soon as you can."

I salute her and take off in a sprint. I spot Angela, who is seated on a rock by the lake. She's decked out in a sunhat and oversized sunglasses.

"Aren't you playing?" I ask.

She slides the sunglasses to the tip of her nose and peers over the top at me. "I made sure to get bitten right away. Now I can enjoy the sunshine without interruption. You?"

"I'm on a recon mission."

She squints. "Is that so?"

"Yes." It isn't a lie. The recon, however, is for my client and not for the human survivors of a fake apocalypse.

Her gaze skims me from head to toe. "I won't reveal your whereabouts if you don't reveal mine."

"Deal."

She slides the sunglasses back into position and tips her face skyward to absorb those UV rays. I take that as my cue to carry on.

I disappear into the thick of the woods. Once I'm clear out of eyesight and earshot of everyone else, I open the PDFs of the property records saved on my phone—I assumed the Internet would fail me out here—and study the images. According to the records, I've almost reached the farthest point of Courtney's land. If there's anything that's been missed, any violation or issue that could be used as leverage against her, I might find it here off the beaten path.

I stop in front of what amounts to a woodland wall. The trees have grown so close together in this section that they seem to be forming a blockade. Is this considered a fire hazard, having trees clustered like this? One forest fire could blaze through here in a matter of minutes. If Courtney was forced to clear some of the trees, it would cost a small fortune—a fortune I happened to know she didn't possess.

Uncertain, I snap a few pictures just in case, then instinctively glance over my shoulder to make sure Angela didn't follow me. I feel a strange sensation in my stomach as I tuck the phone into my pocket. At first, I worry that I ate something I shouldn't have, until I realize I've experienced a twinge like this before.

It isn't indigestion; it's guilt.

Here I am, actively working against the people who are currently actively working to protect me and the others from a zombie invasion. It doesn't matter that it isn't real. If it *was* real, I have no doubt they would be out there, working to defend the community they've built, while I'm secretly working to destroy it.

I feel sick.

An uncomfortable realization sinks into my bones. This is about more than my fear of getting caught. If I'm being honest with myself, the truth is I don't want the campers to think less of me. I like them. They're nice people, with the possible exception of Hunter, who may, in fact, be a sociopath disguised as a nerdy firearms enthusiast.

I hear a garbled growl behind me and turn to see Fiona stalking toward me wielding a five-foot branch.

"That seems excessively large," I tell her.

"That's what she said." The zombie cracks a smile, and I see she's blackened a few of her teeth. I admire her commitment to the role.

"Zombie brains lack the capacity for humor," I remind her.

"Right. Grrr. Argh," she says, slipping back into character.

When she pulls back to take a swing at me, the top end catches on the branch behind her. I seize the moment to slip past her toward the campground. I'm unprepared for the adrenaline rush that comes with dodging a zombie attack, fake as it is.

My survival instincts kick in and I race toward the picnic area with Fiona hot on my heels. Up ahead, I see a group has already gathered there. The second whistle sounds as I reach a table.

"I almost had him," Fiona says, panting. "I tracked his footprints to Endor Forest, but he had a little help from the trees."

Adam whips toward me. "You were all the way out by Endor Forest?"

"That's against the rules," Bradley adds.

Gloria rushes to my defense. "It isn't his fault. Nobody explained the boundaries before we started." She turns to me. "We don't go as far as Endor Forest. If somebody were to get lost trying to hide in there, it would be almost impossible to find them."

"Noted," I say. And not at all surprised. At least they took sensible precautions. "Why are you all here?"

"Hunter got us," Olivia complains, casting a steely eye at the camo zombie. "Are you the only one who didn't get bitten?"

I survey the group. "I guess so."

"Charlie's the winner!" Bradley crows, yanking my arm skyward in triumph. I feel uneasy accepting any accolades, knowing the real reason I managed to successfully dodge the zombies.

Olivia looks at me, eyes shining. "What does he win?"

"He gets to be first in line in the cafeteria for the next three meals," Gloria announces.

"Lucky," Adam says with a hint of resentment.

I don't feel lucky though. I feel more like our undead opponents—a monster.

For the remainder of the afternoon, I can't stop thinking about Stefan's joyful transformation and how happy everybody was to witness it. It was almost as moving as Courtney's wistful gaze whenever she talks about the camp. I wish I had more of that in my life.

Following a Lego meetup where every participant built an iconic movie scene (there was a shark Lego, so I chose

Jaws), I agree to participate in a tabletop game. I get so caught up in reading the rules to avoid making a mistake that I don't realize how many hours have passed until I get a message from Jeannie requesting proof of life, and that's when it hits me.

I haven't checked in with the office all day.

I've been so immersed in camp life that I failed to check emails, voicemails, or messages. My chest tightens and I find it difficult to breathe. I excuse myself from the game and race back to my cabin before I have a full-blown panic attack in front of a group of trolls and elves and whatever else they're supposed to be.

"Charlie? Is everything all right?"

Shit. I slow my pace. "Hey, Courtney. Yeah, everything's fine."

"You don't look fine. You look green, and not in a cool Hulk way."

"I needed fresh air."

"You're in luck. We have that in abundance here. Still on for movie night?"

I manage a nod. "Six, right?"

"On the dot."

"Why so early?"

"Have you seen the other campers? They're not exactly night owls. Besides, I prefer an early night so I can get up for sunrise yoga."

I bark a laugh. "You get up before the crack of dawn to stretch outside?"

"Don't mock it 'til you try it. It's a great way to start the day."

"I'm not mocking it. I don't see the point."

"Does there need to be a point? Can't I do it because I enjoy it?"

I have no clue how to respond to that. In my world, every action worth doing has a reason, whether it be a goal or a prize. I wouldn't be here now if it weren't for the goal of making partner. Courtney's camp is simply the means to an end.

"Don't let me interrupt your commune with nature," Courtney says. "You're clearly desperate for it. Pretty sure you left scorched earth in your wake."

Not yet, but I may very well do that the day I leave camp.

I grunt something unintelligible and continue to my cabin, drawing deep breaths along the way. Once my heart rate slows to a nonfatal rhythm, I return Jeannie's call. She picks up before it manages to complete a full ring.

"Where have you been?" she hisses into the phone.

"Is there an emergency?"

"Yes, the emergency is you've been incommunicado. I was worried they tied you to a tree and left you for the crows."

"They wouldn't do that." Well, Hunter and Olivia might.

"Joel and Matt have both been sniffing around. From what I heard, Matt's client is having to delay their negotiations."

"He must be pissed."

"He isn't happy, that's for sure. It's probably a good thing you're not here for him to torment."

"Has LandStar called?"

"No, but your mother has. Twice."

"In less than twenty-four hours?"

"Yep. I suggest checking in."

"I'd rather not. The service up here is spotty."

"Sounds fine to me."

"It's unreliable. The call might get cut off, and then she'll worry."

"Call your mother, Charlie. It'll take two minutes and you'll both feel better."

My mother only wants to ask me about the promotion. She's probably preparing the speech for their anniversary party and wants to know which impressive details to include.

Unfortunately, I have no impressive details to share at the moment.

By the time I finish my call with Jeannie, leave a voicemail for my mother, and review all my outstanding messages, I realize it's five minutes to six. Great. I've missed dinner and I'm about to be late for the movie.

My hand hovers over the knob as I reach the door. If Courtney is in the movie cabin with everybody else, maybe now would be a good time to search her office.

No. Too risky. Courtney isn't stupid. She'll notice if I'm the only one not in attendance and probably come looking for me. If she catches me rooting through her files, she'll send me packing. Then again, if I never look because I'm scared of getting caught, how do I expect to find anything?

My heart starts to race again. I wasn't cut out for this sort of work. I'm great in an office setting, complimenting the morning pastries or charming a new client. What I'm not great at is infiltrating what is essentially a family in order to destroy their lives. If I wanted to do that, I would've become a divorce lawyer.

I delay my plan until tomorrow and walk to the cabin designated for movie night.

"You-hoo, Charles. There's a free seat next to me."

My gaze swings to the left, where Angela is patting the

empty chair beside her. An older gentleman tries to sit, and Angela pushes his leg, her predatory smile still fixed on me.

"I've got you, boo," Courtney says, sweeping in and steering me to another row. She sits and hands me a bag of popcorn. "I thought you might be hungry. Missed you at dinner."

"Yeah, I fell asleep," I lie.

"Fresh air will do that to you."

I stare down at the popcorn and, on cue, my stomach rumbles. "Thank you."

"Welcome."

Someone switches off the lights and darkness blankets the room. I'd fully intended to look up the movie in advance, but between my mad dash to the cabin and my catchup conversations, I'd completely forgotten. I remain buried in thoughts until colorful animated characters appear on the screen.

"Hey, this is a kids' movie," I whisper.

"No, *Inside Out* is a movie for all ages. You'll see."

The characters are personified emotions like Anger, Fear, Disgust, and Sadness.

And Joy. The only one I can't relate to.

Everything in my life has always been so serious. So Very Important. I prefer the version of childhood that's on the screen.

As the credits roll, I wipe a stray tear from my eye and hope I was discreet enough that no one notices.

"Hits you in the feels, right?" Courtney's smile tells me that she didn't miss it. Of course not. The woman notices everything. She's like Poirot, Miss Marple, and Nancy Drew all rolled into one adorable package.

Did I call her adorable? Thank God that was in my head and not out loud or I'd never live it down.

"I enjoyed it. Thanks for inviting me."

"You're a camper now, Charlie. Everyone's invited."

The campers file from the building to head to the firepit, but I'm not in the mood to be social. I decide on an early night and head into the darkness.

"You're not joining us?" Courtney's voice catches me off guard.

When I turn to answer her, my breath catches in my throat. Backlit by moonlight, she's practically aglow. The effect is stunning.

I force myself to speak. "Not tonight. See you in the morning, Cricket."

I swear under my breath as I turn away. I called her Cricket instead of Courtney. The woman is getting under my skin. I can't have that.

I change course and stride toward her office. It's now or never. If there's leverage to unearth, now's the time to find it.

"Beautiful night, isn't it, Charlie?"

I ground to a halt outside the office. Adam's black costume is barely discernible in the darkness. I notice a flash of red and see Chewy at the end of a leash. "It is. I didn't see you at the movie."

"Not my kind of story. I prefer space opera or fantasy."

Chewy trots closer to sniff my shoe, and I instinctively jerk my foot away.

"No need to worry. He won't pee on them or anything. He likes to sniff."

I relax and let the small dog continue his investigation. "How old is he?"

"Thirteen."

"Is that old for a dog?"

"Not for his breed. You didn't have a dog growing up?"

"No, my parents didn't want any pets. We were too busy with all the sports and activities."

"I guess that's fair. It's worse to get a dog and then neglect them." He scoops the Yorkie into his arms. "Chewy wouldn't let me ignore him even if I tried. He's very demanding." As if to demonstrate the point, the dog licks the side of his black mask.

"He seems sweet."

"Don't know what I'd do without him. So, how are you enjoying camp so far?"

"It's great. Nothing like I expected."

"I saw you at Lego club today. Nice *Jaws* creation."

"Thanks. I assume yours was a scene from *Star Wars*."

"Actually, it was from *Guardians of the Galaxy*. Have you seen it?"

"No."

"The main character is Peter Quill or Star-Lord. He's a professional thief because of his messed-up childhood. He's also sort of an asshat, but that's another story."

"And Star-Lord is the villain?"

"No, he's the hero."

"Doesn't sound like one."

"That's the great thing about this kind of story. The unlikely hero."

"I'll bite. How does the thief become a hero?"

"I'm so glad you asked, Charlie. Peter becomes a hero when he develops a genuine connection with others. In this case, a ragtag group of aliens. They bring out the positive traits within him. Thanks to their bonds of love and devotion, Peter begins to make better choices, ones that aren't steeped in greed and misguided loyalty."

"And then he stops being an asshat?"

Adam's gaze flicks to the office and back to me. "That remains to be seen. Have a good night, Charlie."

"You too."

He continues his evening stroll with Chewy, and I stand outside the office feeling like the worst kind of human imaginable. I'm not a villain; I'm a good person.

But if I walk through that office door, I'm definitely an asshat.

I return to my cabin and let myself in. It feels strange not to have to unlock the door. Although my house isn't in a crime-filled neighborhood, I wouldn't dream of leaving the front door unlocked. It seems like asking for trouble.

Maybe there's a way to satisfy both parties without subterfuge. I could try to have a real conversation with Cricket instead of trying to cram a check down her throat.

I strip off my clothes and brush my teeth. It's too hot for anything more than boxer briefs. The fan is doing its best, but it's only capable of circulating the hot, humid air that already plagues the cabin. Too bad Cricket doesn't have the funds to invest in air conditioning for the cabins. I wonder whether she sleeps in her underwear too.

I try to block any further thoughts of Cricket in her underwear, but another feeling is making that difficult, and this one is of the physical variety. Groaning, I return to the sink and splash cold water on my face. Courtney Abernathy is a thorn in my side. An obstacle to mount. A mountain to climb.

Nope. Not helping.

I try to focus on a different subject, like partnership and the fact that Matt's deal suffered a setback. I still have time to work my magic on...

Forget it. I refuse to think of her. She's already permeating my every waking moment. No need to add her to dreams too.

I'm still deep in thought about Cricket when I climb into bed—which is why I don't immediately notice that I'm not alone under the sheet.

My side brushes against something and my body reacts faster than my mind. I launch out of bed, not quite screaming but not exactly mute either. More of a Muppet sound.

I peel back the sheet to reveal an ugly-ass doll with menacing eyes. Is that the Chucky doll from the horror movies? In addition to his blue overalls and striped shirt, he's wearing a green tie. On closer inspection, I realize it's a Philadelphia Eagles tie. Nice touch.

At first, I place Chucky under the bed, out of sight, but after a few minutes with my eyes wide open, I realize I won't be able to sleep with him right underneath me. I get up again and relocate Chucky to the bottom dresser drawer and shove the chair in front of it. One can't be too careful.

Admittedly, I don't sleep well that night. I dream that Michael Myers, Chucky, and Jason Voorhees show up at the camp. We ride in a pontoon and drink beer together, but the whole time I'm wary that they have an ulterior motive.

The next morning, I pull on a T-shirt and shorts and add the Eagles tie. "Never let them see you sweat," as both the deodorant commercial and my father always say. Take that, nerds. I can quote things too.

I venture to the cafeteria and load my plate with scrambled eggs and bacon, then head to the picnic area where most campers are enjoying breakfast.

"Go Birds," someone says with a fist pump as I approach the group of tables.

I offer the natural response. "Go Birds."

Cricket is seated at a table with the usual suspects. I plant myself at the end of the bench. Cricket's gaze goes straight to the tie, and I notice her mouth twitch.

"Fly Eagles fly," says Ben.

Olivia squints at the tie. "It isn't football season."

"The Eagles are always in season," I tell her.

"Sleep okay?" Cricket asks with a mischievous twinkle in her eye.

"Best night I've had yet," I answer. "Camp is infinitely more fun with a bunkmate."

Ben spits his coffee back into his mug.

"You got a bunkmate?" Angela asks. "Lucky you."

"I am," I say with a wide grin. "So lucky. It's great when you can borrow each other's clothes, and he said later he'll show me how to use a knife. Apparently, my grip is all wrong. Who knew?" I shrug and bite a slice of bacon.

I glance at Cricket and see that she is smiling ear to ear. Warmth spreads throughout my body. I want to give credit to the coffee, but I haven't had any yet.

"I'm glad you two hit it off," Cricket finally says. "I'm sorry I didn't run it past you first, but we're fresh out of beds."

"No worries. I had no idea how badly I needed a cuddle buddy until last night."

Cricket buries her face in her hands, shoulders shaking. Making her laugh feels good. I realize I want to do it again.

"Historically I haven't been into redheads," I continue, "but I'm open to it now."

Angela tilts her head. "As it happens, I keep a red wig in the trunk of my car."

"I bet that's not all she keeps in there," Gloria mumbles.

"Why do you keep a wig in your car?" Olivia asks.

"I like to play dress-up," Angela replies smoothly. "Keeps life interesting."

"I stopped playing dress-up when I was six," Olivia says.

"Did you enjoy it?" Angela asks.

"I guess so."

"Then you'll come back around to it eventually."

Ben clears his throat. "Olivia is into books and science, and I wouldn't have it any other way."

"And animation," Olivia adds. "I love Omori."

"What's Omori?" I ask.

"An RPG about a boy and his alter ego. You get to explore the real world and his dream world."

"Wow. Games sure have changed since I was a kid. I think my generation either shot things or jumped over them. There was no story."

Olivia fixes her expressive brown eyes on me and it's like I'm deep in conversation with Bambi. "What games did you like to play?" the doe asks.

"Sports," I reply.

"No video games?"

"I wasn't allowed to play video games."

There's a collective intake of breath at the table.

"None at all?" Olivia asks.

I shake my head. "My parents consider them unhealthy distractions."

Olivia reaches across the table and gives my arm a 'there, there' pat. "You're a grown-up now. You can do whatever you want."

"I wish," I say with a wry smile.

"You never played games at a friend's house?" Adam asks.

I shake my head. "If my parents found out, I would've been punished."

Angela gasps. "It's the video game version of *Footloose*. You poor deprived child."

Cricket jumps to her feet and extends a hand. "Come with me if you want to live."

I notice her T-shirt. "Geek Chic today, huh?"

"I mean, honestly, it's every day." She wiggles her fingers, encouraging me to take her hand.

"Where are we going?"

"I know a place."

"Is it a place that involves yarn and needles? Because that's what's on the schedule."

"Forget arts and crafts. I'm taking you somewhere more important."

I feel an instant jolt as I slide my hand in hers. Her skin is smooth and soft. I'm slightly disappointment when I'm on my feet and she lets go.

I grab my banana off the table and follow her outside. Her pace is quick and determined and I'm forced to lengthen my strides to keep up with her. She's a woman on a mission and somehow that mission involves me.

Cricket stops outside a cabin not far from her office and opens the door. "This, my deprived friend, is the arcade." She flicks on the light switch. Inside the cabin are multiple computer screens with game consoles, as well as two traditional arcade games—Pac-Man and Donkey Kong.

"This is nerd-vana," I say, almost speechless. "Why didn't I see this on the tour?"

"Because I skipped it. It's a free space, so anybody can come in here to play between the hours of noon and eight p.m." She motions to the Pac-Man machine. "But I've decided to make an exception for you this morning."

"Because of my sob story?"

"Yes. Which one would you like to try first?"

I hate to admit that I have no idea how to play any of them.

"Games aren't really my thing," I start to say, but she pushes me toward the consoles.

"You've told me how competitive you are. You're tailor-made for these games. Pick one now or I'll pick for you."

I almost tell her that her bossy attitude is a turn-on but manage to swallow the words before they come out. This isn't a date. I'm supposed to be mining this place for information, not wasting time on frivolous games. My parents were right. In under five minutes I'm letting them distract me from more important matters.

"I appreciate you showing me this cabin, but I'm not really—"

She grabs me by the shoulders and steers me to another machine.

"Sit."

I sit and she squeezes into the seat beside me. "This is a race. You take the wheel and drive the car first, then it's my turn. Fastest time without crashes wins. Got it?"

She's so close that I can smell her skin. Rose petals. Not that cloying sweetness like some rose scents. This one is only a touch. It's nice.

"Earth to Charlie." She knocks on the side of my head. "Ready?"

"I don't know what to do."

"I just told you, silly." She takes my hands and places them on the steering wheel. Leaving her hands on mine, she nudges my foot aside and taps a pedal. "Now drive!" She guns it, and the video car skids into action. In truth, I figure out how to play in about three seconds, but I enjoy touching her too much to say so.

When it's her turn, she bumps me aside with her hip. I loom over her, watching as she races with abandon, cursing at the other cars and acting like a general menace.

I love every second of it.

"I don't see myself getting in a car with you anytime soon," I say, once the game ends in a crash of fatal fury. "Do you always make up your own curse words?"

"I like to be creative." She tilts her head back to look up at me. "They get my point across."

I laugh. "Without a doubt. Those other racers didn't know road rage until you screeched onto the scene."

"Do you want to play something else?"

I realize with a start that I do. Thanks to Cricket, the competitive juices are now flowing freely. I spin around to investigate the other options.

We play Pac-Man, then Donkey Kong. As I dodge my last fireball, the door swings open and Olivia appears. "It's twelve on the dot," she says.

It's been over two hours already? I check my Apple watch to make sure. Yep. It's noon.

"Come in, Olivia. Charlie and I were just finishing up. Is there something you'd like to play with me?"

"No thanks. Grandpa is on his way. He wants to play Pac-Man again."

I hook a thumb toward Cricket. "Word to the wise: do not ever race this one. She's a maniac."

Olivia musters a smile. "Everybody knows women are the best drivers."

"Did you see that?" Cricket whispers as we leave the cabin. "She actually smiled."

"I know. I wasn't sure if it was a trick of the light."

She nudges me with her arm. "I know you don't think so, but you're very funny, you know."

"I'm a comedic genius. Why do you think I became a lawyer? We have more jokes than any other profession."

"I'm dead serious about how funny you are."

"That's kind of you to say. Thank you." I bow, uncertain what the appropriate response is in this situation. Women don't generally find me funny. Sexy. Smart. Successful. But not funny. I wonder if it's a bad sign. Maybe funny is what puts guys in the Friend Zone.

Why would I care if Cricket puts me in the Friend Zone? I have to shake this off—whatever *this* is. She's clouding my judgment worse than any video game ever could.

"Are you ready for lunch?" she asks. "I have it on good authority that the hotdogs today are all beef."

As tempted as I am, I force myself to decline. "I should probably take a nap. I'm pretty beat from last night."

Another smile appears. "From your all-night cuddling sesh with your namesake?"

"What can I say? He's very fidgety. He nearly pushed me off the bed more than once."

"I don't doubt. I hear he has an aggressive nature."

I grin at her. "Sounds like someone else I know."

She gives me a playful shove. "That was a video game. You're supposed to act ridiculous."

"I'll see you this afternoon," I say, lengthening my strides to increase the distance between us. Against my will, I register her scent as I walk toward the residential area. I glance at my hands, remembering how good skin-on-skin contact felt. Her skin, specifically. I seriously doubt I'd be having the same response to Ben's hands. Her laugh is something special. Wicked, bawdy, triumphant, and sexy as hell. No wonder she thinks I'm funny. I now seem hellbent on triggering that laugh at every opportunity.

I catch sight of Gloria and Angela over by the ring toss and give them a friendly wave, but I keep walking at a brisk pace. I don't trust myself to have a casual conversation right now because I know exactly where it will lead.

To Cricket.

At this camp, all conversations lead to Cricket. They're either about her, instigated by her, or include her. She isn't under my skin; she's everywhere, like the Force.

Fuck me. I just made a *Star Wars* reference.

If a *Star Wars* reference is made in Endor Woods, does anybody hear it?

By the time I arrive inside the safety of my cabin, I am falling to pieces. More to the point, I am falling for Courtney Abernathy.

Chapter Seven

Cricket

After a lakeside lunch, Gloria and I heed Esther's call for 'all hands on deck' in the arts and crafts cabin. We collect our trash, careful not to leave anything that might attract wildlife, and amble through the residential area.

I slow my pace to listen. "I hear singing."

Gloria's brown eyes widen. "I think it's coming from Charlie's cabin."

We exchange excited looks and creep toward the source of the sound. Sure enough, it's Charlie's voice raised in song.

Even better, that song is "Defying Gravity."

We lean against the exterior wall outside his bathroom to listen. Gloria whips out her phone and hits record.

"Do you think he'll go for the high notes?" she asks.

"We'll find out soon enough."

His voice strains and squeaks.

We burst into hysterical laughter. "He's taken that song to new heights," I say.

"Should I share the video in the group chat?"

"That seems cruel." I pause. "Yes, let's do it." At the very least, we can hold on to it as leverage in the event we need any. No matter what he says, I don't fully trust him. He's a man, after all, and a lawyer to boot.

"Angela will be very pleased with herself," I say. "That seed she planted has borne fruit."

"He was really belting it out," Gloria adds. "I think he was enjoying himself."

I snort. "I guess we know what his karaoke song will be."

"If he doesn't sign up, we'll do it for him."

My stomach pinches. "Do you think this is hypocritical of us? Camp is supposed to be a safe space."

"And Charlie came here to take that safe space away from us. We could do a lot worse than sharing his impressive vocal range."

My resolve strengthens. "You're right."

We enter the arts and crafts cabin to find a small crowd gathered.

Wendy pushes a basket toward us. "Come on, ladies. These plushie penises aren't going to crochet themselves."

"I overcommitted, I know," Esther says. "I won't do it again, I swear."

I hold up my hands. "We all know micro-coordination isn't my thing." The smaller the movement, the harder I find it.

Hunter glances up from the table with his usual intense expression. "If I can crochet a dick, anybody can."

Esther studies me. "Cricket's right. I remember the time she tried to use the emergency sewing kit on Ben's shorts." She offers me a curt nod. "You're excused from duty."

I don't wait to be told twice. I exit the cabin and head

straight to my office to get through a few more administrative tasks. I constantly put them off, which means they continue to build up into an insurmountable mountain of work.

Not for the first time since he arrived, Charlie's face flashes in my mind. Gone is the cocky, hitched-up mouth, replaced by something far more earnest and, as much as I hate to admit it, far more appealing. The more vulnerable Charlie gets, the more dents he puts in my emotional armor, that bastard.

I will not soften toward Charles Widmore Pennyloafer VI. He isn't one of us. In fact, he's worse. He's the *antithesis* of us. Charlie represents the establishment. The status quo. He's the kind of guy who would've mocked us to his jock friends in the high school cafeteria for sport. For the hundredth time, I remind myself that he's only pretending to be interested now because it's the means to an end. I refuse to be fooled by another man pretending to be someone he isn't. Been there, got the oversized Mumford & Sons T-shirt he left behind.

I open the drawer to the filing cabinet, and my eardrum is punctured by a scream. I quickly realize it's coming from me and clamp my mouth shut.

From the depths of the drawer, two evil eyes stare back at me, glassy and unrepentant.

"What the hell, Chucky?" I wrench the doll from his hiding spot and glare at him as though he might actually offer up an explanation. If any doll was capable of such a feat, it's Chucky.

I tuck him under my arm to return to his rightful owner. I sort of wish Chucky *could* talk, if only to tell me about the Charlie he glimpsed when no one was looking. Was the rest of his body as rock-solid as his chest, not that I was scoping him out? Everybody here has noticed his physique, and Charlie has talked about his athletic past.

"Why am I trying to justify having a set of working eyes?" I ask Chucky.

The doll only stares in response.

"What's it like sharing a room with him?" I picture Charlie making his bed in the morning, complete with hospital corners. I think of my own bed, unmade with the sheets in a ball at the foot of it. Where I kick them to in the middle of the night is where they stay.

I march toward Charlie's cabin. Before I get there, I'm intercepted by Adam out for a walk with Chewy.

"What are you doing with Chucky?" he asks.

"Charlie decided to get back at me for my prank by leaving him in my file drawer."

Adam laughs. "I didn't think he had it in him."

"I know, right?"

"So you're going to give the doll back and let him do it again?"

Adam makes a good point. "I'm listening."

"What if we hide him? We'll make a game of it."

I contemplate Chucky. "Bury him like treasure and draw a map?"

"More like a ransom note. We find a spot to stash the doll and make Charlie work for it."

I like this idea. "What if he doesn't?" I wouldn't blame Charlie for leaving the doll wherever we chose to hide him. We'd give him the ideal excuse to abandon Chucky without losing face.

"I bet you anything Charlie's too attached to let the doll go for good. He'll take the bait."

I smooth back Chucky's red hair, and the ends stick

straight back up. "Okay, but let's not bury him. That seems cruel."

Adam observes me. "You know that's a doll, right? He can't breathe."

I cover Chucky's ears. "You wouldn't feel the need to point that out if I was holding a Yoda doll right now."

"Point taken." He glances over his shoulder. "You should hurry before you run into Charlie. I saw him leave his cabin about five minutes ago. Not sure when he'll come back."

I waste no time sneaking into Charlie's cabin. I take a second to digest the state of the interior. He's exceptionally neat and tidy, which shouldn't surprise me given the condition of his shoes. His laptop is open on the small table, and I resist the temptation to sneak a peek. Besides, the Internet is garbage here anyway. With my luck I'd try to glimpse his socials and end up freezing his screen on some Instagram model's boobs.

I quickly brush off the notion. Charlie doesn't actually seem like the kind of guy who follows models on IG. He seems far more likely to follow businesspeople he admires.

Do successful businesspeople post on Instagram? I have no idea. I'm only on there for the dogs in costumes.

I set Chucky up with a kitchen knife in Charlie's bathroom sink. It isn't easy to get the doll in position, especially with the knife, but I finally manage it with an ingenious use of the toilet plunger and duct tape, which truly is the greatest invention since the printing press, as my grandfather espoused.

Outside the cabin, I hear Charlie's voice and freeze. The front door clicks open, and I look around frantically. There's only one place to hide. I dart into the shower and cower behind the curtain. I fervently hope he doesn't choose now to have a bowel movement.

His footsteps head straight toward the bathroom. Shit.

No! Don't manifest shit by thinking the word.

"Damn, Chucky," Charlie says. "Not you again."

Okay, he doesn't sound terribly frightened. I can expose myself without giving him a heart attack. I poke my head out from behind the curtain.

"Charlie..." As I start to emerge from the shower, he unleashes a blood-curdling scream. I grab the boat-inspired curtain with such force that I manage to yank it off the clips. I fall out of the shower and onto the bathroom floor, wrapped like a nautical mummy. I'm battered and likely bruised, but I cannot stop laughing.

"Holy shit, Cricket. Is that you?"

I emit some sort of sound that's a cross between a snicker and a cry of pain.

Charlie tugs at the curtain until I'm able to emerge from my makeshift cocoon. "What in the hell are you doing in my bathroom?"

I catch my breath. "I was setting up Chucky when you came back. I didn't know where else to go. I couldn't exactly climb out the window." When I dare to glance up, I see him grinning at me.

"Would you like a hand?"

"Only if you washed it first."

"I haven't been to the bathroom yet. That's why I came in here before I was scared out of my wits." He pulls me to my feet with his clean hand.

"I only intended for Chucky to scare you. I planned to be long gone." I pause. "Or at least outside your cabin listening to the sounds of discovery."

"And recording them for posterity I would imagine." He actually sounds amused.

"I'm sorry for sneaking into your cabin. I know it isn't very professional."

"I believe it violates several camp rules and regulations."

I lower my head. "I know. Again, I'm very sorry."

"Do you promise not to do it again?"

I look from Chucky to Charlie, reluctant. "If you insist."

"I'd like to keep Chucky with me from now on, if you don't mind."

"Like a hostage?"

"Something like that."

"You really are attached to him," I murmur, recalling Adam's insight. I'm surprised, but I'm more relieved that he isn't going to make an issue of my trespassing. I take the win.

"You won't do anything horrible to him, will you?"

Charlie gnaws his lip. "You're worried I'll do something horrible to the doll threatening me with the butcher knife?"

"Technically it's a vegetable peeler..."

He holds up a hand. "I solemnly swear to do no harm to Chucky. Will that do?"

"Yes." Now that the uncomfortable has passed, I realize we're crammed together in his tiny bathroom. Cue new uncomfortable moment.

"In exchange for one thing."

"What's that?"

"Twice now Ben has mentioned a mysterious prank that I won't see coming. Could you kindly make that go away? Every time I turn a corner, I expect to be confronted with some crazy prank I can't even predict." He gestures to the shower. "I'm not a big fan of surprises."

"No promises, but I'll see what I can do."

"Great. Would you mind giving me some privacy?" he asks, motioning to the door.

"Of course. Sorry." I observe the curtain in a ball on the floor. "I'll bring you another shower curtain later."

"No need. This one's fine. I can hang it back up."

It's only when I leave the cabin that I hear his rollicking laughter, and I can't help but smile. My embarrassment aside, it's a good sound. One I'd very much like to hear again.

Chapter Eight

Cricket

Trivia night is one of my favorite events during camp because what nerd doesn't love a knowledge-based competition?

We divide into groups and summon the Ubers for those intending to drink. Somehow Charlie ends up in the back of a sedan sandwiched between Angela and Esther, which I am fairly confident Angela orchestrated. If he were older, I'd worry for his safety, but Angela has always preferred older men, at least when it comes to husband hunting.

The bar is only a seven-minute drive. I've been coming here since I was a teenager, but those early years mainly involved driving my dad home at the end of the night.

Charlie gazes at the squat building in wonder when we arrive. "Nickers? Is that a pun?"

"You aced the test. Most people think Nickey's was misspelled, and he was too cheap to change it."

He continues to stare at the building. "This is a dive bar."

"Very good. Now identify this." I point to a nearby bush.

"I was expecting more of a sports bar, the loud kind with big TVs."

I nudge him forward. "What's the matter? Are you afraid you'll burst into flames upon crossing the threshold?"

"No, I'm worried they won't accept AmEx."

"You're right, they won't. Not to worry, we have enough cash between us to cover the bill. As I'm sure you can surmise, the beer here is inexpensive."

The bar's owner bounds toward us with a Labrador's enthusiasm. "Cricket. Great to see you, honey."

"Hi Nick. I reserved seating for trivia night."

"You sure did. Manny will be here soon. You want pitchers for the tables?"

"Please." I lean over to Charlie. "He's talking about beer, not baseball."

He bites back a smile. "I'm familiar with the concept."

"I'll help Nick with the pitchers and glasses," I say. "You all go ahead."

"I'm sticking to you," Charlie says, following me to the bar.

"Nick and I can handle it."

"No, I mean there's so much residue on the floor, the toe of my shoe has adhered to your heel."

"Hardy har. Be prepared. You'll leave this place tonight with more molecules than you came with."

Charlie recoils. "I don't even want to know what that means."

I try to see the place through his eyes. There's a U-shaped bar in the middle of the room dotted with stools. To the left is a jukebox, a dartboard, and a pool table. To the right is the seating area where we're headed, with a few booths that line the wall and a smattering of square tables. The floor is covered in sawdust and it's anybody's guess whether it's a design choice or leftover debris from construction. The lighting is dim enough to make everyone look reasonably attractive but not so dark that you end up canoodling with your own brother. I've always liked it here, not that I frequent bars very often. I'm more of a pajamas-by-eight-and-bed-by-ten person.

Nick slides a tower of glasses across the bar to me. "Is that enough?"

"Two more."

While we wait, I notice Charlie's gaze lower to my chest, which seems pretty brazen until he asks, "Do you own any item of clothing that isn't trademarked?"

I pretend to think. "Nope. Even my underwear is DC."

He blinks. "Washington?"

"The comics. Wonder Woman."

"Right."

"They had a thong version, but I think Diana Prince would opt for full coverage, don't you?"

He shifts awkwardly. "Can we stop talking about your underwear now?"

"You brought it up."

"I was talking about your T-shirt."

I glance down at the Tree of Gondor design. "This one is lucky. I wore it last year on trivia night and my team won."

"In that case, I'll plant myself right next to you."

I smirk. "It's trivia, not a lawsuit."

"I already told you, I'm not a litigator."

"Maybe you should've been. Seems like winning is important to you."

He doesn't answer. We're greeted by cheers when we deliver the pitchers to our section.

"If I'd have known beer could garner such a positive

response, I would've had a keg delivered to the camp," Charlie says.

Gloria lifts her chin. "We don't negotiate with blackmailers."

"Technically it's bribery," Charlie says.

"Oh, in that case, you should have."

"There's still time," Angela quips. She pulls a pitcher closer to her and unwraps a straw. "What's everybody else having?"

Angela doesn't need Charlie's keg. I'm convinced she stores bottles of alcohol under the floorboards of her cabin. She would've made an excellent smuggler during Prohibition.

We divide into teams and Charlie makes good on his promise to stay close to me. He slides into the booth and immediately pats the empty seat beside him. For some reason, it doesn't occur to me to object, so I dutifully slide in beside him. Ben and Laura join us.

We agree to call ourselves Balrog's Revenge. Correction: we all agree except Charlie, who abstains because he doesn't know what a balrog is.

Laura covers her face. "I have secondhand embarrassment right now."

"What happened to the judgment-free zone?" Charlie asks, although he doesn't actually seem bothered.

"This is a field trip," Laura replies. "We're free to be as judgy as we want until we get back to the campground."

"In that case, I'd like to comment on the decor." He points to a life preserver affixed to the wall. "Why is there a nautical theme in a mountain bar?"

"Oh, that's for emergencies. There's a pond out back. Once in a while someone drinks too much and wanders into the water."

"That seems like a lawsuit waiting to happen."

"Only you would see opportunity in someone else's tragedy," Laura says.

"Except it won't end in tragedy because your man Nick thought ahead." He points again to the life preserver.

"There's also a canoe outside," I add, "although once in a while someone takes it out on the water when they probably shouldn't."

Charlie stares at me. "I'm starting to think there might be an issue with overserving customers in this establishment."

"You don't come here unless you intend to be overserved," Laura tells him. "Nickers is best observed through the lens of beer goggles."

"Yes," Charlie says slowly. "I'm beginning to get that impression."

I elbow him in the ribs. "I happen to be very fond of this place. You might as well settle in because you'll be spending the next few hours inhaling the secondhand smoke."

"There's no avoiding the smoke," Laura agrees. "It's like an alien species. You could hold your breath all night and it would still find a way to seep into your pores."

"Gee, this place gets more appealing by the minute. Anything I should know about the restroom?"

I cringe. "Oh, I'd recommend going outside."

My suggestion amuses him. "That pleasant, huh?"

"The smoke gets everywhere, but so does the sawdust." I rock in my seat. "Trust me. It's very uncomfortable."

"I'll take it under advisement."

"Welcome back, campers," a booming voice says.

I look up as Manny places a Sharpie and paper in the middle of the neighboring table. "There you are. How's it going?"

"Excellent. I'm glad to see you here. Every year I worry it'll be the last." Manny drops paper and a Sharpie on our table. I snatch the purple pen before Charlie gets his hands on it. I'm the captain of this ship.

"I have no intention of letting that happen," I say. "Can't say the same for this guy." I bump Charlie with my elbow.

"At what point will you decide that I'm on the level?"

"At the point where you no longer represent Cricket's archnemesis," Laura answers.

The ends of Charlie's mouth hitch up in amusement. "Riggieri is your archnemesis? Why didn't you say so? I wouldn't have passed along his proposal if I'd realized you were mortal enemies."

My face feels flushed. "Laura is exaggerating. I don't have any enemies. I love people."

"Clearly. That must be why you isolate for ten months," Charlie quips. "All that love for everybody."

"Not Patrick," Laura says. "There's no love lost there."

If there is a god, the crack in the booth would open up right now and swallow me whole.

Ben fills Laura's half-empty glass. "Here you go, Laura. Something to keep your mouth busy."

"Who's Patrick?" Charlie asks.

Before anyone can answer, Manny officially kicks off trivia night. Inwardly, I'm relieved. I was having fun. No need to throw a rotten apple into the bunch and spoil it.

Manny is like the lovechild of a game show host and an auctioneer. He says many words in a short span of time and manages to sound like your biggest cheerleader, even if you're not convinced he remembers your name.

"First category of the evening is Influential Television Shows."

The announcement is followed by high fives and fist bumps. This group slays TV shows, which means the competition will be fierce.

Laura's gaze rests on Charlie. "Well, we know who the dead weight will be for this category," she mutters.

I try to look on the bright side. "Hey, if there's a sports category, we're golden."

She perks up. "Good point. Last year they had that run of questions about tennis, and nobody answered a single one correctly."

There are five questions in each category. We write down the answers after conferring with our teammates, and then Manny goes through them at the end of each round. The noise level drops by a few decibels because no one wants a neighboring table to overhear their proposed answers, unless you're deliberately trying to mislead your competitors, which is Hunter's style, so we know to tune him out.

"I've only seen one of these shows," Charlie comments, once we jot down the fifth answer.

"Which one?" I ask.

He taps *Bill Nye the Science Guy*.

"I wouldn't have pegged you for a science nerd."

"I'm not. My younger brother Michael is, though. He's the reason I ended up watching it."

"Did he become a scientist?" Laura asks.

"A surgeon."

Ben's eyebrows perform a dance of approval. "Your parents must be very proud."

Charlie hesitates. It's brief but I notice. "Yeah, of course," he says. "Three successful kids. What parents don't want that for their children?"

"What does your other sibling do?" Ben asks.

"She's a professional golfer."

Ben nods as he guides his glass back to his lips. "Your family gatherings must be so fascinating."

"That's one way of describing them." Charlie dabs his forehead with a cloth napkin. "Does this place have air conditioning? It's sweltering."

"Who wears long sleeves in summertime?" I shoot back.

"We're in the mountains. I expected the temperature to drop at night." He unbuttons his sleeves and pushes up the fabric to expose a pair of well-toned forearms. I don't often see muscles like that at camp. Most of the men are more interested in lifting their comic book collection than weights.

Unsurprisingly, all the teams nail the television category, so it's on to the next one. By now Charlie has polished off two beers in quick succession and I realize his khaki-clad thigh is pressed against mine. I can't decide whether it's deliberate on his part. If I move over an inch, half an ass cheek will be hanging off the seat. Then again, I kind of like the way it feels, being this close to him, not that I would admit it out loud. That's what my mother would've called an 'inside thought.'

Charlie surprises us by helping with two answers during the round on British Royals.

"Why, Charles Dickens Darwin the Fifth, I did not expect you to be the dark horse on that one."

His grin seems to be powered by beer and joyful satisfaction. "You can thank my mother. She's obsessed with the royal family."

"What has this generic draft beer done to you? Normally you have an excellent poker face, but right now you're very transparent."

He leans closer, his expression bordering on devilishly sexy. "Am I?"

I flick his forehead. "Yes."

He straightens. "Well, you have one of the worst poker faces I've ever seen. I can tell when you know the answer before you even open your mouth. It's written all over your face."

I don't take it as an insult. "Deception isn't one of my strengths."

"We lawyers have to play our cards close to the vest. It's part of the job."

"Well, not that you asked, but I prefer this Charlie, the one who wears his feelings on his face." I don't know what possesses me—probably the beer I finished—but I pick up the purple Sharpie and write across his forehead. To my delight, he laughs and calls me nuts.

The next category is announced—Flora and Fauna. I lock eyes with Ben and smile. He's a plant aficionado and Laura is an animal expert. This round should be a bloodbath.

As Manny fires off the first question, Charlie leans forward and scrutinizes my face to the point where I'm worried he's noticed a zit that hasn't surfaced yet.

"What is it, Mr. Thorpe? Does my face tell you I know the answer?"

He leans back, continuing to study me with an intensity that makes my head buzz, or maybe that's the alcohol.

"No," he finally says.

"Aha! You can't read my face." I jot down the answer.

"Just because you're confident doesn't mean you're right," Charlie whispers, and his mouth is so close to my earlobe that it sends an involuntary shiver through me.

"You seem chilly," Charlie says. "Maybe you should wear a long-sleeved shirt next time."

"You're hilarious." Then it's my turn to laugh when the answers are announced and mine is correct.

I raise my empty glass. "Victory never tasted so sweet."

He touches his forehead. "This washes off, right?"

"I'm sure it will … eventually." I lean forward so that my nose is close to his. He somehow manages to smell minty fresh in the midst of all this stale beer and smoke. "What are you feeling right now?"

His blue-green eyes meet mine. "Drunk."

"That's not a feeling,"

"I beg to differ. Have you ever suffered from bed spins?"

I pull back to regard him. "I'm talking about emotions, Chickie. How do you feel right now?"

He shrugs.

I sigh. "Angry? Sad? Disappointed?"

"None of those things."

"That's good at least."

Laura raps on the table between us. "Pay attention, you two. The final category is Geography."

I'm mildly disappointed. I was hoping for sports so we could make better use of Charlie.

Ben leans forward. "Remember, we only need three correct answers to win."

Laura grimaces. "I'll have to defer to the rest of you. I've always struggled with geography. The best I can do is the seven continents."

I look at Ben. "You know country flags, right?"

He nods. "And the oceans."

Charlie gives a dramatic clearing of his throat. "This might be my time to sparkle."

"In that case, I should've used Angela's marker. Theirs has glitter."

The first two questions stump us, but Charlie seems fairly confident in his answers, so we stick with them. He jots down answers to the remaining questions without hesitation, although his penmanship is dubious at this point.

"You're sure?" I ask.

He caps the Sharpie as a sleepy grin overtakes his face. "Care to wager?"

"Thanks, I'll pass."

Turns out Charlie was right about the first two questions. Unfortunately, so is Gloria, which means InGloria's Bastards are now tied with Balrog's Revenge. The pressure is on.

"The answer to number three is Czechoslovakia."

Charlie pounds his fists excitedly on the table, nearly knocking over his glass in the process, not that there's any beer left. He polished another one off during the round.

Gloria's team moans, which is a good sign.

Our answer to number 4 is also correct, which leaves one to go. We huddle together, waiting for the answer.

"The final answer is the Ganges river."

"We won!" I reach over to hug Ben, but he's already hugging Laura. I turn and slap hands with Charlie instead.

"Of course we won. I'm a Thorpe. It's in my DNA." He looks around the room with droopy eyes. "What do we win anyway?"

Manny drops a book of coupons on the table. "Great game, everybody. See you next year."

Charlie stares at the coupon book. "This isn't a trophy."

"No, this is better. They're all local establishments. I'm sure they would appreciate the business."

He picks up the book and thumbs through it. "What's a Peter Pan Pizza? Do they sprinkle it with fairy dust?"

"Pixie dust," I correct him. "Tinker Bell is a pixie."

"Can I see?" Laura asks. He slides the coupon book across the table to her.

"Will it help if I buy you a beer?" I ask.

"I've probably had enough of those for one night. It's a long walk back to my cabin from the parking lot. Wouldn't want to fall in the lake on my way there."

We split into Ubers, and Charlie and I end up alone in the backseat of a Volkswagen Beetle, which seems even more compact when your fellow passenger is the size of a lumberjack. I was sure he only had four limbs until this moment. Now I'm questioning everything I thought I knew about his bodily structure.

"How do you know so much about geography?" I ask. I'm pressed up against him in a way that makes conversation awkward yet necessary.

"I was in the geography bee in high school. Made it to the state championships."

"That's impressive."

"I guess it would've been, if that hadn't been the year my brother won an international science and engineering competition." He scratches his cheek. "Funny, I haven't thought about that in years."

"You should invite your brother here next year. Sounds like he might fit in."

Charlie blows a drunken raspberry. "Michael is too busy being an uptight prick to enjoy robot dog races."

"Well, congratulations on a well-deserved win. We wouldn't have won without you."

The driver drops us off in the parking lot. Charlie staggers toward the woods and I manage to redirect him toward the cabins instead.

"This was a fun night, Cricket. I'm glad you talked me into it." He hesitates. "How'd you get the name Cricket anyway? Were you into insects as a kid? Or maybe a big fan of Jiminy Cricket?"

"No. I was so quiet, my family didn't realize when I'd spoken. My dad would ask me a question and think I didn't answer him." I pause for effect. "Crickets."

He shakes his head. "Does not compute."

"What do you mean?"

"Your dad must've had a hearing problem because I can hear you fine." His arm makes a sweeping gesture, nearly catching me in the ribs in the process. "You're confident. You're whip-smart. And you're the best kind of loud."

"You're right."

"I know I am."

"Not about me. I mean that you're definitely drunk."

"I can be drunk and still be right about *you*." He boops my nose. "Some people say I'm more honest when I drink. Loose inhibitions and all that."

"Who are some people?"

"My brother and sister. They have categories for me when I'm drunk. I'm either Sleepy Charlie or Chatty Charlie."

"Which one are you now?"

He rubs his head. "Kinda both."

"Good thing we're getting you to bed then. You can chat to Chucky until you fall asleep."

"Or I could chat to you." He sways toward me, walking with loose limbs like the Scarecrow in *The Wizard of the Oz*. "I like talking to you."

I nudge him upright. "What do you like about it?"

135

"It's easy-breezy. We have a connection." He casts a sidelong glance at me. "Do I sound crazy?"

"You sound like you've had one too many beers." I steer him toward the door of his cabin. "I agree with you, though. It's been a fun night, Charlie Thorpe. Sleep it off and I'll see you tomorrow."

"Not if I see you first." He salutes me and walks straight into the closed door of his cabin.

I hold in my laughter until I'm sure he's unharmed, then I snort-laugh all the way to my cabin.

Chapter Nine

CHARLIE

I wake up the next morning feeling more hungover than I would've preferred. I'm not much of a drinker. One beer at a work event and I'm ready to head home. And if it weren't for the corporate culture, I'd skip the event altogether. It's not like I enjoy them. They're perfunctory, like most things in my life. As much as I tried to escape the life my parents planned for me, somehow I ended up in a similar situation. Same archipelago, different island.

Except last night. Last night was arguably a work event, but I'd been in no rush to leave. Why didn't the law firm host trivia nights? I tried to imagine my department in a dive bar guessing answers to inane questions. Matt would be competitive, but his knowledge would be limited to sports, cars, and world wars. Zach would complain that another team cheated and grovel for points. Abby would get drunk and overshare about her sex life, or lack thereof. Joel would take the game too seriously and suck all the fun out of the room. And they'd all be sore losers.

The memory of Cricket's laughter rings in my head. It was a wicked, bawdy laugh that ought to belong to a gangster's moll and not the bespectacled woman in the Tree of Mordor or Gondor or one of the 'dors T-shirt who was seated beside me all evening.

With great effort, I swing my legs out of bed. That's when I see two missed calls and a message from Jeannie.

Meeting at 10. Get here.

My heart drops to the floor. What meeting? I pick up the phone and call my assistant.

"I'm sorry. It's a last-minute change to the schedule." She's speaking in a hushed tone. "I think this is Matt's doing."

The bastard is trying to sabotage me. "What's the meeting about?"

"Call me from the road and I'll fill you in, but you should get moving or you'll miss it, which I'm sure is his plan. Did you pack a suit? If not, I've got the one I took to the dry cleaners for you."

"I've got one, but thanks, Jeannie. You're the best."

"From your lips to payroll's ears."

I check the time. I'll have to skip the shower, or I won't make it. I'll be pushing the clock as it is. I'd have to skip breakfast, too, and miss out on Bernie's gluten-free chocolate chip pancakes. Bummer. I would've inhaled the hell out of those.

After wearing casual clothes all week, my suit feels stiff and uncomfortable. I spend the next hour with my foot on the gas, listening to Jeannie's rundown of events. The firm's annual meeting with LandStar got bumped up to this week. The only reason Jeannie knows about it is because she's good friends with Joel's assistant.

I don't know how he managed it, but this schedule change has Matt's fingerprints all over it. It doesn't surprise me that he would try to find another way to take out the competition. He's worried I'll secure the LandStar deal, so he has to undermine me another way. Joke's on him because I currently don't see a way of making my client happy. All his shady tactics will have been for nothing.

Jeannie glances up from her computer screen with a bright smile when I arrive. "Good morning, Charlie. Glad to hear it."

I give her a quizzical look. "Glad to hear what?"

"That you're happy."

"Am I?"

She points to my face. "They say you can tell when a lawyer's lying when his lips are moving, but they don't say anything about his forehead."

Now I'm thoroughly confused. "I have no clue what you're talking about."

"In that case, you might want to take a look in a mirror. Your meeting starts in five minutes, by the way. I don't recommend walking in like that."

I hurry to my office and shut the door, whipping out my phone for the camera. Across my forehead in bright purple marker is a single word.

Happy.

It takes a second for the memory of last night to snap into focus. A purple Sharpie. A mischievous gleam in Cricket's eye. I'd been too drunk to remember it by the time I reached the cabin. The ink was apparently strong enough to withstand good old-fashioned soap and water.

Shit.

I rub the ink, which I know is a futile gesture, but I have to try. No way can I walk into the meeting looking like I slept in a frat house.

Jeannie appears at my door holding a bottle of nail polish remover and a cotton ball.

"You're a lifesaver."

"Whatever you did last night, you should do it more often."

"Really? My body feels like I walked through a cheese grater."

"Well, your spirit says you're walking on air."

"Thanks, Jeannie. I needed the pep talk." Especially before entering the lion's den.

"It wasn't a pep talk," she calls after me, but I am already gone.

The meeting is dull but necessary. The saving grace is the selection of bagels and pastries that save me from hunger pains. I smear cream cheese on a bagel and down two cups of coffee to keep myself awake, both from the hangover and the meeting itself.

Riggieri nods in my direction, and I can tell he's desperate to jump me for an update the second the meeting is adjourned. Matt knows I have nothing to offer the client, which is why he somehow managed to orchestrate this early reunion. Lyman shouldn't even be in attendance, let alone allowed to influence a change in the schedule. If I had a purple Sharpie, I'd write 'pissed' across my forehead this time.

Relief floods my system when the meeting comes to its merciful conclusion. As expected, Riggieri and Joel intercept me before I can exit the conference room.

"Hey, Thorpe. How's geek week?" Joel asks. "Mr. Riggieri mentioned before the meeting that he hopes you brought a signed contract with you today."

"I'm working on it, sir."

Riggieri doesn't bother to disguise his disappointment. "Well, what have you found so far? There's got to be something damning."

"Everything appears in order so far, but there's a filing cabinet I haven't been through." It isn't a lie. Cricket's office only appears to hold one filing cabinet and I haven't combed through it.

"Then what are you waiting for? Get back up there and find my leverage, kid."

Joel snorts his derision. "Who are all these adults with enough time on their hands to attend summer camp, am I right?"

But Riggieri is no longer interested in our conversation. He exits the conference room without another word.

I answer Joel anyway. "They're a broad mix of people. Teachers, retirees, a dog groomer, a caretaker. Some of them save up all their vacation days so they can splurge them on these two weeks at camp. These people are committed."

Joel eyes me carefully. "Watch it, Thorpe. You sound like you're drinking the Kool-Aid."

"They actually serve Kool-Aid in the cafeteria. This week's flavor is cherry."

Joel shakes his head. "As long as you lock down that deal, you can drink Tang for all I care."

"I love Tang. My parents used to give it to us when we were kids. They were hoping one of us would become an astronaut."

He claps me on the back. "Instead, they got a future partner at Melvin, O'Reilly, and Gaines, quite possibly the youngest in our history."

"Shoot for the moon and you'll still end up among the stars," I say, trying to match his level of enthusiasm.

"You up for a round of golf on Saturday? I've got a tee time with Brandon and Lawrence at nine. Could use a fourth."

"I'd love to, but camp doesn't end until Sunday. It

wouldn't look good to the client if I skipped a full day of sleuthing to go golfing."

Joel aims a finger gun at me. "And that level of commitment is why you're going to be our next partner." He grabs a bagel on his way out.

A long shadow passes over me as I reach my office.

"Hey, Matt."

"Didn't think you'd make it, Chucky."

"I know." I bite into my bagel and chew. "Good thing my assistant likes me."

"You look like hell, and you smell even worse."

"It's called fun, Matt. You should try it sometime." I bump his arm aside and enter my office. I figure while I'm here, I may as well catch up on emails and other messages. I spend the next hour working until I'm sure there's nothing else that requires my immediate attention.

The landline buzzes and Jeannie's voice cuts through the quiet. "Your mother's on the line. Should I take a message?"

I pick up the phone. "Hi, Mom."

"There you are. I've called you a couple times, but you haven't answered."

"I'm working offsite for a client. Cell service isn't great."

"I hope this client is the one that makes you partner. Your brother won an award. Did he tell you?"

"No. I haven't spoken to him recently."

"You should ask him about it," she says. "Very prestigious." And then she proceeds to tell me every detail known to man about the award. I put her on speaker and manage to change out of my suit and back into camp clothes before she finishes.

"I'm glad for him." I mean it. Michael is smart and

ambitious. My parents may pit us against each other, but that doesn't mean I can't be happy for his achievements.

"When can we expect to announce the happy news about your partnership? The anniversary party?"

"It's out of my hands, Mom. You know that."

"Well, it would be nice to make some sort of announcement. It won't be fair to you if we're extolling your brother and sister's virtues and leaving you out. What will people think?"

I already know all of this has more to do with impressing their peers than my well-being, but she could at least try to hide it better.

"I'll be at the party, that's as much as I can promise you. Listen, Mom, it was nice catching up, but I need to go."

Jeannie is in the doorway when I hang up. "Does that woman ever tell you she loves you?"

"In her own way."

Jeannie's expression conveys that she knows I'm full of shit but is too polite to say so. She has a maternal quality that I appreciate. She doesn't try to act as a stand-in for my mother though. More like a no-nonsense aunt who would throat-punch a pack of hyenas to protect me.

"Tell me about camp."

"What do you want to know?"

"I was checking out the website. It actually looks fun."

"I mean, it isn't the kind of place I would've chosen for myself, but it has a certain appeal."

"Are there any Trekkies there?"

"Not that I know of, but maybe I haven't met them yet."
I tell her about the Star-Warlord and Chewy.

Her face lights up. "Do you have a photo?"

"No, but I can send you one."

"Please. It'll make my day." She leans the side of her

head against the doorjamb. "I'm a little jealous. I wish they would've sent me with you. Camp sounds like a dream. Do you roast marshmallows at night and sing songs?"

"There's a bonfire and apparently singing in the shower. There's karaoke too."

Jeannie claps her hands. "What will you sing?"

"Nothing. I'll wear my earbuds and clap politely."

She narrows her eyes. "That's not very community-minded of you."

"I'm not very community minded."

"Nonsense. I watch you buy Girl Scout cookies every year."

"Because their cookies are delicious."

"You can get delicious gourmet cookies from the firm cafeteria for free any day you want. You go out of your way to support the Philadelphia troop and buy cookies from them specifically."

I look up and realize Jeannie is staring at me. "What?"

"That's the third time you've checked your watch since we started talking. Is there another appointment I should know about?"

"No, I'm wondering whether I'll make it back to camp in time for combat archery. They've been hyping it up so much, I'd hate to miss out."

"If you leave now, you should bypass the worst of the traffic."

My gaze lingers on my desk. "What about Matt?"

"That piece of garbage in human form? Don't worry about him. He's not the one at camp. You are. Go back and shoot some arrows or whatever combat archery involves."

I crack a grateful smile. "I'll let you know when I find out."

. . .

The drive back to camp is a *Mad Max: Thunderdome* exercise and I can't wait to park my car and leave traffic behind for another week. It takes an extra ten minutes to get here, and my body feels every second of it. As soon as I exit the vehicle and hear the birdsong, my muscles relax.

My phone pings with a message from Elizabeth. There's no text, only a photo of an empty pickle jar.

You owe me, I reply.

I'll replenish your supply when I get back from Florida.

Good luck, not that you need it.

Thanks, big bro. xxx

On the way to my cabin, I cross paths with Ben. "Hey, Charlie. You're headed in the wrong direction. The big game is this way." He hooks a thumb over his shoulder.

"I just got back from a long drive. I should probably hit the bathroom before I head out to the field. Sounds like it'll be a long afternoon."

He slaps an arm across my shoulders. "Listen here, young man. If this seventy-five-year-old prostate can handle a couple hours, so can yours." Before I can object, he steers me toward the field. "You're gonna love this event. Combat archery is one of my favorites."

"What do you like about it?"

"It's dodgeball, paintball, and archery rolled into one. What's not to like?"

The teams are in the process of being formed when we arrive at the battlefield. I'm the last to join Adam's team. Cricket manages to look both sporty and sexy in a white tank top and jean shorts. The white frames of her glasses are shaped like hearts.

We all don protective face masks, including Adam, who swaps his helmet. The bows are real, but the arrows have foam tips. Nothing sharp.

Cricket holds up a whistle as she addresses the gathered players. "When I blow this, you run."

I survey the field. "Run where?"

"It's like *Hunger Games*."

I stare at her blankly.

Frustrated, she smacks her forehead. "The arrows are in a pile in the center of the field, and you all run for them at once."

"This is where the dodgeball part comes in," Ben explains. "The players run to grab as many arrows as they can, but you run the risk of being shot by someone faster than you."

"So you want to grab your weapons and then seek coverage," Hunter adds. "But if I catch your arrow, which I probably will because I excel at this game, then I can choose to bring an eliminated teammate back into the game."

"Last player standing's team wins," Ben says.

It quickly becomes clear that Hunter and Olivia are the team to beat. Hunter is faster than I anticipate; I can tell he has experience aiming and shooting. I try not to think about what's normally at the other end of his sharp eye.

Wendy and Esther are eliminated first. I'm fairly certain they get hit on purpose, and my suspicions are confirmed when they disappear. I hear Cricket say something about plushies.

I hit Bradley next, and he paces the sidelines calling for Hunter and Olivia to catch an arrow so he can reenter the game.

It doesn't happen.

Hunter shoots both Gloria and Angela. Olivia shoots her grandfather in an epic showdown.

Eventually only four of us are left. A golden opportunity presents itself when Hunter stumbles over a tree root and drops his arrow. I don't have a clean shot, but Adam does.

"Come on, Adam!"

The warlord lets his arrow fly. It sails over Hunter's head, giving our opponent time to reclaim his weapon.

I cry out in exasperation. "That was a straight shot! How could you miss?" The moment the words leave my mouth, I regret them. Adam crumples like I've humiliated him in the presence of Yoda *and* Luke Skywalker. "I'm sorry, buddy," I say quickly. "Heat of the moment. I didn't mean it."

"These games are only for fun," Cricket reminds me gently. "The winners are those who play."

And suddenly I understand the point of participation trophies. If you know you have zero chance of ever winning, why would you ever try? You'd sit out every game and miss the chance to enjoy yourself for the sake of it. Miss the chance to bond with your teammates and, sometimes, even your competitors.

My father's skin would crawl if he could hear my thoughts right now. In his mind, participation trophies are the equivalent of athletic pacifiers. If you're not good enough to win, you deserve to leave empty-handed.

Needless to say, my dad is a dick, and for a brief moment, I was too.

The game continues with everyone in good spirits. My arrow hits Hunter behind the knee. He goes down, arms and legs splayed like a starfish. Olivia seizes the moment and uses Hunter's fallen body as a springboard. She leaps into the air with not one but two arrows. She tries to take us out in quick succession, first Adam, then me, but I loose another arrow at the last second. Our arrows collide in midair. We both race forward to grab our respective weapons and throw them at each other. My arrow makes contact, hitting Olivia's thigh. Hers pegs me in the forehead. It all happens so fast, I'm not clear on which one hit first.

I drop to my knees, simultaneously laughing and gasping for air. "Did I win?"

"Who cares?" Ben says, not unkindly.

I peer up at him. "Isn't that the point?"

"No, kid. The point is to have a grand old time, which we did." He offers me a hand and helps me to my feet. I'm careful not to grip him too tightly. He's built like a reed. One overzealous tug and he'd be sprawled on top of me.

"It's been a long time since anyone's referred to me as a kid."

"You're what? Thirty?"

"Thirty-five."

He examines my face. "Once you hit the ages of twenty-five to sixty-five, I find it hard to tell. As far as I'm concerned, anybody under the age of forty is a kid."

I chuckle. "That's a long childhood."

"Meh. We could all use a longer childhood, don't you think? I started working my first job when I was fourteen and didn't stop until last year. That's a lot of hours devoted to work."

"Do you regret it?"

He shrugs. "How can I? Didn't have a choice. If I wanted to earn a living, enough to pay bills and take a vacation once a year, then I had to dig in." He draws a deep breath. "And now I get to spend part of the summer here every year until I die. Couldn't imagine a better place to cap the end of my days."

Threads of guilt form a knot in my stomach. "You love it here that much?"

"How can you not? As far as I'm concerned, this place is paradise on Earth."

Cricket blows the whistle. "Dinnertime!"

Everyone plows ahead like the stampeding dinosaurs in *Jurassic Park.* Angela pushes through us. "Excuse me. Future wife coming through." She surges ahead, a heat-seeking missile that has identified an unknown target.

When I reach the cafeteria, Cricket is lingering outside. "Did you have fun?"

"I did. It was more exercise than I expected." I gesture to my sweaty skin. "Hence the well-moisturized body."

"I'm glad you enjoyed it. Every year I think we'll try something new, but the campers threaten to revolt."

"Wouldn't want that, now that I've seen them on a battlefield."

She gives my arm a gentle smack. "Hey, before I forget. I just want to say that I appreciated your apology to Adam earlier."

I squirm a little, uncomfortable that she's opted to draw attention to my brief moment of assholery instead of sweeping it under the proverbial rug.

She appears to notice my discomfort. "Did I say something wrong?" Her face relaxes. "Oh."

Her 'oh' grabs me by the balls. "What?"

"You're embarrassed that I mentioned it."

She's right. I am.

Her hand flutters to her chest. "I'm sorry. I wasn't trying to make a big deal out of it."

I stuff my hands into the pockets of my shorts. "It's okay. I'm not used to it, that's all. People usually only comment when I do something wrong."

"That's terrible."

I shrug. "My parents were all about the stick and not the carrot. I can't say my law firm is much different."

"It makes sense if that's how you grew up, that's what you'd gravitate to. It became your comfort zone. It probably feels strange when somebody compliments you."

"Or I wonder what they want from me."

She cocks her head. "Is that what you thought about me? That I only said it because I have an ulterior motive?"

"No," I say in a tone of finality. "Not you. Giving out compliments seems natural for you. I'm more like a dragon. I hoard them like rare treasure."

"It costs nothing to be kind," she says matter-of-factly.

"Then why do people find it so difficult?"

"Because they view it as a sacrifice instead of an offering."

I frown. "Is that a line from a movie? Because if it isn't, it should be."

She breaks into an engaging smile. "See, Charlie? Seems like you're capable of doling out compliments after all. Oh hey, don't forget to bring something for swag swap later," she calls after me, as I enter the cafeteria in search of Bernie's famous chili with a side of cornbread.

I spin around. "What's swag swap?"

"Everybody brings an item they're willing to exchange for something else."

"We trade our possessions?"

"You give something a new lease on life by giving it a new home."

"Or you could toss it if you don't want it anymore."

She shrugs. "One person's trash is a trash panda's treasure."

"That's not how the saying goes."

"Just bring a belonging you're ready to part with, Charlie. Don't overthink it."

Chapter Ten

CHARLIE

I overthink it.

I drag every one of my limited belongings into the middle of the cabin and debate the pros and cons of trading each and every one, including my laptop, which is ridiculous because it's a firm-owned device loaded with confidential files, but that's how seriously I decide to take swag swap.

In the end, I tuck Chucky under my arm and carry the doll to the lakeside picnic area where the activity is set to take place.

Cricket is already there, barking orders and looking both adorable and sexy in a white sundress. This is the first time I've seen her in anything without a licensed character or a logo. The white fabric accentuates her natural tan. She looks ethereal. A delicate angel. If I observe her long enough, I imagine she'll sprout gossamer wings.

I know it's an illusion. If there's one thing I've already learned about Cricket, it's that she is far from delicate.

The sun slips below the horizon, casting us all in shadow, but Cricket is prepared. She hoists a giant flashlight on the table and switches it on. Buffy immediately appears in the halo of light, wings spread, prompting a burst of laughter from Adam.

"Quick," he says with false gravitas. "Call the Mayor of Gotham City. It's the Bat Signal."

"For the last time, Buffy isn't a bat." The sugar glider zips to Gloria to rest on her shoulder. "She doesn't like bright lights." Gloria coaxes the timid animal into her pocket and gives the exterior a gentle pat. I'm amazed how attuned she is to her companion. I'm not sure I have the capacity. Whatever her issues with her mother are, Gloria managed to pick up a few enviable traits.

"Who would like to go first?" Cricket asks.

Olivia raises her hand. "I will." She produces a plushie of a character I don't recognize and sets it in the center of the table.

"Look, it's my favorite color," Angela declares. "Penile-erection purple."

Ben claps his hands over Olivia's ears. "Must you?" he hisses at her.

Angela tips up her chin. "It's basic biology, Benjamin. I thought you were guiding your granddaughter toward a career in STEM."

Ben grows flustered. "You and I have very different ideas about what constitutes science."

"But my ideas are far more fun," she replies with a sultry wink.

Olivia shakes off her grandfather's hands and addresses the group. "I've outgrown this pony, so she's up for grabs."

"Bullshit," Angela interjects. "I can tell a lie when I hear one."

"You love that doll," Ben agrees.

Olivia's face scrunches up and I can almost feel the kid's discomfort, which triggers my own.

"I remember when your parents bought her for you. You named her Glowy and brought her everywhere," Ben continued.

"Pony plushies are for babies," Olivia insists. "I don't need her anymore."

"But just because you don't need something anymore doesn't mean you can't want it," Angela tells her. "I don't need another pair of diamond studs, but it doesn't stop me from wanting them."

Olivia looks her grandfather dead in the eye. "Is this swag swap or isn't it?"

Cricket leans over to Ben and whispers, "She's trying to let something go, Ben."

The older man's shoulders slacken in response.

"I think it's obvious who should adopt her." Angela plucks the plushie from the table and passes it to Ben.

Olivia nods her approval. "She'll be in good hands."

"And you can visit her whenever you like," Ben says, clutching the toy to his chest. I'm pretty sure there are happy tears glistening in his eyes.

As a lawyer, I was taught that you know it's a good deal when both parties leave the bargaining table feeling slightly disappointed. This moment seems to contradict that lesson. From where I'm standing, both Olivia and Ben appear pleased by the outcome.

Ben's swap is next, to make room for the penile-purple pony in his life. He contributes a coin commemorating the Apollo 11 moonwalk that a couple people argue over until they decide to flip for it, which seems apt.

Cricket donates a Mumford & Sons T-shirt that looks far too big for her. Nobody queries the size differential. I suspect they know the original owner's identity and have a silent pact not to mention his name. Anger flares inside me that some guy could hurt someone like Cricket, but then I remember I'm here to do exactly that. I have no right to cast stones at the Mumford fan. He may have broken her heart, but if I achieve my objective, it will break her spirit. Somehow that seems even worse.

Gloria swivels toward her neighbor. "What about you, Angela?"

Angela sets a silver flask on the picnic table.

"Is that monogrammed?" Laura asks.

"It says 'No You Can't Have A Sip.' My ex gave it to me for my birthday. He liked to tease me for refusing to share drinks."

Bradley releases a reverberating snort. "I'm surprised you don't share fluids, Angela. Seems right up your alley."

She shoots dagger eyes at him before turning back to the rest of us. "Anyhow, I've been carrying it around for years, but I'm ready to let it go."

Stefan twists off the lid and sniffs inside. "Smells clean. When's the last time you used it?"

"I never drank from it, dear. I only carried it around because Paul gave it to me." Her shoulders lift and fall as she expels a deep breath. "But I found out he got married last month, so I figure I might as well lighten my load."

Her admission shifts something inside me. Angela has been carting around that flask as a symbol of hope. Now it's only the memory of unrequited love.

"I don't blame you for trading it," Gloria says. "You deserve better than Paul. He's the one who cheated on you with your own co-worker, isn't he?"

"Is that who he married?" Laura asks.

The lines of Angela's angular face soften. "No, this is a

new woman, and she won't be the last, I'm sure. A tiger doesn't change his stripes." Angela sounds a little sad when she says this, and I get the sense that she believed Paul might have changed his stripes for her.

"People only change if they want to," Cricket says. "Nobody can force them into it." It's the first time she's spoken in a while, and I wonder if there's a reason for her silence.

Gloria surveys the group. "I'd like the flask, unless somebody else is desperate for it." She waits a beat and then says, "And I have this to offer." She tosses a comic book on the table. "I got this at New York Comic-Con."

Cricket rubs her friend's shoulder in a supportive gesture. "Proud of you, G."

Gloria allows herself a tiny smile. "Letting go isn't easy."

The comic book seems innocuous enough. "I didn't know there were Buffy comics."

"That's because you're not a true fan," Laura remarks, which results in a hissing sound from a couple of the others.

"We don't pop-culture shame in this family," Cricket reminds her. "Everyone has their own level of interest and investment."

Laura's arms snap into a folded position. "That wasn't Adam's attitude when I told him I don't get the love for Grogu."

"Grogu is Baby Yoda," Cricket whispers to me, anticipating my ignorance.

"Din Grogu must be protected at all costs," Adam shoots back.

"If that's your position, then you're in the wrong mask," Laura says. "You ought to be wearing a Mandalorian mask."

To my utter shock, Adam rips off the black helmet. "You're right. I have one in my cabin. I'll get it." Adam's hair is matted to his head thanks to excess sweat. I suspect he may have showered with the helmet on.

"You carry a spare?" I ask.

"The Mandalorian is my second favorite," Adam explains, pulling out his phone. "I have a ranked list if you'd like to see it."

Cricket nudges his phone away. "Your rankings are special to you, remember? For your eyes only."

I get the distinct impression they've had this conversation before. As usual, Cricket impresses me with the kind and careful way she redirects Adam. The guy would've had no hope of developing his passion in my household. My parents would've shamed him until he buried his interests in a place too deep to access.

Finally, it's my turn. I swipe Chucky off the ground where he's been concealed by darkness and place him directly in the spotlight.

Olivia pinches her grandfather's sleeve. "Please don't take Chucky. I don't want him in our cabin."

Ben pats her hand. "I have no intention of depriving the young man of Chucky's company."

"Even if someone else takes him," Angela chimes in with a knowing smile, "I have a feeling he'll end up right back in Charlie's cabin."

Cricket can't quite conceal her shit-eating grin. "I think Chucky is yours for the duration. Sorry about that."

"You can only swap something that belongs to you," Gloria says. "Otherwise, it's cheating."

"Well, we can't have that." I may have many flaws, but being a cheater isn't one of them. As I pat my pockets in search of another option, an idea flares. I open my wallet and produce a baseball card, slapping it on the table next to Chucky.

Bradley whistles. "Cal Ripken Jr. Absolute legend."

Stefan picks up the card and studies it. "Is it worth money?"

"I imagine so."

"Then why would you trade it?"

"It isn't worth a fortune, and the sentimental value... It doesn't have any, not anymore."

"What's the story with this?" Stefan asks, flicking the card.

"Does there have to be a story?" I lob back.

"You said it had sentimental value, but now it doesn't," Gloria jumps in. "That implies a story."

"Are we here to swap possessions or stories?" I ask.

Cricket catches my eye. "Both."

As much as I want to point out the lack of story surrounding the Mumford T-shirt, I'd rather not press Cricket's buttons—not about that anyway. I'm here to be cunning, not cruel.

"We've all shared," Laura says. "It's your turn, Charlie." Her statement is followed by heads bobbing in unison.

How did I get myself into this? Oh right. In a desperate attempt to earn my parents' love and approval, I volunteered for this emotional torture. Lesson learned.

Another look at the card stirs up uncomfortable memories. "I played baseball when I was a kid."

"Were you any good?" Stefan asks.

"Of course he was," Angela replies. "Look at those arms." She reaches toward my bicep, but Gloria smacks her hand aside.

"I was, which was unfortunate because that meant I was there to win, not to play."

"Isn't that the point of a baseball game?" Angela asks. "One team wins. Gets a trophy and a Super Bowl ring."

"That's football," Olivia says in a stage whisper.

Angela waves a hand airily. "Who cares? They're all men in tight pants as far as I'm concerned." She offers a flirtatious smile. "I'm picturing your butt in tight pants right now."

I make a noise at the back of my throat and continue, "My father expected me to be the next Cal Ripken Jr., hence the card. I carried it around like a talisman."

"You were trying to manifest that player's success," Laura says.

"Something like that, except at a certain point, I realized I didn't want it. Too much pressure and very little enjoyment, so I gave up baseball."

"But not the card," Ben says gently. "You were holding on to something."

"Yeah. The memory of my father's support, but it wasn't real support. It was only a projection of his own needs. There's no reason to cling to something firmly embedded in the fantasy realm."

The returned Mandalorian taps his new helmet. "Nothing wrong with the fantasy realm."

"My attachment to the card had no basis in reality, and it no longer has the meaning I gave to it." I hesitate for a split second. "But I'm ready to let it go now."

Somewhere in the background, Idina Menzel belts out the famous refrain from *Frozen*. One sharp look from Cricket and the music cuts off.

Slowly, John reaches toward the card as though I might change my mind. He gives me another look for confirmation, and I nod.

"Thank you," he says, admiring the way the foil hits the light. "I'll give it a new meaning now."

"You can sell it if you want. Don't feel like you have to keep it."

"No way. I'm not that hard up, and I always keep the mementos from camp. I have a shelf in my collectibles room where I display them so every time I pass by, I think of this place and my friends here."

"I have mine encased in glass," Ben admits. "I couldn't fit last year's though. Too big." He looks at me. "I got a Gandalf-inspired walking stick."

"Sounds awesome," I tell him.

Cricket slaps her hands against her thighs. "Welp, looks like we're finished. Thank you for another successful swag swap, everybody. You never disappoint."

"Because we all have great taste," Angela says.

I reclaim Chucky and make a beeline for my cabin. I expected people to unload shit they didn't want. What I didn't expect was for swag swap to become so personal. In my world, negotiations and deals are numbers-driven. Emotion and sentiment don't factor into the decision-making. I can see why LandStar has hit a snag in its attempt to acquire Cricket's property. Riggieri is wholly focused on numbers whereas Cricket is wholly focused on emotions. I'm more of a numbers guy myself, although I hate to think I'm anything like Riggieri.

I hear the quickening of footsteps behind me and crane my neck to see Cricket hurrying to catch up. "Hey," she says.

"Did I forget something?"

She gestures to Chucky. "Not the most important thing." When I don't laugh, she continues, "I wanted to tell you that I'm proud of you, of the way you participated tonight."

"Everybody participated. It would've been strange to sit this one out."

"I know, but you shared. You really shared. I'm glad."

I feel a tightening in my chest. "Cool. Well, I'm nothing if not a joiner."

"I'm sorry you didn't get to take anything. The numbers aren't always even."

"I don't mind." I notice the Buffy comic book in her hand and gesture to it. "What's the story behind this one? Gloria didn't elaborate, but everyone seemed to understand."

Cricket seems to have forgotten about the comic she's clutching. "Oh, this? Gloria's dad bought it for her. She held on to it for years as proof that her dad knew her better than her mom. Her mother wouldn't have bought one for her. Comics are for children," she says, presumably mimicking Gloria's mother.

"Then why let it go?"

"Because her dad sucked worse than her mom. He left them when she was eight and only came around once a year or so. He'd bring a favorite toy or a beloved present and then ride off into the sunset again, leaving her mom to do all the real work of raising a child without support, which is the main reason Gloria is determined to support her mother now."

I got the gist. "She's releasing the fantasy version of her father."

Cricket nods. "Her dad died a few years ago, and she's held on to this idea that he would've been the better parent to her, but the truth is he had every opportunity to improve, he just didn't take it." She flicks the cover of the comic. "And even a stopped clock is right twice a day. This proved nothing."

I try to think of the gifts I received from my parents over the years. If I were to draft a list, I'd bet good money that most of the presents reflected my parents' needs and wants, or were designed to make them look good when the anecdotes were shared at cocktail parties or on social media.

"You all seem really close for people who only see each other once a year," I tell Cricket.

"We have a group chat. That helps." She falters. "We can invite you if you want, but I figure I've got you pegged."

My eyebrows lift. "Excuse me?"

Even in the shadows, I can see spots of crimson dapple her cheeks. "God, no. Not urban dictionary pegged. I mean that you don't seem like the type of guy who enjoys..."

"Pegging?" I offer.

She swallows hard. "Group chats." She rubs the back of her neck. "Good grief, I'm glad Olivia isn't here right now."

"Not to worry, I'm sure Angela will explain it to her at some point in descriptive detail."

The spots of crimson fade. "If you ever want to talk about your dad in more descriptive detail..." She gestures behind her. "You won't be alone. As you can see, most of us have a story of parental hardship."

My stomach clenches in response. "I'm good, thanks. Chucky and I are hitting the hay now. We'll see you tomorrow."

The crushed expression on her face as I turn away is like a punch in the gut. I don't know why I'm so short with her. It was a nice evening. She didn't do anything wrong, yet I don't want to rehash the event. I want to be alone. Well, with Chucky.

I retreat into the cabin and close the door behind me. It feels strange to know such intimate details about the lives of strangers, and now they know something about me too.

Something deeply personal that they can use against me at a later point. It's like I gave away a piece of my soul and I can't control what happens to it now.

It's unsettling.

I push the thoughts aside and undress. My mind conjures up an image of Cricket in her sundress. One strap kept sliding down to rest on her arm, exposing her bare shoulder. Each time she tugged it back into place, it would slide down again. I imagine what it would feel like to press my lips along that curve of skin.

In the shower, I think more about Cricket in her sundress, about peeling down both straps until the bodice slips to reveal a pair of perfect breasts, which is a mistake when all I want to do after this is sleep.

At least the water is cold.

The temperature doesn't dip in the night, and the humidity is stifling, so I awaken drenched in sweat. I glance at my Apple watch. Five-fifteen. As much as I would've liked to sleep longer, no surprise it's impossible. A quick look outside reveals ribbons of bright golden light filtering through the trees. Sunrise.

I'm up anyway. Might as well see what the fuss is about.

I pull on a pair of shorts and a T-shirt and wander down to the lake. Cricket is already on her yoga mat with her face tilted toward the rising sun. I stop at the edge of the lawn to observe her. Without her usual oversized T-shirt, you could actually see her body.

I wish I hadn't. More fodder for bedtime.

She's more toned than I realized, not that it matters. I'm not interested in Courtney. She is the vampire I'm desperate to stake.

Shit. Never mind.

She stretches toward the cabins and spots me. Her whole demeanor changes in the blink of an eye. Gone is the lithe, graceful woman. She wobbles on one leg before falling smack on her ass.

The geek is back.

I hurry toward her. "Are you okay?"

Flat on the mat, she rubs her backside. "I wasn't expecting to see you—or anyone."

"Sorry. I should've shouted."

"Not at this hour. Someone might think it's a wildlife emergency."

I help her to her feet. "I didn't sleep well, so I decided to watch the sun rise since you seemed so enthusiastic about it."

"It's beautiful, isn't it? Check out those colors."

I follow her gaze to the burning rays of light rippling across the water. "I can see why you like to do this, but sunset is every bit as pretty."

"Except everybody's awake at sunset." She inhales deeply. "This is my quiet time. When it's me and Mother Nature kicking it old school."

"I'll tell you who else is kicking it old school. I saw Bradley outside smoking a cigarette. Can you believe that guy sleeps in striped long johns? He looked like a candy cane."

Cricket bursts into laughter. "Are you serious? No, I had no idea."

I like her laugh so much, I find myself wanting to hear it again, but I can't think of anything funny to say. Not without caffeine first.

"I remember he posted a picture in our group chat in

March when we all celebrated Pi Day. I thought I caught a glimpse of candy stripes but figured it was a shirt."

"You can eat pie whenever you want. Why do you need a special day?"

She slams the heel of her hand against her forehead. "Not the pastry, dinkus. The mathematical equation."

"Wait. Did you call me a dinkus?"

"What's the problem? Is it too early for insults?"

"Hey, I'm not the one throwing math parties."

"You obviously like to learn or you wouldn't have gone to law school."

I snort. "Yeah, that's why people become lawyers, a love of knowledge."

She blinks. "Then why did you?"

"Parental pressure. Societal pressure." I shrug. "Pressure."

"Huh."

I give her a searching look. "What does that mean?"

"Nothing. I didn't take you for the kind of guy who makes life decisions based on the opinions of other people."

"You don't exactly strike me as someone who was in open rebellion against her parents. You're even running the family business."

"Because I wanted to. Nobody had to force me into it."

"Have you even tried doing something else? What if you discover there's something better for you out in the big wide world?"

She spreads her arms wide. "This is the only big wide world I need."

"You're not interested in travel?"

"Sure, especially in the winter. But travel only makes me appreciate this place more. I'm always happiest when I'm home."

"Huh." I don't think I've ever felt that way about anywhere, not even my childhood home.

"Do you travel?" she asks.

"Not as often as I'd like. I have to meet those billable hour requirements each month."

"I would hate that. Your whole life is dictated by numbers."

"Isn't everybody's? We all need to make ends meet somehow. That's capitalism for you."

"I consider myself lucky. I inherited my house and my business, and I live within my means."

"But think of all the money you could have if you sold the land. No financial worries. You'd be set for life."

"I'm already set for life, Charlie. This camp is magical. How many people can say that about the place where they work or live? I have both."

"You don't get lonely out here when everybody's gone for the season?"

"The Poconos are popular in the winter months too. People drive out here to ski or snowboard."

"But you're not doing those things. You're hibernating in your house all by yourself. You don't even have a Chewy or a Buffy to keep you company."

"I'm fine with my own company. I don't need anyone else."

She's holding back on me; I can feel it, but I don't want to pry. "I have confidence LandStar would up their offer if you want to squeeze more out of them before you agree."

She looks at me like I grew a second head in front of her eyes. "Are you ever going to give up?"

"It's called exploiting your weaknesses."

"It's called being a dick."

I've pushed her too far. Time to retreat. "I'll leave you in peace."

"Now that you've destroyed it. Gee, thanks." She gives her head a small shake. "You know what, Charlie? I take it back. You have your job to do, and I have mine. I get why you brought it up again, but let's agree that it was the last time. If you don't accept my answer is final, then I'd like you to leave."

I contemplate her for moment. I can tell she means every word.

I'm also not ready to leave.

"I apologize," I tell her. "I was being an asshat. It won't happen again."

To my surprise, she smiles. "I like a man who can admit when he's wrong."

I clutch my chest over my heart. "Did I hear you right? Did you admit that you like me?"

"Don't get too excited." She pauses. "Why did you cry?"

"Excuse me?"

"You told me the last time you cried was when you were a kid. I'm wondering what happened."

"I have no idea."

"But if you remember the last time you cried, you must remember the reason for it."

"No. I don't even know how old I was. I only know that I haven't cried since then."

"What do you do when you get upset? You're not one of those rage-induced men, are you?" She seems genuinely horrified at the prospect.

"No, I tend to take everything in stride."

"So if someone cuts you off on the highway, you shrug it off?"

"I might mutter a string of curse words."

"What about when you lose a client?"

"Hasn't happened."

"When your dog died?"

"No pets."

"When your favorite sportsball team loses their big game?"

"I say they'll get 'em next year and move on."

She regards me. "Huh."

"What?"

"That all sounds healthy."

"But...?"

"But not crying isn't healthy. It's important to feel negative emotions."

"I feel them. I just don't do anything about them."

"Then you're repressed, like a Jane Austen character."

"Am I the heroine or the hero in this scenario?"

"Does it matter?"

"Just curious. For the record, I'm not repressed. If the right emotion came along, I'd express it."

She laughs. "That's not how that works. You don't sit there watching the emotions pass in front of you like sushi on a conveyer belt. Ah yes, I'll take the sashimi sadness." She mimes lifting a plate from an imaginary belt.

"I thought this camp is supposed to be judgment free."

"I'm not judging you. I'm helping you."

"I agree. You're helping me feel inadequate."

She slaps a hand over her mouth. "I'm so sorry, Charlie. That isn't my intention at all."

"I didn't come here for a therapy session."

She angles her head and a sheet of chestnut hair dips alongside her face. "Then why did you come?"

"I told you. I wanted to experience the things you told me—a home away from home."

"And how are we doing so far?"

My gaze sweeps the campground. "I'm starting to get it."

"Are you?" She sounds uncertain.

"What will it take to convince you? I'm still here, aren't I?"

"Yes, and I've got to be honest, it surprises me. I expected you to pack up after the second day, once you realized you couldn't persuade me to sell."

"I'm fitting in, enjoying all that your camp has to offer. I mean, where else can I crochet a penis?"

She cringes. "Esther roped you in, huh?"

I shrug. "One more skill to add to my resume."

"Speaking of which, you know what I realized? You haven't had a turn to feed Buffy."

Now it's *my* turn to cringe. "Not sure how I feel about that."

"What do you mean? She's sweet, adorable, and completely harmless."

"She's a rodent with wings. And not even cute butterfly wings."

"Would that make you more inclined to feed her?"

"Not really," I admit. "Why a sugar glider? Why not a cat or a dog?"

"Gloria says Buffy is easier to care for. She already has her mother, so she couldn't be outside walking a dog multiple times a day."

"How about a cat, though? They seem low maintenance."

"Her mom is allergic."

"Oh. That's too bad."

"Not really. She adores Buffy."

"Did you ever have a pet?" I ask.

"We had a dog, Taffy. She was a golden retriever."

"I'm surprised you wouldn't want a dog now, living in an isolated area by yourself most of the year."

"I considered it, but I didn't want to get attached again. Taffy lived until she was seventeen. That's old for a dog."

I point at her. "Aha! I'm not the only one who has issues dealing with negative emotions."

She opens her mouth to object, but no sounds come out.

"I'd ask if the cat got your tongue, but we both know you don't have one."

"This?" She sticks out her tongue.

"I'm talking about a cat, silly." The 'silly' slips out. It has an intimate ring to it, like we're close friends who've known each other forever and are comfortable with tacking on lighthearted nicknames. I feel a pang of embarrassment, but Cricket doesn't seem to notice.

We're not friends, my inner voice insists. I've infiltrated Comic-Camp as a tactic to get my client what he wants so that I get what I want.

Except the longer I stay here, what I want and why I want it are beginning to fade from memory.

Chapter Eleven

Cricket

I'm relieved to finally be rid of the Mumford shirt. I'm also glad no one mentioned its origin. I wouldn't have wanted to explain to Charlie, which I realize is somewhat hypocritical given how much I've pushed him out of his comfort zone.

Big deal. I'm a hypocrite. There are worse things to be in life, like a liar and a cheater.

After yoga I shower and check messages. Adam's toilet won't stop running and it's upsetting Chewy, so I swing by his cabin for maintenance. Thankfully, it's an easy fix.

"You're a lifesaver," Adam says. He's seated on the edge of his bed cuddling Chewy on his lap. For once he's in regular clothes.

"It's no big deal, unlike Charlie trying to unload Chucky at swag swap last night."

Adam strokes the Yorkie's silky hair. "Don't be so quick to judge. He had that baseball card ready and waiting at his fingertips. I think subconsciously he wanted us to object to Chucky."

"Huh. You're more insightful than people give you credit for, you know that?"

"It's the helmet. Everybody underestimates my capacity for compassion, but if they really knew anything about Anakin, they'd know..."

I tune out, as I tend to do whenever Adam goes off on a *Star Wars* tangent. I'm a genuine fan, but for Adam the franchise is an obsession. He can recite Anakin Skywalker factoids until you lose sensation in your limbs. Ask me how I know.

"What time is karaoke tonight?" Adam asks.

"Later than I'd prefer, but Melody was only available at ten."

"Ooh, that's past our bedtime." He holds up Chewy. "Isn't it, little guy?"

"You can make an exception for one night. I have an indoor and an outdoor activity planned to keep everybody occupied until then."

"I vote for indoor."

"I thought as much, that's why I'm playing *Empire Strikes Back* in the cabin."

"Out of curiosity, but what's the outdoor activity?"

"Capture the Flag: After Dark edition."

Adam snorts. "Let me guess: Hunter's request."

"Of course."

Adam is quiet for a moment. "I like Charlie."

"That's all part of his evil plan. Makes everybody like him and then bam! Ruin our lives."

"Do you honestly believe that?"

The tension eases from my shoulders. "I honestly don't know."

"Has he given you any reason not to trust him?"

I arch an eyebrow. "Apart from the whole registering under false pretenses?"

"If there's one thing we know it's that bad guys can turn away from the dark side. Try to remember that."

"I'll bear that in mind. See you later, Adam."

Capture the Flag starts after sunset. Olivia opts for movie night with Ben and Adam, but the other campers choose the outdoor activity.

As soon as I finish explaining the rules, Charlie objects. "I'm a lawyer. I can't steal."

"Funny words from a guy who's trying to steal my land out from under me."

"Point taken."

We split into two teams. My team has a Care Bear flag and Hunter's team has a Smurfs flag. I offer a brief overview of the rules for Charlie's sake, explaining that each team stores their flag at their hidden headquarters. Members of the opposite team have to find the location and steal the flag. Whichever team returns to their headquarters with the other team's flag first wins.

I offer to hide our flag, and my teammates offer to act as decoys and defense. To my surprise, Charlie chooses to accompany me to the hiding spot and act as a lookout.

"I already know where I'm hiding it," I tell him as we traipse through the woods. We share one flashlight between us.

"You can pick any tree," Charlie says. "It'll be impossible to find a scrap of material in the middle of these woods in the dark."

"You only say that because you haven't played in the pitch black with Hunter. I swear he has night vision."

"More like night-vision goggles."

"Fair." I become acutely aware of his presence beside me. We're walking so close together that his arm keeps brushing against mine.

"What happened with the Mumford guy?"

His question throws me for a loop. "What?"

"The former owner of the Mumford T-shirt. Ex-boyfriend?"

I steal a glance at him. "You caught that, huh?"

"It was hard to miss." He shines the light under his chin and produces a monstrous laugh.

I don't give him the satisfaction of a reaction. "Is that supposed to be scary?"

He shifts the flashlight away from his face and I scream.

"What?" he shouts, clearly unnerved by the high-pitched sound. I don't blame him. I scared myself.

"It's a tick!" I flick the insect off his arm before it has a chance to burrow.

Charlie stares at the red mark on his skin. "Where've you been hiding those fast reflexes? That was superhero level."

"Any superhero in particular?"

I can see his gears churning as he struggles to come up with an answer. "Um, Batman?"

"Batman relies on gizmos. He isn't naturally gifted."

"How about Spider-Man?"

I nod. "That's a good one."

He scratches his arm. "Should I be worried about this?"

"I don't think so. It didn't get under your skin."

He looks harder at me. "Why do I sense a but?"

"But there could be more that we can't see."

His eyes narrow. "Can't see because they're so tiny that they're practically invisible?"

"This time of year they're bigger, but they like fleshy, warm places."

He grimaces. "Fleshy?"

I move to stand behind him. "Lift up your shirt." He passes me the flashlight, and I shine the light on his bare back. I didn't realize how sexy a back could be until this moment.

"Anything?" he asks.

"No, just a freckle."

"I have a freckle?"

"Right above your hip bone." I press my finger against the freckle, causing him to jump.

"Cold hands," he says.

I laugh. "It's eighty degrees."

"Fine. I'm ticklish."

"Why didn't you say so? Or is being ticklish somehow emasculating?"

He doesn't respond. I continue my examination and somehow manage to hold the flashlight steady as I focus on his arms. Those biceps deserve a spotlight. It's a shame they're regularly hidden beneath layers of designer suits. The corporate world's loss is my gain.

"See anything?"

His question snaps me back to the task at hand. "Not yet."

"You said warm, fleshy places."

"I did."

"Then shouldn't we check...?" He drags his gaze lower.

I take a step back. "No way."

"How do you expect me to look there? I'm not a contortionist and unless you have a mirror." He stops. "Hold up. We can use the camera on my phone."

My mouth runs dry. *"You want me to take photos of your balls?"*

"Not to keep."

We stare at each other.

"If the head gets buried..."

I wince. "Please don't say head while I'm staring at your nether regions."

"No need to stare. Give them a quick look and we won't ever speak of this again."

"A vow of silence?"

He nods, somber, and reluctantly exposes himself.

I lower myself to my knees and shine the light at his groin. Great Mississippi River!

I snap to my feet, unable to speak.

"See anything?" he asks as he hikes up his shorts. His anxious tone brings me back to earth.

Holy Gandalf's walking stick, yes, I most certainly do.

"No ticks," I squeak.

"I should check you now, right?" he asks. "Unless you have a natural immunity to tick bites."

"That's not a thing."

"Then what's the issue? You checked me. Let me return the favor."

Even in the pitch dark, I don't miss the pleased quirk of his mouth. Return the favor, indeed.

I can't afford Lyme disease. My health insurance isn't good enough. And yet the prospect of Charlie poking around the hidden parts of my body while we're alone in the woods... It has sexy times written all over it.

Or slasher movie. Maybe both.

"Okay." I drag out the word, still reluctant.

"Lift up your shirt," he says. "I promise to be quick."

"Just what a girl likes to hear," I joke.

"Trust me, Cricket. If this were another sort of naked party, I'd take my time."

His words seem to graze my bare skin, and I strain against a shudder.

I close my eyes and do as I'm told, fully aware that this exceptionally hot man is currently scrutinizing every inch of my back. I swallow a whimper. "You should check under the bra line. They like to squeeze underneath things."

I expect him to shift the underwire. Instead, he unhooks it, and a small gasp escapes me.

He hears my surprised reaction. "Sorry, is that not what you meant?"

"It's fine." I feel under my boobs for any tiny bumps.

"Do you want me to aim the light at your ... underboob?"

"No," I say, "but also yes. Think of it as a breast exam, like you're a professional looking for suspicious lumps."

I expect him to crack a joke about playing doctor, but he seems to take his task very seriously, which I appreciate.

His thumb skims my bare breast, and my nipple hardens at the attention. "Nothing here," he says in a voice that sounds huskier than normal.

"That's a relief." I drop my shirt, mortified by the moment of vulnerability. I'm grateful for the blanket of darkness between us.

"Anywhere else I should look?" he asks.

"I'm good, thanks." The elastic on my underwear is tight enough to leave indentations on my skin. No way is a tick crawling past the border.

"While we're busy baring ourselves," he says, "I have a confession to make."

My mind scatters into a thousand possibilities, each one more awful than the next. I brace myself for an answer that involves either a wife and three kids at home or a preference for pineapple on pizza. "What is it?"

He hesitates, as though reconsidering.

"What is it, Charlie? Do you see something?"

He switches off the light. "I haven't seen *Star Wars*," he finally says. "Or *Lord of the Rings*, for that matter."

His admission strikes me speechless. My jaw refuses to operate. It doesn't even drop to the floor; it stays clamped shut like an oyster holding tight to its pearl.

Charlie studies my face in the shadows. "Have I done it? Have I finally broken you?"

I regain control of my mouth. "It'll take a lot more than your pathetic childhood to break me."

He scoffs. "Pathetic? I'll have you know my childhood was idyllic."

"No one's childhood was idyllic. The only people who think that are the ones who weren't paying attention."

He whistles. "Wow. That has to be the bleakest view of humanity I've ever heard. No wonder you hide away in your nerd camp every summer. Why bother to take a chance on people when you already know they all suck?"

"I've taken plenty of chances with people." And they burnt me like toast. Never again.

"Do you even have friends in real life?" he asks.

"What's that supposed to mean? The camp *is* my real life."

"I'm talking about the other ten months of the year. Do you even leave your house? Catch a movie with another local?"

"I watch movies with friends," I say carefully.

"I'm not talking about watching a movie at the same time as someone in another state. I mean sitting in a movie theater next to someone you know, sharing a bucket of popcorn."

"Why does it matter whether my friends live near me?"

"Because living your life online isn't actually living a life."

I cross my arms. "Is there where you tell me to touch grass? Because I spend the entire summer doing exactly that, thank you very much. And I don't need a lecture on how to live outside technology from a guy who probably keeps his ringer on all night in case a client calls." Annoyance flickers across his face. Another bullseye.

"You act like I'm the one who doesn't step outside of my comfort zone, but you're the one who built an entire business around staying in hers."

I bark a laugh. "Nice try. I love what I do, unlike you."

My comment rankles him. "What makes you think I don't love being a lawyer?"

"It doesn't take a law degree to read between the legalese." His expression hardens, and I realize that I have, indeed, hit a nerve. I decide to guide the conversation back to a lighter space before he leaves me stranded in the woods without a flashlight. "Listen, I have a confession, too." I suck in a breath and hope the others don't kill me for this later. "There's no prank."

His eyes narrow. "What do you mean? You've been pranking me all week."

"I know. Those were obviously real, but the one Ben mentioned... It's a fake out. The prank is to make you worry about a prank that doesn't exist."

He stares at me, gobsmacked. "That's genius."

I can't resist a smile. "I know, right? The most harmless prank is also the most effective."

"You have no idea how this has affected my bedtime

routine. I check behind every door, under every object." His shoulders slant lower. "This is a relief. Thank you for telling me."

"You deserved to know the truth. You've been a good sport too." He has. If we had done this to someone else, like the Prick, he would've threatened to take his ball and go home. "Anyway, we're not always the most mature group. I'm sorry."

He arches an eyebrow. "Are you, though?"

"Okay, not really. They've been amazing, and I'm sad it's over."

He pats my shoulder. "Honesty is always the best policy."

"Ironic policy for a lawyer. Now, how would you like to remedy your pop-culture deficiency?"

"You want me to watch more movies?"

"You sound disappointed. Do you have a problem with movies in general, or only the ones you've refused to see so you can maintain your Too Cool for School demeanor?"

"It isn't a badge of honor. My family was more partial to westerns and political thrillers."

"*Stars Wars* is basically a space western. What about in college or law school? Are you telling me not one nerdy friend insisted that you watch these movies?"

"Not that I recall."

I eye him closely. "You didn't have any nerdy friends, did you?"

"I did. Greg Chumley. He was a bio major. We were roommates."

"Let me guess. Your first year."

"How did you know?"

"Because he was assigned your roommate, but you

didn't choose to room with him after that. Did you stay friends?"

He's silent for a beat. "I wouldn't say we established a friendship. We got along okay, but there was no bond."

"And who did you bond with?"

Vertical lines appear between his brows. "No one."

"Not a single person?"

"I had friends. Guys I hung out with. Girls I dated."

"But you didn't bond with any of them?"

"I don't keep in touch with anyone from college or law school, so I guess that answers the question."

"Why not?"

"Don't know. It wasn't a conscious decision. We didn't keep in touch, that's all."

"What about the law firm? Any close friends?"

He snorts. "Only a frenemy. Matt Lyman. He and I are both gunning for the lone partnership spot this year."

"Ooh, I love a good frenemy. Who has the edge?"

His expression crumples. "You know what? I don't really want to talk about work."

"Because you're having too much fun?" I poke him in the stomach, expecting a soft landing. Instead, my finger immediately makes contact with the slab of granite that doubles as his abs. I'm surprised I don't sprain my finger.

"I wouldn't say too much," he tells me. "Just enough."

Warmth floods my body in response to the quasi compliment. As much as I hate to admit it, I'm glad he chose to accompany me into the woods. I'm also glad he felt me up, even if it was under the guise of saving me from an incurable disease.

CHARLIE

I'm partially relieved when Cricket and I emerge from the darkness of the woods. I say partially because the greedy side of me wanted nothing more than to stay in that quiet, isolated space with her for a few more hours. Outside of the campsite, I felt like we were in our own protective bubble. The world fell away, along with all its demands and problems. It had nothing to do with the sanctity of the woods and everything to do with Cricket.

"You should move Hugo. You parked him right underneath a tree with weak branches. If there's a storm, your car is screwed."

It takes a moment to register that she's talking about my car. "Why is my car named Hugo?"

"Because it deserves better than douchemobile, and I'm confident you haven't already named it."

"Why would I name my car?"

"Why wouldn't you?" she shoots back.

I scan the parking lot. "What's the name of your car?"

"Rhonda."

"Is there a reason for that choice?"

"When I'm running late or the car is giving me trouble, I can sing 'Help Me, Rhonda.' You know that song? My grandparents used to play it all the time."

"Is there a song for Hugo?"

Her eyes turn to sly slits. "If there were, would you sing it?"

Inanimate objects don't need names. She's trying to

make a fool of me somehow, yet I don't feel like a fool. I feel... like I'm having fun. Again.

Maybe I'm giving Cricket too much credit and I need to commit to more time away from work. I spend the majority of my waking hours holed up in my office. It's possible that a walk to the art museum would produce as many endorphins as this conversation.

"I'm not much of a singer."

"So you say. I guess we'll find out for sure tonight."

Laughter booms from my chest. "Like hell you will. I'm an observer only."

"No such thing at Comic-Camp. Everybody sings. You don't have to sing alone, but you have to get up onstage and participate."

I remain noncommittal. I could always ditch the evening, although the prospect of sitting front row for a Cricket performance is too enticing to resist.

"What's your song?" I ask.

She shrugs. "You'll have to stay long enough to find out."

"Are you any good?"

"Nope. Terrible. That's why it's both fun and entertaining."

"You're not embarrassed to get up there and bomb?"

"Firstly, the crowd consists of my friends. They're my safe space, and I know we're all there to have fun and support each other."

"And secondly?"

"It's healthy to step outside of my comfort zone, even if it's only once a year. I know I suck, so I get nervous beforehand, but I do it anyway."

"That's what alcohol is for."

Her smile is pure mischief. "You might want to consider

"Defying Gravity." I have it on good authority you can nail those high notes."

I'm not a fan of catastrophe movies, but I would be perfectly happy for one of those giant meteors to crash into Earth right this moment. "How long have you been sitting on that one?"

"Since I stood outside your cabin and recorded you singing."

The look on her face erases any mortification I was inclined to feel. She's absolutely delighted to finally share this nugget with me.

"You've been holding this card for days."

Her smirk solidifies. "Oh, I know."

"How does it feel to show your hand?"

"Tremendous." She rests her hand on my arm. "So, will you sing it? I promise it'll bring down the house."

"I'll take it under advisement."

She smiles up at me. "Not a no then. It's a start."

I can't get over how much I enjoy her company. She's easy to talk to—I found myself touching on subjects I never would've mentioned to anyone else. I know the camp has this whole 'no judgment' vibe, but Cricket personifies it. Whatever I say, I know she's simply listening, taking it all in and that feels amazing.

There isn't a single person in my life that I could describe in the same way, not even my mother or my siblings. My father is an obvious no. The man emerged from the womb judging the squalid conditions. My mother's criticisms are subtler; they're glimpsed in the tilt of her head and the squint of her eye. You feel them rather than hear them. My brother will tell you what he's thinking, although his delivery is generally less harsh than our father's. My sister will beat around the bush until you drag her thoughts out of her, but she makes it clear she has them.

When we arrive back at camp, we're immediately surrounded by campers.

"What happened to you two?" Hunter demands. "I tried to track you, but I ended up by the creek."

"That was a successful decoy move," Gloria says with satisfaction.

Bradley cuts through the shadows and holds up the Smurf flag. A collective cheer follows. I'm swept up in the moment and feel a satisfying thrill that people care so much about this stupid game.

No, not stupid.

Fun.

"Don't forget! Karaoke at ten in Cabin Twelve," Cricket announces. "I need to shower first. My head feels itchy."

"I'm covered in mosquito bites," Fiona adds. "Does anybody have calamine lotion?"

Cricket starts toward her cabin, and I instinctively fall into step beside her. "The game was fun. We should do it again sometime."

The squint in her eye tells me she's wondering whether I mean the game or the woodland encounter.

"It's only a two-week camp, Charlie," she finally says. "'Sometime' is fairly limited."

The karaoke deejay is, appropriately enough, named Melody. I'm hardly a karaoke regular, but I can tell Melody is a pro. She seems to know the right order for the songs and how to keep the crowd engaged, not that this group needs any encouragement. They're all happy to be here, and even happier to be in each other's company. The positive vibes are palpable.

Adam hums the *Star Wars* theme song as he takes a seat.

Cricket leans over and whispers, "I told you everybody sings."

"I'm not sure that one qualifies."

"The helmet makes it difficult for him."

"He can always take it off."

"He will when the time comes."

Angela slips me a gummy. "You seem like you're in dire need of this."

I don't typically indulge in gummies, but I make an exception tonight for karaoke. My mind continues to hum with memories of Cricket's bare skin and the soft curve of her breasts. It's hard to focus on much else.

Stefan sings "Immigrant Song." Bradley and Hunter perform a surprisingly good duet of "Creep" by Radiohead. Fiona, Gloria, and Laura sing "Girls Just Wanna Have Fun." Cricket's song is the biggest surprise of the night, with an entertaining rendition of "The Warrior." Not sure about her vocals, but the gestures and gyrations are on point. I would've assumed Joel put me off finger guns, but apparently not.

Cricket drops into the chair next to me and holds out the microphone. "You're up, Charlie Brown. What's it going to be?"

I wave her off. "Nobody needs to listen to me."

"Imagine what your career would look like if you said that to your clients." She thrusts the microphone into my hand. "You're one of us now, Charlie. Nobody leaves this cabin without making a fool of yourself... except Stefan."

"Yeah, he was incredible. I need him to give me some tips."

"Have fun with it. That's the tip."

Someone starts chanting my name and soon the whole cabin reverberates with the same two syllables. I make a last-minute change to my selection. I don't feel capable of "Defying Gravity," so I go for "Take Me Home, Country Roads" by John Denver. My stomach would be in tangles if it weren't for the gummy. Well, make that two gummies.

I only manage to get one line into the song before the whole bar joins in. Before I know it, I'm in the middle of a sing-along and can't even hear my own voice, despite the microphone. I'm perfectly okay with that outcome.

The song ends with hoots and hollers. I'm carried off the stage on a cloud of euphoria. My head is cloudy but not so muddled that I'll forget the way this moment feels tomorrow. As with everything related to camp, this evening is good-natured fun with nothing to be gained except pure, unadulterated enjoyment. What a novel concept.

Melody closes out the evening with "Sweet Caroline," always a crowd-pleaser. Afterward we pour out of the cabin, sticky with sweat. The humidity outside doesn't help.

"Midnight swim!" Fiona yells. She takes off in the direction of the lake.

My eyes meet Cricket's. "If I offer to race you, will you come?" she asks.

"You challenge me," I blurt. "Nobody else does that."

"Are you sure? It sounds like your dad spends a lot of time doing exactly that."

"What he does is different." I have no interest in talking about my father—how he belittles and berates me. All the be's. "You call me out on my shit, but you do it in a way that doesn't feel threatening or critical."

"Well, thank you. As far as compliments go, that's a good one."

"You're also very pretty."

Her eyebrows slide to her hairline. "Did Angela slip you a gummy?"

I hold up two fingers.

"Right. Never mind. Running or swimming tonight would be ill-advised."

A bloodcurdling screech interrupts our moment. At least I think it's a moment. Then I hear the words that inject adrenaline straight into my veins.

"It's a bear!"

Chapter Twelve

Cricket

A stampede follows the human alarm. Specks of dirt invade my eyes, kicked up by Stefan, who is probably halfway to Harrisburg by now.

"I'll take care of it," Charlie says without hesitation.

How does he intend to take care of a bear? Blind and confused, I stumble forward, uncertain which way to go to avoid being mauled to death.

My vision finally clears, and I see Charlie doubled over, shoulders shaking. It takes me a second to realize that he's laughing.

I look around. We're the only two left in the clearing—unless you count the raccoon currently scampering into the woods.

"False alarm," Charlie says, recovering his breath and retuning to an upright position.

"What did you intend to do if it *was* a bear?"

He blinks in rapid succession. "I don't actually know."

Charlie wasn't just heroic. He was *manly*, a realization that fuels a deep thrum in my lower abdomen. I silently berate my body for this betrayal. He's the enemy. The Kylo Ren to my Rey.

On second thought, not the best analogy.

Charlie cups his hands around his mouth. "It's safe to come out. It was only a raccoon."

Campers slowly emerge from their hiding spots like the Lollipop Guild after the house falls on the Wicked Witch of the East.

"It looks like somebody left trash outside the bins," I announce. "I'm not going to ask you to out yourself, but I *am* going to ask you to never, ever do that again. Proper storage of trash is essential to the health and safety of this camp." And I can't afford any issues, not with LandStar hovering like a vulture and waiting for any sign of a carcass.

Olivia promptly bursts into tears.

Gloria flings an arm around her. "What is it, little bit?"

"It was me. I dropped a napkin and then I couldn't find it. I thought it blew away."

Gloria kissed the top of her head. "The raccoon wasn't attracted to a napkin, hon."

Olivia sniffs. "What if the napkin had ketchup on it?"

Ben wraps his arms around her. "That wouldn't be enough."

Adam removes his helmet and wipes aside the damp strands of hair stuck to his forehead. "I think it was me. I'm so sorry, everyone. I put a few bits of hotdog in my pocket at dinner. I intended to give it to Chewy before bed."

Olivia stops crying. "Maybe it was the smell of the ketchup and hotdog together."

Laura clears her throat. "I think it was my fault. I might have dropped a buttered roll."

Charlie leans over and whispers, "Is this going to become a Spartacus situation?"

I bite back a laugh. He's right—now they're clambering to take responsibility for the mishap.

I love my campers.

Gloria pulls a tissue from her pocket and passes it to Olivia. The girl wipes her eyes with such vigor, I'm afraid she's going to rub her eyeballs raw. I'm relieved when I see Ben urge her to be gentler.

"She's tired," Ben says with regard to his granddaughter. "It's well past her bedtime."

"Mom and Dad don't let me stay up until midnight," Olivia crows.

"Let's keep this between us, shall we?" Ben steers her toward their cabin.

"Still want to race to the water?" Charlie asks. His bright eyes hold mine for a beat longer than necessary, and I feel that pesky tug in my lower abdomen. I do not support the reaction my body seems to be having to him. In fact, I strenuously object.

"Let's do it. On the count of three. One..." I sprint toward the lake. Unfortunately, I start laughing at Charlie's shocked response, which causes me to lose my lead.

We splash into the water at the same time, fully clothed.

"You laugh like you've been smoking menthols since you were ten years old," Charlie says.

"Rude."

"It's a compliment, Cricket. Take it."

"In what world is that a compliment?"

"I'm telling you your laugh is sexy as hell. Take the win."

"So you're telling me you think a ten-year-old who smokes menthols is sexy? Gross." Despite my response, my insides begin to heat up like the core of a volcano.

He knocks on my head. "Are you being deliberately obtuse? That's not remotely what I'm telling you."

I cling to the word 'sexy' like it's wreckage from the *Titanic* and I'm a woman without a lifeboat. I've only ever been referred to as sexy one other time, and as I've stricken that other time from the record that is my brain, I shall consider this the first time.

"I've never smoked," I say, apparently determined to miss the point. I know I have a hard time accepting a compliment—it's one of my flaws—yet my resistance seems even worse when that compliment is coming from Charlie Thorpe.

"That makes two of us," he says.

"Really? Is that an athlete thing?"

"Maybe? No idea."

"What about pot?"

"Nope."

"Gummies?"

"Only tonight." He squints at me. "Is this a character assessment?"

"No, we don't judge here, remember?"

"In that case, I like nothing more than to snort cocaine off the well-worn fur of my childhood teddy bear."

I fold my arms and glower at him. "There's no way that's true."

"No?"

"No. You're not sentimental enough to keep a treasured childhood toy."

"Shows how little you know. Mr. McRibbons is currently occupying the middle shelf in my spare room closet."

"Mr. McRibbons? Was this name inspired by the famous McDonald's sandwich?"

"Not at all. He wears a red ribbon around his neck."

"Then why is he Irish?"

"No idea. I was two. I didn't exactly have the vocabulary to name him Othello."

I snort-laugh. "Othello? That would be the adult choice for your bear's name?"

"No, it would probably be Bryce Harper Bear."

"Should I get the reference?"

He shakes his head. "Probably not. He's a baseball player." His attention shifts to Ben's cabin. "Olivia was more upset than I would expect. Most kids don't fully grasp consequences and responsibility."

"It wasn't about the napkin or the raccoon," I admit. "Her parents are getting a divorce. That's why she's here. Ben usually comes alone, but he was unexpectedly saddled with a plus-one." Not that he minded in the least. The sun rises and sets on Olivia as far as Ben is concerned.

Concern creases Charlie's brow. "I didn't realize."

"It's not contentious, but Olivia is taking it hard."

"As one would expect."

"Yeah," I say. "It came as a shock to Ben too. He didn't know how unhappy they were. He feels guilty for not being as attuned to his son as he thinks he should've been."

Charlie falls silent. Finally he says, "Ben shouldn't feel bad. He's a good dad. I can tell."

"And a good grandfather too."

"My father wouldn't have a clue if I was having problems."

"Because he isn't attuned to you or because you hide them from him?"

He shoots me a curious look that I don't quite understand. "Both. My father isn't interested in feelings, only achievements. Our conversations consist of whether I finalized any big deals and when I can expect to make partner."

"That's a fairly limited conversation."

"I prefer it that way."

"I'm sorry," I say.

His head swings to me. "Why are you sorry? You're not my father."

"I'm sorry that your relationship with him isn't what it should be. You deserve loving parents."

He ponders me. "I get the sense you had loving parents."

Now it's my turn to grow quiet. "My mom was amazing."

"How old were you when she died?"

"Sixteen."

"You must have good memories of her."

"Yes and no. Sometimes they're hazier than I'd prefer. When you don't have anyone to reminisce with, it feels harder to keep those memories alive."

He looks like I killed his favorite plant. "You don't have any family?"

I imagine my smile is as rueful as I feel. "No blood relations. I'm an only child, and so were my parents."

He takes a minute to process this and then says, "Well, family isn't everything. Sometimes they're downright shitty."

"Oh, I know, believe me. Ask around. Plenty of campers have horror stories. I wouldn't wish Gloria's mother on my worst enemy."

"She's the one with dementia?"

"Alzheimer's. But I'm not talking about that. I'm talking about the kind of mother she was before she developed the condition."

"Are we talking Medea or Matilda's mom?"

I laugh at his literary references. "She's a momster. Repeatedly told Gloria she wished she'd not had a child. That if it weren't for Gloria, she would've been a Broadway star. That getting pregnant ruined her life."

Charlie lets loose a low whistle. "Yet Gloria has dedicated her adult life to wiping the drool from the chin of the woman who treated her like that?"

"Because she's a saint in sheep's clothing. In a twisted way, Gloria prefers this version of her mother. She's kinder and seems to appreciate Gloria more than the younger version ever did."

He drags a hand through his hair. "That's gotta be rough for her."

"Why do you think she lives for these two weeks at camp? Once she goes home, it's another year before she does anything for herself. The memories of the fun she had at this year's camp will help sustain her for the next twelve months."

He releases a breath. "What about the other campers? Do they all have stories like that?"

"Everybody has a story, Charlie. That's why it's so important to cut people some slack. You never know what they've been through. Ben's wife died a few years ago while he was battling cancer."

"What happened to her?"

"She went for a walk on a windy day. Got hit by a tree branch and died."

Charlie falls silent. I don't blame him. It's a tough story to hear. The brutal randomness of it. I marvel that Ben found the strength to keep fighting, but he did.

"These aren't secrets, by the way. They're very open about their struggles."

"This isn't a nerd camp. This is a wellness retreat."

I feel my body relax. "You're finally getting it."

"Thank you for telling me. I feel like I know them a bit better now."

"And they'd like to know you better, too. Everybody likes you, Charlie. Swag swap was an excellent start, but we both know there's a lot more to you than a cherished baseball card."

I feel the shift in energy the moment I mention the baseball card. His eyes shutter and I wish I could snatch back the comment. I was finally chipping away at that wall of his and now this one offhand remark would set me back a few bricks. Lesson learned.

"Sorry, I didn't mean to upset you."

"It takes far more than that to upset me, Courtney."

His use of my real name isn't lost on me. Despite his protestation, he's resetting a boundary. One more brick firmly back in place.

"It's late. I should get some rest," he says abruptly. "Stefan challenged me to a wizard duel for tomorrow. I have to prep."

"How do you prep for a wizard duel?"

"For starters, find out what it is. If I need my own wand, I'm SOL."

"Wands are provided, so don't worry about that." As much as I long to recover our lost ground, I recognize that I need to let him go. Charlie isn't someone you can push. The more I press him, the more resistant he'll become. I know this because I do the same thing, and the last time I let my guard down for someone I found attractive, I paid the price.

He exits the lake, his clothing stuck to his skin. I wait a couple minutes before following suit, to give him space.

"You two have gotten chummy. I guess he isn't working

for the Empire anymore," Fiona says as she strides past me with her clothes tucked under her arm. Her Batman glow-in-the-dark camisole and underwear are dripping wet.

"I guess not," I say, but I honestly have no idea.

No surprise that tonight I dream about Charlie. This isn't the first time he's been featured by my imagination, but it's the first time his appearance involves sexy times. I think it's because of his recent vulnerability. Of course, afterward, he reverted to his robot form and acted like we'd been formally introduced over a tray of caviar, or whatever they served at fancy lawyer parties.

He finds it hard to share his feelings, that much is obvious. Based on what he's revealed about his family, I get the impression that he didn't hear the words "I'm proud of you" very often, if ever. And I *was* proud of him for sharing at swag swap and for participating in karaoke. He was clearly reluctant, but he joined in, and even better, he was authentic, and that's all I wanted for him. Maybe he'd feel better about our lake conversation in the light of day.

On the other hand, maybe I should consider his behavior a warning not to get emotionally involved. If he's determined to be an island, let him be one instead of trying to establish a peninsula or an archipelago. I already serve as a bridge to my campers. If Charlie wants to join civilization, he'll have to build his own.

Chapter Thirteen

CHARLIE

Last night was ... a lot. I'd never wanted to kiss a woman more in my life while simultaneously wanting to run from her. Cricket confuses the hell out of me, or more accurately, my own feelings confuse the hell out of me.

I manage to avoid her by spending the morning with the fan fiction club. To my surprise and relief, I find myself enjoying the collaborative nature of the work as well as the creative process. I may not have watched *Supernatural*, but I know enough about Sherlock to contribute. Of course, Fiona insists on showing me social media clips from *Supernatural*, allegedly to give me a better understanding of the show, although I suspect she simply likes ogling the actors. When the Internet connection acts up and we're forced to abandon what must be the fortieth reel of two admittedly good-looking guys exchanging quips, I act disappointed.

When the activity block ends, I walk outside to heavy cloud cover and my phone bleeps with a weather alert for heavy rain, which Cricket must've also received because she cancels the evening's fireside chat. Everyone decides to cram into the Danger Zone cabin. I'm not a fan of crowds in tight spaces, so I opt to go back to my cabin. Avoiding Cricket may also be a factor in my decision.

I catch sight of her entering the cabin with Stefan as fat raindrops begin to fall. No one's outside at this point, which makes it the ideal opportunity to snoop in Cricket's office. I make a beeline for the vacant cabin.

The moment my hand makes contact with the door-knob, I freeze. This camp is all she has in the world. The last connection to the family she lost and the only connection with the one she created for herself. My client doesn't understand any of that, not that he'd care. If it doesn't involve dollar signs, he isn't interested.

But I am.

Very interested, if I'm being honest, and it's a problem. Cricket's need for this camp conflicts with my need to secure this deal. To become the youngest partner in the history of the firm. To be on equal footing with my siblings and make my parents proud.

Still, I can't do it.

I release my grip on the doorknob and abandon my plan. I want to make Cricket laugh again, not cry. Maybe another Chucky prank will mend the fence I built between us last night.

I return to my cabin and retrieve Chucky. She won't expect to see him in her filing cabinet a second time. I only hope someone is there to witness the moment when it happens.

I sneak back into the office and open the drawer of the filing cabinet. I pose him with a glimpse of his arms and head sticking out and hear a crunch of paper as I adjust his position.

Shit. I hope I didn't rip anything important. I yank

Chucky from the drawer and feel around the bottom. The files are so tight, it's like trying to fix a paper jam in the printer.

With delicate precision, I manage to extract the paper from the drawer. Relief ripples through me when I see it's all in one piece, quickly followed by another emotion when I realize what the document is.

A smoking gun.

I scan the details and immediately shift into lawyer mode. I know exactly what this is and what it means for both Cricket and my client.

I wish I hadn't stepped foot inside this office today.

My throat tightens as I consider the options. I've only known Cricket for a blip in time, yet I feel like I've known her forever. If only I could figure out a way to satisfy us both. If I turn this over to LandStar, it would destroy her. Standing here right now and confronted with this reality, I realize that I don't want Cricket to be even a little sad or disappointed, and I certainly don't want to be the reason for it. That woman deserves full-blown happiness handed to her on a silver platter.

Based on the state of her files, I doubt she knows this document exists, let alone its implication. I fold the paper and stuff it in my pocket before repositioning Chucky. As soon as I finish, I rush from the office, feeling more like a criminal than a prankster.

I hurry back to my cabin and pull out my laptop to try to focus on work. The Wi-Fi is even worse than usual, if that's possible. I assume it's the approaching band of bad weather. I give up and focus on the files on the hard drive. I click open the LandStar folder and start reviewing the files related to the camp, not because I intend to exploit a loophole. Instead, I'm looking for that magic answer that solves both our problems. It's probably wishful thinking, but I'm a determined guy. The upside of being raised by pushy parents. Maybe I would've become driven and determined without their constant pressure—who knows?

I hear a downpour outside as I revisit the client's brief, the reasons for wanting this land in particular, and what LandStar intends to do with it. The location makes sense. The camp sits on a gorgeous piece of property. You can't beat the lakeside setting and acres of pristine forest. It would be a shame to cut down Endor Forest to make space for tennis courts.

I'm so immersed in my mental gymnastics that I almost miss the stream of water sliding under my door. I set my laptop on the bed and peer out the window. The area outside my cabin looks like a swamp. I throw my belongings into my duffel bag, including the expensive shoes on my feet, and exit the cabin barefoot.

Water splashes around my ankles as I wade farther inland toward drier land. The flooding seems concentrated around my cabin, probably because I'm farthest from the other cabins and closest to the lake. I'm soaked to the bone by the time I knock on Cricket's door.

"Holy crap, Charlie! Get inside!" She practically yanks me forward and slams the door behind me. "What are you doing?"

I set my duffel bag on the floor. "My cabin is starting to flood."

Her eyes widen. "You're kidding me. That's not good." She turns toward the window. "The cabin closest to you is on an incline. It's probably okay, but I'll check with Ben."

"If you can get through."

She gets through. Ben's cabin is fine. She types a message in the group chat and asks everyone to remain in their cabins for their own safety and to leave at the first sign of flooding.

"I guess it's you and me tonight, roomie," Cricket chirps.

My gaze drifts to the one and only bed in the cabin. "Why don't I bunk with Adam?"

"Chewy will bark at you all night like you're an intruder."

"Stefan?"

"Vikings don't share cabins." She picks up my bag and moves it to the other side of the room. "Relax, Charlie. It's one night and we're both adults. No need to make it weird. We'll dry out your cabin tomorrow and you can return to your self-imposed isolation."

"I wasn't isolating."

"Sure you weren't." Cricket's phone buzzes, breaking the tension. Probably for the best. She taps the screen. "Hey, Gloria. Everything okay?"

I can't hear the words, but I can tell from Gloria's tone that everything is not okay.

"I'm sure she's fine, but if it would make you feel better, I'll see if I can find her." Cricket's eyes meet mine and she mouths the word 'Buffy.'

I understand the problem before Cricket hangs up. The sugar glider is outside in the deluge. With that small body, her wings are likely vulnerable during a downpour.

"I'll let you know when I find her." Cricket tosses me a look. "Buffy flew outside and hasn't come back. Gloria is worried sick."

"I heard your end. Let's go. I'll help you."

She blinks. "You want to help me?"

"Why not?"

"You came here to get out of the rain."

"I know how important Buffy is to Gloria. Besides, I'm

already soaked. Where's your flashlight? We'll flash a Bat Signal."

"Good thinking."

She dashes to the corner of the cabin and grabs the light from underneath a chair. "Let's go!"

The rain is even worse than when I arrived at Cricket's cabin. The downpour has become torrential. There's no way Buffy could glide in these conditions.

We run toward the woods, calling Buffy's name and splashing muddy water everywhere.

If I were an animal, where would I hide to ride out the storm? Childhood memories bob to the surface. I was obsessed with animals as a kid. I read every zoo plaque and watched every nature program I could find. It was only when I was old enough to play sports that my interests were squashed by my parents.

I have a distinct memory of being enthralled by a David Attenborough episode on National Geographic. My father marched in and turned it off, ordering me to go outside to practice throwing and catching because he wasn't raising any tree huggers. I remember the shame I felt, as though I'd been caught watching porn. My parents weaponized shame against all three of their kids, but they needed to use it less with my siblings. Michael and Lizzie were far more likely to fall in line before any shaming was necessary.

Cricket switches on the flashlight and aims it the dark sky. I let loose a shrill whistle and yell Buffy's name. Raindrops pelt my face. If I look in the mirror right now, I have no doubt my skin will be covered in red splotches from the intensity.

"I can't see anything," Cricket says.

I turn to look at her. "That's because you need windshield wipers on those glasses."

She takes them off and attempts to stuff them in her pocket, but her fingers are too slick. The frames fall straight into a fast-moving stream of water.

"Your glasses!" I rush to retrieve them, but I'm too late.

"Leave them. It's fine."

"You won't be able to see."

"I can see fine, Charlie."

"Who wears contact lenses and glasses at the same time?" My face snaps to hers as the realization slams into me. "You don't need them to see."

There's no need for verbal confirmation. Her expression tells me I'm right.

"I can't believe this."

"I like the way they look, okay? They're fashion frames. I have perfect vision."

A gasp escapes me. "You're not even near-sighted?"

She drops her gaze. "I'm sorry. I have perfect vision."

"You talk about authenticity, yet here you are walking around like you're half blind."

"I never said I couldn't see without them."

"It's implied by the wearing of them on a daily basis."

"So what does that mean? That I've entered into some sort of contract with the public to be visually impaired?"

"There's a certain expectation, yes." I give her a rueful shake of my head. "You're a fraud, Cricket, if that's even your real name."

"You already know it isn't."

Laughter bubbles up to the surface and I don't bother to resist. I let it pour out of me.

Her hand rests on her hip. "I'm glad you're enjoying this moment. You should really savor it. Care to take a video for posterity?"

"Would you object?" I hold up my phone and she swats it away.

"Of course I would object." Something catches her eye, and she shushes me.

"You're the one talking," I point out.

She motions behind me. I turn around and squint in the gloaming. It takes me a second to spot her. Buffy is atop a branch curled against the trunk of an oak tree. She's shivering. She's too high to reach without climbing, which doesn't feel particularly safe at the moment.

"Aim the light at her," I tell Cricket.

The second the light hits Buffy, she glides toward me in search of safety. I guide her into the pocket of my hoodie, which is soaking wet by now, but the sugar glider doesn't seem to mind.

Cricket switches off the light. "We found her."

As much as I want to celebrate this victory, I can feel Buffy's vibrations through the wet cotton. "We should get her dry."

Cricket takes off in the direction of Gloria's cabin and I follow at a slower pace, exercising caution. One slippery step and I could crush the very creature I'm trying to save. I try not to think about that.

My heart is thumping like an erratic drumbeat by the time Gloria's door swings open. Cricket ushers me inside first so that I can deliver the precious parcel. Gloria's face is streaked with tears when I tug open my pocket to reveal Buffy.

Gloria throws her arms around me and breaks down, choking out relieved sobs. I don't care about anyone as much as Gloria cares about this tiny animal. I feel in awe of her emotions, but mostly, I feel deprived. Why have I not grown that attached to another living creature? Where's my Buffy or my Chewy? My Olivia?

My anyone.

She scoops Buffy from my wet pocket and carries her to a blanket where she wraps her delicate body in warmth.

"Thank you both," Gloria says.

"It's no problem," I say. "I'm glad we found her."

"She took refuge under a tree," Cricket adds. "I bet she would've stayed there until the rain passed."

Gloria seems to really see us for the first time. "Look at the state of you. You're both saturated."

Gloria spends fifty weeks a year helping someone else without support. I have no desire for her to feel guilty about asking for help now. "Nothing a couple towels can't handle," I say. I feel Cricket's eyes on me, but I resist the urge to meet her gaze.

"Maybe you should wait here until the storm is over," Gloria suggests, but neither of us seems keen to stay.

"We're already a wet mess," Cricket says. "And we're making puddles on your floor."

"Thank you again," Gloria tells us. She looks ready to cry all over again.

"Have a good night," I say. We leave before the fresh batch of tears begin to flow.

As we reenter Cricket's cabin, I realize why I didn't want to see the gratitude in her eyes. It's the same reason I felt uncomfortable with Gloria's praise.

Because I don't deserve it.

And not only because I registered for camp under false pretenses. It's more than that. Deeper.

I shove the feelings into a mental trunk and slam the lid shut. I can't think too hard right now. I am drenched and exhausted, and I want to sleep, which will prove difficult in a confined space with Cricket.

She waits until we're both showered, dried and dressed for bed to speak. "I appreciate you braving the weather with me. You didn't have to do that." She's wearing cotton shorts and a Geek Chic T-shirt yet somehow manages to look sexy as hell. It's a gift, one that I wouldn't mind unwrapping under different circumstances.

"I didn't do anything special," I object. "Anybody here would've done the same."

"I know, but you haven't been 'anybody here' until recently." She waves a hand at the desk. "Feel free to take your stuff out of your bag and let it dry. I'm sure some of your things are wet."

"Thanks." I place my laptop on the desk and spot a pack of scratch-off lottery cards wrapped in a rubber band on the corner of the desk. "If you're saving those for a rainy day, I have good news. The time has come."

She musters a smile. "I'm in the process of relocating them."

"You don't plan to scratch them off?" Cricket clearly needs the boost to her bank account.

"I found these in my dad's secret stash after he died," she says. "I've held on to them because ... Well, I'm not sure why, honestly."

I dig through my pockets for a coin. "You can use a little luck."

Cricket barks a laugh. "My dad was many things, Charlie, but lucky isn't one of them."

I realize in that moment that Cricket has spoken more about her grandparents than her parents and perhaps there's a reason for it—that life at Lake Willa wasn't as idyllic as it seems. The lawyer in me should be salivating at this small revelation, knowing that a chink in Abernathy armor could be useful to LandStar, but the human in me feels only empathy for Cricket. Those lottery cards obviously hold some emotional weight.

"Why not give them up at swag swap?"

"I considered it, but I wanted to get rid of the T-shirt more." She climbs into bed and inches over until she's against the wall. "There's room for you. It isn't much, but it's better than the floor."

Heat rises in my gut and spreads to all my appendages, and I do mean all of them. "I don't mind the floor."

"Don't be ridiculous. It isn't the floor of the Ritz. It's a hard wooden floor that's going to be cold and damp right now." She pats the side of the bed. "I promise not to try anything."

It isn't her I'm worried about.

I debate my options, which are basically the floor or the bed. There isn't even a bathtub to consider.

"I'm six-four," I tell her. "I'll take up way more space than you."

"I'll manage. Come on. I'm sure we're both dead tired. It'll be fine."

Reluctantly, I join her in the twin bed. It's instantly like a game of Twister, where we each struggle to find agreeable spots for our limbs that don't encroach on the other person. As she attempts to relocate her arm, her hand grazes my side, and I jerk back. Unfortunately, that swift reaction fails to take into account the lack of bed space and I land on the floor with a thud.

Cricket's head appears over the side of the bed. "Omigod, are you okay? I'm so sorry. I forgot you were ticklish."

I climb back into bed, my pride more bruised than my

tailbone. "It's not your fault." I hear the sourness in my tone and wish I could snatch it back.

Cricket notices, too, but instead of sweeping it under the bed, she asks, "Lots of people are ticklish. Why does it embarrass you?"

Not for the first time, her directness catches me off guard. I find myself matching her candor. "My dad thinks men need to be tough under any and all circumstances."

"And that includes the ancient art of tickling?"

I nod. "Laughter is a weakness. A loss of control."

She whistles. "Your dad must be a good time in the sack. I don't envy your mom."

I feel myself cringe. "Thanks for that mental image right before I fall asleep."

"No wonder you find it so hard to let your hair down. I suppose your dad thinks that fun isn't manly either."

"If I play something, the primary goal is to win. If it isn't a competition, then there's no point."

Pain seeps into her features. "That explains a lot."

I narrow my eyes at her. "What's that supposed to mean?"

"Your response to my comment about your dad yester-day." She props herself up by an elbow. "You must feel conflicted about him. On the one hand, he's your dad and you love him. On the other hand, he's an asshole. Trust me, I understand more than you know."

Her comment triggers my lawyer brain, which quickly makes the connection between the lottery cards and the paper I found. I'm tempted to present the document to her right here and now, except that I left it tucked under my mattress for safekeeping. I also don't want to upset her. It's clear she had unresolved issues with her father, and I have no desire to show her exactly how much he sucked.

"What happened when you didn't win?" she asks.

"A variety of punishments. My favorite was the silent treatment because at least I didn't have to listen to him critique my performance in excruciating detail."

"Good grief, Charlie. That's monstrous. You were a kid. You didn't deserve to be treated like that."

I stare into the darkness, remembering how trapped and helpless I felt when being subjected to one of my father's 'helpful' critiques. I'd leave a game walking tall, only to be reduced to the size of an ant by the time the car rolled into the driveway.

"The messed-up part of it is that I thought the whole thing was normal. That all parents were as tough as mine."

"Your mom too?"

"They tend to operate as a team when it comes to parenting, so it's hard to know when they actually disagree." Either way, she was complicit in his behavior.

Cricket strokes my arm. "You deserve to feel joy, Charlie."

"Why?"

"Do you need a reason?"

"I'm not the sugar glider-saving man you think I am."

"Of course you are. I just witnessed it."

"It's out of character for me."

"Helping another human being in need is out of character for you?"

"It is when there's no payoff."

She shifts position again, and I become acutely aware of the length of her body alongside mine. I'd managed to avoid it until now. My heart beats faster and I try to slow it down through sheer force of will.

"Are you trying to tell me everything with you is transactional? Because I don't believe that."

"You barely know me," I say.

"Then educate me. Tell me something about you that I can't observe with my own two eyes."

"You mean your own two fully functional eyes?"

She elbows me in the ribs.

I fix my gaze on the eggshell white ceiling. Anything to avoid looking at the woman next to me. "If I don't get this promotion, then I'll be a failure, and my mother and father will feel like they failed as parents."

"Can't you get a promotion next year if you don't get one this year?"

"It isn't about that. It's about bragging rights. This year is an achievement. Youngest lawyer in the firm's hundred-year history to make partner. Next year, I'd be tied with the youngest."

"And who was that?"

"Jerry Larkin in nineteen-sixty-seven."

"Pffft. Jerry Larkin sounds like a knob."

I feel a smile tug at the corners of my mouth. "Apparently he was kind of a jackass."

"Is that the kind of legacy you want? To have some lawyer talking about you in fifty years, that you were the youngest partner in the firm's history and also a giant asshat?"

"I would hope that isn't my reputation."

"Well, if you ask me, your parents already failed."

My head jerks toward her. "What makes you say that?"

"Because they made you think that achievement is more important than your own happiness."

"You think I'm unhappy?"

She lets loose that bawdy laugh. "Charlie, you're downright miserable."

I turn back to the ceiling. "Gee, thanks."

"I'm not trying to give you a hard time, I swear. It's the way you talk about your job and making partner. None of it seems to bring you joy."

"Then I guess we're both joyless freaks," I say.

She slides to a seated position. "I'm not the one walking around like a robot in the wild."

"Maybe not, but I get the sense that you're like Gloria, marking time until this camp opens every summer. That's no way to live either."

"I love this camp."

"I know you do, but what about the other months of the year when the camp is closed?"

"Not a fan, I'll be honest. Saddest day of the year is the day I close up for the season. I let myself have a good cry."

"What do you do the rest of the year?"

"I work at the reception desk for a ski resort in the winter."

"Why not get creative? Try to find ways to extend the season."

She knocks my arm with her own. "You're supposed to be sweet-talking the camp out from under me. Here's your big chance to tell me how much better my life will be if I take your money."

"Not my money. LandStar's money."

"Whatever. If you plan to become a big shot, you need to work on your persuasion techniques because from where I'm sitting, you're on my side."

"That's only because I'm squeezed next to you."

"If the lawyers at your firm could see you now."

"They'd be jealous," I blurt. At first, she laughs, but then her smile melts away like heated snow. "What's wrong?"

"I can't tell if you mean it."

"Why wouldn't I mean it?"

"Because you're trying to play me. Charm me so that I'll sign over the land."

Now it's my turn to prop myself up by an elbow. "Do you really think that?"

"Isn't that the real reason you registered? To find a way to make me sell?" Her eyes are downcast. "It's okay to admit it. I won't be mad, as long as you don't intend to follow through with it now that you've spent time with us."

I think of the document tucked under my mattress. I'll have to destroy it. There's no way I would do that to Cricket —or any of the other campers. I see how important this camp is to them, and I can't imagine the rustic cabins being replaced by luxury condos or anything else. Nerd camp belongs right here in this safe, idyllic space.

"Charlie?"

This is the moment of truth, literally. "I fully intended to find leverage to use against you to get my promotion."

"But you've changed your mind," she says matter-of-factly.

"How can you be so sure?"

"Because you're kinder than you give yourself credit for." Her lips soften into a sad smile. "And I forgive you."

Relief floods my body. I can't believe how important it was to hear her say those words. "You're not going to kick me out of camp? Or more imminently, out of this bed?"

"I'm also kinder than you give me credit for." She slips back down to rest her head on the pillow. "And so you know, there's nothing you could've done that would've convinced me to sell. Not a single thing on planet Earth."

"No kidding. I've been around you long enough to know that I can't make you do anything you don't want to do."

She studies me closely. "If you already decided not to find dirt on me, then why are you here? Why haven't you made an excuse and gone back to the city?"

"I guess I want them to think I'm giving it my best shot. If I leave early, they'll wonder if there wasn't more I could've done."

"You could lie. Tell them I caught you snooping and kicked you out, or would that be considered a worse failure than finding nothing at all?" She hesitates. "Do you really think there's anything to find?"

She's presented me with the perfect opportunity to tell her about the document, yet I can't bring myself to do it. It wouldn't be fair to add to her negative feelings toward her father, a man no longer alive to confront. The negative emotions would fester inside her and I don't want that for her. As they say, ignorance is bliss.

I shrug. "I guess we'll never know."

My answer generates a wide smile that warms me from the inside out. I want to say something equally worthwhile to keep her smile in place. "There is one thing I'm wondering though."

"What's that?"

I dare to make eye contact. "Did it work?"

The shine in her eyes tells me she knows exactly what I mean. "Does it matter?"

"I'm curious. It's the lawyer in me."

Her earnest expression tugs at heartstrings I didn't know were part of my anatomy until now. I expect her to defuse the moment with a joke.

Instead, she says, "Like a charm."

We stare at each other. This is a complication I didn't anticipate. Because as much as I want to pretend otherwise, I like her too. A lot.

Too much, in fact.

"Thank you for your honesty. It means more than you know." She pulls the sheet to her shoulder and turns to face the wall.

"You're welcome," I say, because I don't know how else to respond. I'm taken aback by my willingness to share things with her that I've never told anybody. She didn't even need to pry it out of me. I just—said it.

It takes me another forty-five minutes to fall asleep. I wait until I hear her breathing change and know that she's drifted off before I can do the same. Courtney Abernathy might be the only obstacle in my life I haven't wanted to overcome.

Chapter Fourteen

Cricket

Charlie is gone when I wake up. The rain has stopped, thank goodness. I'll have to make sure none of the other cabins flooded during the night and assess the damage to Charlie's cabin.

I get out of bed and pad to the bathroom, grateful for the return to privacy. Having Charlie in my space was tough—for multiple reasons. I brush my teeth, unable to get the image of him out of my mind. At one point in the night, I woke up in a twisted position to find my leg crossed over his. I swung it back to my side and pressed my back against the wall to keep it from happening again.

Our talk last night was the most open and honest one we've had since his arrival. I'm grateful he felt like he could talk to me. A small, critical voice in my head wonders whether to believe him, that maybe his vulnerability is part of the con. It wouldn't be the first time a man used my compassion against me. I found it hard to trust after that, especially when it's someone I'm attracted to. Maybe the attraction is coloring my perception. I'd have to talk to Gloria or Ben, except then they'd know I had the hots for Charlie. I can't share that information with the others.

Angela might be a good candidate for a confession. She's no-nonsense when it comes to men. If she thinks Charlie is full of shit, she won't hesitate to say so.

I resolve to speak to her in private the next chance I get, but without divulging the specifics. I don't want to break Charlie's trust just because he might be breaking mine.

The more I think about it, the more I think his stories were real, especially the one about his father's critiques. He actually seemed surprised by the memory, like maybe he'd repressed it. I have no doubt there's an unhealthy amount of repression going on in the Thorpe family.

I bring a stack of towels to Charlie's cabin and leave them on the floor to soak up the remaining water. He's already returned his duffel bag to the room, but there's no sign of him. No one else reports flooding in their cabins, so I decide to knock on Angela's door before breakfast.

"Come in, honey."

I open the door and enter the cabin. "How did you know it was me?"

Angela pokes her head through the bathroom doorway. "I didn't, but everyone here is 'honey' to me."

That tracks.

I stand in the doorway as she puts on her makeup. She peers at her reflection in the mirror and groans.

"What?"

"I look like I have two of Tom Selleck's mustaches above my eyes."

"How could Tom Selleck have two mustaches?"

She glares at me in the mirror. "You're missing the point. My eyebrows look like very hungry caterpillars that have eaten their way through a picnic."

"Think of it this way then: soon they'll transform into beautiful butterflies and fly away. Problem solved."

She squints at herself. "You're not wrong. I've seen makeup artists on YouTube do amazing work with eyebrow pencils." She starts to dig through her makeup bag. "I don't think I brought one."

I lean against the doorjamb. "I need your advice."

She whirls around to face me. "This is about Charlie, isn't it?"

My head jerks up. "How did you guess?"

"You can't be serious. You two have been circling each other like horny sharks all week."

I don't love the image of horny sharks. "How do I know whether I can trust him?"

"Oh, sweetie. Is this about Patrick?"

I shrink back at the mention of his name. "No, I'm asking about Charlie. Why would you bring up He Who Shall Not Be Named?"

"Because that's why you're wondering. You trusted Patrick, cared for him, and he betrayed you. Now you've developed feelings for Charlie, and you're scared." She flicks a finger. "Been there many times over."

"You?" I laugh. "You've never been scared when it comes to men."

"I'm like a duck, darling. All you see is me gliding across the surface. What you don't see are my little webbed feet splashing frantically beneath the water."

Her confession shocks me. It hadn't occurred to me that Angela would be afraid of anything.

"You're thirty-two, darling. When was the last time you went into the city or had a date?"

"As a matter of fact, I had a doctor's appointment in the city."

"And when was that?"

"Last year."

Her look is pointed. "Sweetie, you're the hobbit who refused to step foot out of the Shire."

Is Charlie right about me? Do I keep my life in a holding pattern fifty weeks of the year? "What's the difference between a hobbit who got to stay in the Shire and Samwise Gamgee?"

"Courage. To be afraid and jump off that cliff anyway, despite your fears, instead of slinking off to comfort and safety and forever wondering 'what if?'" She pokes my arm. "Patrick was the worst kind of coward, but you, my darling, have courage in spades."

I'm not convinced. "What makes you say that?"

"Do you really not see yourself? You were a baby when your father died and left you this place, yet you rose to the occasion and made it something better than it was."

"I wasn't a baby. I was in my twenties."

She pinches my cheek. "Still a baby, and we both know you were the one who kept this place going even before your father passed. You could've crumbled in the face of all that adversity."

"But I didn't."

"No, you did not."

"And what about Charlie?" My face ignites at the mere mention of his name. "Do you think he has courage?"

"I'd have to know him better. What do you think?"

"I'm really not sure."

She clasps her hands in front of her. "When I met Bob, my second husband, I was terrified that he wouldn't be interested in a woman like me. I mean, I thought he saw me as a good-time girl, but not necessarily a long-time one. His first wife had been Betty Crocker. She loved to play caretaker, and we both know that isn't my vibe. I was convinced he'd ditch me when a Martha Stewart came along."

"He obviously didn't."

"Let me finish my story, darling. One night we'd gone back to his house after a night of dancing. I looked at Bob standing in the kitchen and thought, *This is home.*"

"His kitchen was that nice?"

"Oh yes, but that's not the point. The point is that Bob was home for me, wherever that was, and so I decided to speak up right then and there and tell him how I felt. We were married the very next month."

"You move fast, Angela."

"I'm glad I did. He died a year later. Imagine if I had waited. We would've lost that precious time together." She shakes her head. "I could've asked and gotten a different answer, of course, one I didn't like, but it still would've been worth asking because I would've known to stop wasting my time on someone who wasn't willing to commit."

"Thanks for sharing that with me. It helps." I smile at her. "Any prospects for your next husband?"

"No, but I'm having a grand old time anyway."

I lean my head on her shoulder. "I'm glad you're here. Every year I think you might not come back."

In a rare display of affection, she drops a kiss on the top of my head. "Only Robert Redford himself could keep me away." She pauses. "Unless it's the Robert Redford from the Marvel movies. I didn't care for him."

"He was playing Alexander Pierce, not himself." I straighten. "I should go. People will wonder where I am."

As I reach the door, Angela says, "At the very least, I hope you get to test drive him. If he can make you blush like that when he isn't even in the room, imagine what he's capable of when he is."

I flee the cabin before she starts rattling off a list of descriptive suggestions.

CHARLIE

The cabin floor is disappointingly damp. I can't manage another night in Cricket's bed. I feel like I was offered the One Ring and was strong enough to refuse its call.

Hold up.

I, Charles Owen Frederick Thorpe IV, made a *Lord of the Rings* reference.

I stare at my reflection in the bathroom mirror to make sure I still recognize myself. Same face. Same hair, albeit slightly more disheveled than usual.

Very different thoughts.

I still can't believe how open I was with her. I talked about my parents, my career, my *feelings*. This isn't me.

What have I done to myself? What has Cricket done to me?

If I'm being honest, though, I like who I am when I'm with her. It's a scary realization that makes me deeply uncomfortable. When my phone buzzes, I answer it without looking, grateful for a distraction from my confusing thoughts.

"Hey, buddy. How's Nerds 'R Us?"

I shrink inside at the sound of Matt's voice. "Going great. What's up?"

"Wondering whether you've sealed the deal yet."

"Not yet, but I'm close," I lie. No way am I giving Matt Lyman an inch.

"Then I guess that means you won't make it to the charity auction tonight."

I pinch the bridge of my nose. I forgot all about the event. People from LandStar will be there, as well as other clients. Clients who Matt will not hesitate to schmooze in my absence.

"I guess I'll have to miss out," I hear myself say. "Say hello to Riggieri for me."

"No problem. Enjoy the rustic lifestyle. Hope those Gucci loafers can withstand the dirt."

"They're holding up. I'll see you next week." I hang up before I have to listen to his voice one more time. The thought of being back in the office with Lyman and everybody else ... It seems like a galaxy far, far away.

Damn. The campers have infected me with their love of pop culture. Soon I'll be collecting bobbleheads and sticking them on Hugo's dashboard.

I search for the nearest hardware store and grab my wallet. Cricket intercepts me in the parking lot as I'm reversing out of my spot.

I roll down the passenger window. "Hey."

"Hey. Where are you off to?"

"There's a hardware store a couple miles away. Thought I'd buy a space heater for my cabin to try to dry it out."

"Good idea. You drive. I'll buy." She slides into the passenger seat before I can object.

"It's my cabin. I'll buy the heater."

She folds her arms. "It's my camp. I can buy the heater."

It feels like we're on a first date arguing over who pays the check.

I pull out of the parking lot and onto the road. "We can split it."

Her silence seems like acquiescence.

"Hugo handles well," she remarks once we're cruising along the country roads. It's a beautiful day, with sun-dappled trees and a bright blue sky. A stark change from yesterday.

"Does this mean you no longer think of my car as a douchemobile?"

She pats the dashboard. "He's growing on me."

"This is your first ride. Give it time and you'll want one of your own."

She laughs. "Oh Charlie, I wouldn't dream of spending this much money on a car."

"Why not? You spend more than necessary on shoes. You're wearing special-edition Converse. Those aren't cheap."

"Maybe not, but they're not the price of a luxury vehicle either. I don't deprive myself of all niceties, I choose them carefully and with my limited budget in mind." She pauses. "Which is not remotely the same as yours."

Guilt seeps into my pores. "I'm sorry. I didn't mean to sound like an entitled asshole."

"It's okay. To be honest, even if I had your money, I wouldn't choose to spend it on an expensive car."

"No? Then what would you spend it on? A life-size replica of Gandalf?"

She beams at the thought. "That would be awesome, wouldn't it? Or I could create my own version of Hobbiton right here."

"Might be worth a trip to New Zealand to see the real deal. Seems like a beautiful country."

She nods. "I'd love to see it in person, but I know

myself. I'd spend that money on the camp. It needs work, as you can personally attest, but I probably shouldn't be admitting that to you."

"Why not?"

"You know why not."

I frown. "Do you still worry I'll use it against you?"

She averts her gaze. "I don't know. Maybe."

What would it take to convince her that I won't betray her? "That guy must've really hurt you."

Her face turns to stone as she reaches for the dashboard. "Let's see what Charlie listens to when no one else is listening."

Mozart blasts through the speakers. "Sorry about that," I tell her. "I listen to it as a calming technique."

"No judgment," she says and turns down the volume. "Ever listen to move theme songs? John Williams is a freakin' genius. Let's see if we get service." She taps on her phone. "Check out that French horn. Legend."

"It's the theme song from *Jurassic Park*."

"Damn right it is."

For the remainder of the drive, we listen to recordings of live orchestras play one John Williams song after another. I'm blown away by the number of masterpieces one man has composed, to the point where I'm disappointed to have to park the car when we arrive at the store.

Inside, we purchase a space heater based on the recommendation of the owner, an older man named Juan-Carlo who's known Cricket since she was apparently "knee-high to a grasshopper," which seems apt given her nickname. He gives us a friends-and-family discount and receives a hug and kiss on the cheek from Cricket in return. I can't imagine getting a hug and a kiss from a client because I negotiated them a better deal. She lives in a different world, and I feel lucky to experience it, if only for a little while.

We continue our John Williams concert on the drive back to camp, albeit at a low-enough volume so we can hear each other. Talking to Cricket is like talking to a best friend I've known since kindergarten, except I don't actually have one of those. She manages to extract information out of me that I typically wouldn't share or wouldn't have even asked myself if not for her directness. It's a startling revelation, that I'm perfectly adept at directness in a professional setting, but not necessarily in a personal one.

Back in my cabin, I set up the heater and Cricket heads to the arts and crafts cabin to check on a paint spill. We barely see each other the rest of the day, which I have mixed feelings about. I simultaneously want to spend more time with her but also want to keep my distance. It's a battle of my own wills. I channel that energy into an all-afternoon board game extravaganza where I crush my competition. I even manage to win games I've never heard of before today. I feel a twinge of guilt when Stefan cries after a brutal 7 Wonders loss, but he assures me that it's all good and that he cries regularly, which doesn't strike me as very Viking-like, but what do I know?

I stick close to my board game competitors in the cafeteria, where we enjoy a hearty dinner of chili and cornbread. Bernie's skills are topnotch and today I tell her so. There are restaurants in Philly that would be over the moon to find someone with her culinary talent.

"I'm happy here, but I appreciate the compliment," Bernie says.

"But you could make a name for yourself, not to mention a lot more money in the city."

"And I'd also have to live and work there. No thank you.

I'll take the fresh mountain air any day of the week and twice on Sundays, even in the dead of winter."

"Sit down and eat the rest of your cornbread, Charlie," Gloria urges. "Not everyone prioritizes money."

"Some of us work to live, but we don't live to work," Bernie says, before returning to the cramped kitchen.

I finish my cornbread before I leave, careful not to leave a trail of crumbs that might lead a hungry bear to my cabin door. My phone lights up with a voicemail from my father, and I realize I've kept it on silent all day. I spend the evening returning phone calls, including one to Jeannie.

"What's the emergency?" I ask.

"No emergency. I wanted to hear more about camp."

I sigh. "My cabin flooded last night."

"You're not going to report that to LandStar, are you? I'm sure that jerk would want you to find a way to use it against the camp owner."

"Matt called me to gloat about the charity event tonight."

"I'm surprised you didn't drive down for it."

"I considered it."

"But?"

"I checked the traffic report, and it would've taken me almost an hour longer than usual."

"That sounds like an excuse. The Charlie I know would've done whatever it takes to show up." She pauses. "I like this Charlie better."

"Thanks ... I think."

"Are you still enjoying yourself?"

"It's complicated."

Jeannie chuckles. "No, it isn't, Charlie. It's an easy question. Yes or no."

"Then yes."

"Good. Milk the time for all its worth. You deserve it."

"Except the client is paying me to be here and I'm not doing the thing he sent me to do. It's unethical."

"Then don't bill him for the time. Maybe talk to Joel to write some of it off. You're a smart guy. You'll figure it out. Forget we exist for another few days. It won't kill you."

I smile into the phone. "Have a good night, Jeannie."

I no sooner put down the phone when there's a knock at my door. I hope my visitor didn't overhear my conversation.

I open the door to reveal Cricket. In ripped denim shorts, a plaid red shirt with the sleeves rolled up, and a hint of cleavage, she's giving off sexy farmer's daughter vibes that immediately trigger a throbbing sensation in places I'd rather not acknowledge. I force myself to focus on her face instead.

"No glasses tonight?"

"I don't have a pair that matches my outfit." She crouches down and places her palms flat on the hardwood. "Your floor is still damp. You shouldn't sleep in your cabin tonight."

"It's not too bad."

"What if there are mold spores?"

"I doubt mold grows that fast."

"We should ask Olivia. I bet she knows."

"Is that why you're here? To save me from ingesting a lungful of mold and avoiding a lawsuit?"

"Actually no." She holds out her hand. "Come with me."

"If I want to live?" I ask in my best Arnold Schwarzenegger voice, which admittedly isn't very impressive. I sound more like the Count from Sesame Street.

"No, I want to show you something."

"I saw Stefan's balloon animals at the firepit earlier. Very impressive."

"Not the balloon animals. This is better."

My curiosity is piqued. "It obviously isn't a runaway Buffy."

"Nope. This is a special treat. It only happens on certain nights in the summer, and lucky for you, you're here for one of them."

I clasp her outstretched hand and let her guide me to the dock.

"Your chariot awaits," she says, and points to the double kayak bobbing in the water.

"You want to kayak now? It's dark out there."

"Not for long. You'll see." She offers a cryptic smile. If I'm Superman, her smile is my Kryptonite.

I climb into the kayak and hold it steady while she slides between my legs, which feels more natural to me than it has any right to. Our paddles slice through the darkness as we head toward the middle of the lake. I have no clue what to expect. I hope the Poconos doesn't have its own version of the Loch Ness monster. On the plus side, though, a ferocious beast might persuade LandStar to abandon their plans.

"Stop paddling," she says in a voice that's low and reverent.

Then I spot them. To be fair, they're impossible to miss.

Chapter Fifteen

Cricket

"It's magical, isn't it?" Hundreds of tiny lights hover above the lake's surface. "This is as close as I'll ever get to the Lantern Festival in *Rapunzel*."

Charlie's breath seems well and truly taken as he gapes at nature's own fairy lights. "I've never seen this many fireflies in my whole life combined. My cabin is close to the lake. How have I missed this?"

"It doesn't happen every night. You need the right conditions."

He cranes his neck toward shore. "Where's everybody else?"

I wave a hand in the direction of the campground. "Either asleep or part of an RPG campaign. They'll be holed up for hours." Which means we have the entire lake to ourselves. I tilt my head back to look at him. "What do you think?"

"This is spectacular, truly. Thank you for sharing it with me." He's quiet for a beat. "Why did you decide to share it with me?"

"Because it's part of the camp's charm. I want it to win you over."

"I already told you I won't give any intel to LandStar."

My pulse accelerates, knowing what I'm about to confess. "Okay fine. Maybe *I* want to win over you." I hold my breath and await his reaction.

"Maybe you already have," he says, and wraps his arms around me.

Relief ripples through me as I nestle against his chest. The steady beat of his heart joins the other soothing sounds of the night.

"What's the most romantic night you've ever had?" I ask.

He's quiet for a moment as we let the kayak drift. "It was a Phillies game."

I choke back laughter. "Your most romantic date was at a baseball game?"

"What? We had seats right behind home plate. It was awesome."

"Awesome, maybe. Romantic? I'm not so sure."

"How about you? Anyone ever chase you down in an airport to declare his love?"

"That's neither romantic nor realistic. They'd never get past security."

"No romantic highlights then?"

Not until now, I want to say, but I simply shake my head instead.

"Do you ever sleep outside under the stars?" he asks. "I don't mean in a kayak. With the way you wriggle around in your sleep, that would be too dangerous."

I bask in his playful teasing. Patrick used to tease me, too, but there was often an undercurrent of meanness to it. A putdown buried amongst the ribbing rubble. Charlie is different. Despite his so-called competitive nature, he has a calming energy. It occurs to me that he may not know himself as well as he thinks.

"I've slept outside a few times, but I usually wake up covered in mosquito bites."

"And how many times have you been skinny-dipping?"

"That would be zero."

"Wait one second. Are you telling me that in all the years you've lived here, you've never once been skinny-dipping in this lake?"

"Why is that so hard to believe?"

"Because the lake is right here and you're alone much of the time."

"When I'm alone here, the water is too frigid to swim in, let alone naked. Most of the summer I'm surrounded by children. Skinny-dipping would get me arrested."

"We have to remedy this right now."

I shift to look at him. "Charlie Thorpe, there is no way I'm climbing out of this comfortable kayak to strip naked and hurl myself into a body of cold water."

He sticks his hand in the water. "Bath water. Feel it."

"Why does it have to be skinny-dipping? Can't we go for a moonlight swim?"

"Because it isn't the same. There's something primal about swimming in the nude. You can't die without having done it at least once in your life."

"My parents and grandparents would beg to differ."

"How do you know they didn't skinny-dip?"

"Because it wasn't their style."

"Oh, did they wear baggy Princess Leia T-shirts that hid their bodies, too?"

I grow still. "I don't hide myself."

"Of course you do. Your fake glasses."

"Fashion frames."

"Your fashion frames. Your head-to-toe pop-culture clothing."

"It's called self-expression."

"It's called hiding. I get it. You don't want to be seen." He nudges me. "But I see you, Courtney Abernathy, and you're amazing. Everything about you is amazing."

His bolstering words dance along my bare skin.

"Come on. I've been doing all sorts of things outside my comfort zone. Now it's your turn. If it helps, I'll turn away until your lady parts are submerged in water."

I cast a sidelong glance at him, sizing him up. "And you'll be naked too?"

"Of course. I love it."

How about that? Charlie Thorpe loves naked swimming. I guess I don't know him as well as I think. I would, however, like to know him better. Much better.

"You'll keep your dangly bits away from my lady parts?"

"Your wish is my command."

I stare at the water. "All right. You've been such a good sport about everything we've thrown at you. I'll do it for you."

"Don't do it for me. Do it for you." He picks up a paddle and maneuvers us closer to shore. "You'll thank me later."

I avert my gaze as Charlie strips down first, leaves his clothes in a pile in the kayak, and launches himself straight into the lake. I turn back when I hear the splash.

His head surfaces a moment later. "Feels great. The temperature is perfect."

"Don't look," I tell him.

He switches to his back and floats, staring up at the night sky overhead. With his ears submerged in water and only the stars within sight, I imagine it's the most peace he's experienced in a long time.

I remove my clothes and nearly capsize the kayak in my rush to enter the water before being seen.

"I'm in," I gasp.

"How do you feel?" I ask.

"Chilly."

"Are you kidding? This is bath water." He swims closer to me. "You should float."

"So you can see my boobs? Nice try."

He points. "I can already see your boobs."

I fold my arms to cover my bare breasts. "I can't float."

"What do you mean you can't?"

"I mean it doesn't work. My body sinks like a stone."

"Then you're not doing it right."

I glare at him. "It's floating, Charlie, not rocket science."

"But it *is* science. Come on. I'll help you."

"I'm not floating on top of the water when I'm buck naked."

"What if I promise not to look?"

I feel a sensation against my leg and look down. "I think there's something in the water."

"Like a sea serpent?" he teases.

It touches me again and I jump. The next thing I know, my legs are wrapped around his torso. Without any clothing, the nudity adds an extra layer of complication.

"Your lady part is dangerously close to my dangly bit," he whispers.

My arms tighten around his neck. "Now that we're up close and personal, I'm here to tell you dangly bit is an understatement."

His low chuckle reverberates in my ear, sending shivers down my spine. "Is it gone?"

"Can't tell. I'm afraid to feel anything," I say, and in that moment, I recognize the bald truth of my statement. Our gazes lock and Charlie seems to understand.

That's when he kisses me.

One hand moves to cradle the back of my head and the other wraps around my waist to pull me closer. My boobs crush against his bare chest as the kiss intensifies. I lose myself to the hunger that's been growing inside me since the moment I met him.

Hot, wet, and a little wild—not a description I'd expect to apply to either one of us, yet here we are. The kiss is so electric that, for half a second, I worry about our safety given that we're engulfed by water.

"How about now?" he murmurs.

"I definitely feel ... something." All the things, in fact. Tingling. Aching. Breathless.

"Sorry," he says, and releases me. It takes me a second to realize he mistook my response for a comment on his throbbing erection, which I also felt because it was impossible not to. Sea serpent, indeed.

"No need to apologize. I had no idea you packed your own light saber."

He doesn't laugh. His eyes seem to generate their own heat. My heart pounds as we stare at each other like it's a contest, which maybe in his mind, it is. People talk about being 'in the moment,' but I've never felt as fully present as I do right now. Admittedly, I haven't experienced many romantic evenings in my life, but tonight is top of the charts. I'll still be thinking about our moonlit kiss on my deathbed. Quite frankly, I didn't expect someone like Charlie to be capable of injecting a kiss with that much passion. It feels like a dream. An incredibly pleasant dream.

I'm not sure what persuaded me to give in to his request. I've always been self-conscious about my body, not because I think there's anything specifically wrong with it. I realize that Charlie is right about me. For reasons that I don't need to dig very far to unearth, I'm uncomfortable feeling seen.

And Charlie Thorpe sees me.

Those blue-green eyes are worse than Superman's X-ray vision because they see straight to my emotional core. All this time I've been working on his vulnerability, trying to coax him out of his Gucci shell, when I was hiding behind my geek-chic outerwear.

Charlie clocked me—I don't choose those clothes for style alone. Like the lawyer in his tailored suit, I wear loose Marvel shirts like a protective suit of armor that announces to the world which kingdom I belong to, that way if they reject me, I can blame the kingdom. I can say they failed to get past the armor, so they can't be rejecting *me*. But without a willingness to remove the suit, I also don't give people a chance to know me.

To be seen.

Well, Charlie has seen all of me tonight, more than I ever intended to show him, in fact. It feels scary.

And it also feels really, really good.

If I never have another experience like this for the rest of my life, I'd die a happy woman, but if any falling stars happen to be passing overhead right now, please know I'd really like to have another experience like this, preferably with Charlie and preferably tonight.

CHARLIE

I can't believe I kissed Cricket. It wasn't my intention when I convinced her to skinny-dip with me. I fully expected a flat no to that request, like her response to Land-Star's proposal. The kiss seems to have shocked the entire world around us because absolute silence has descended upon the lake, and I'm too distracted by the taste of her to think of anything clever to say to break it.

Thankfully the water is high enough to keep her covered, although I can see the swell of her breasts, which makes me grateful my lower half is deeply submerged.

I clear my throat to break the spell. "Would you like to try floating now that the moon is behind some clouds? I can only see your silhouette. No sensitive areas."

"How big is the cloud?" She glances skyward.

"Very big and very slow-moving."

"That's what she said."

I crack a smile. "Think of this as a trust exercise."

"Well, that explains why I can't do it."

"You're naked in the water with me. There has to be a certain amount of trust there already or you wouldn't have agreed."

"You did already feel me up in the woods. I suppose nudity is the natural progression of events."

"That was for ticks!"

Laughing, she shifts to her back, and as promised, immediately sinks. My hands catch her lower back, one dangerously close to her bare ass, and lift her toward the surface. Her perfect breasts rise to my eye line. Whose idea was this anyway?

"Relax, Cricket. You're not going to drown. I won't let you."

"It won't look good for you if you do. Naked camp owner found in the arms of the primary suspect." She closes her eyes. "Even your law firm will have a helluva time defending you."

"We don't handle criminal cases."

Her legs start to drift down, and I move my hand lower to buoy her.

"Your hand is on my ass, Charles Xavier Thorpe."

"Is it?"

"Either that or this lake has a small octopus."

"This lake is pitch black. Nessie herself could be living here, and no one would be the wiser." I realize my hand is still cradling her backside. "Want me to move it?"

She turns her head toward me and opens her eyes. "Only if you want to."

Gauntlet thrown. The first kiss wasn't planned; we could write it off as a heat-of-the-moment situation and never speak of it again. This one, however, would be premeditated. This one would say not only that we meant it, but that we liked it enough to do it again.

Challenge accepted.

I lean in for another kiss, removing my hold on her in the process. As my lips reach hers, her head slips beneath the surface.

"Shit! Cricket!"

Her head pops up and bangs straight into my chin. I bite my tongue and my mouth fills with the metallic taste of blood.

"Omigod, Charlie! I'm so sorry. Are you okay?"

I can't speak.

Her lips find mine, soft and searching. When they part, there's a sudden painful reminder that my tongue suffered a grievous wound. I groan, prompting Cricket to draw back.

"Was that a sexy groan or an ouch-that-actually-hurts groan?"

"Can it be both?"

She threads her fingers through mine. "I know first aid. Let me kiss it better." She takes my tongue in her mouth and gently sucks. It takes all my self-control not to—

Pain stabs my calf, and I jerk away.

"Charlie?"

The intensity leaves me breathless, and not in a good way. "Leg cramp," I croak.

She hooks an arm around my chest and pulls me to shallower water. "Do you need me to rub it? Your leg, I mean."

"Let me stretch it, thanks." My calf throbs as I flex my foot forward and back until the cramp subsides.

"A friendly reminder that bananas are always available in the cafeteria," she says.

Leg cramps and bananas. I've definitely ruined the vibe. "It's getting late. We should probably go back to our cabins."

Hesitation flickers in her eyes. "Would you like to stay over again tonight?"

"Because of the mold spores?"

"Because I don't want this night to end."

Her directness sucks the oxygen from my lungs. Hell yes, I want to be in her bed, but sleep is the last thing on my mind.

"Are you sure?"

"We're both consenting adults. I don't see why not." She wades over to the kayak. "But first I'd better put on my clothes. The last thing I need is to give the campers a free show."

"It's worth the price of admission," I tell her.

Cricket showers first. I spend those five minutes pacing the cabin floor and reconsidering whether this is a good idea. I registered for camp under false pretenses. I snooped through her belongings to find evidence to use against her.

Nothing has to happen, I tell myself. We already proved that two people can share the same bed without having it turn sexual.

Of course, that was before the naked kissing.

She emerges from the bathroom in shorts and a T-shirt and with her wet hair wrapped in a towel. "Your turn. Hopefully I didn't use all the hot water."

I kind of hope she did. A cold shower will snap me out of this.

I enter the bathroom and immediately spot two frilly baskets filled with tiny bottles and other paraphernalia that weren't here before. "Where did all this stuff come from?"

Cricket pokes her head in. "Oh, those are from Angela. She wants me to have more of a self-care routine."

I point to the fluffy white slippers on the floor. "Does that involve owning your own spa?"

"You know Angela. Go big or go home." She motions to the mouthwash. "You might want to gargle that too. No clue what lurks in the lake water."

"Good point."

After I shower, I decide to have a little fun with Angela's products. I apply a green face mask that smells like cucumbers, teeth whitener, and slip on the fluffy white robe and slippers. The piece de resistance is the satin pink eye mask I wear like a headband. Anything to hear the sound of her bawdy laughter again.

Cricket is seated cross-legged on the bed when I emerge, and I'm rewarded with a sound so raw and throaty, it lingers in the air like a punchline to a dirty joke. "I'm glad to see someone taking advantage of my gifts."

"I'll be honest. I'm not a fan of the chemical taste of the teeth whitener."

"There's no rule that says you have to use every product all at once."

I nod. "You know what? In the right light my teeth look white enough." I spin back to the bathroom where I peel off the strips and rinse my mouth.

Cricket's smile remains firmly intact when I reenter the room. "If the partners at your law firm could see you now."

"Maybe they can." I glance around the cabin. "Is this a setup to blackmail me?"

"That's what the recording of 'Let It Go' is for. You have only yourself to blame for this."

"Fair enough. I accept full responsibility." I settle beside her on the bed and snap down my eye mask.

"Why are you smiling?" she asks. "Picturing the smooth, wrinkle-free skin you'll be enjoying after that mask washes off?"

"I'm having fun, which if you recall, is something you've encouraged me to do from the start."

"If I'd realized your idea of fun was a cucumber mask and fluffy slippers, I could've hooked you up days ago."

"Admit it. You had fun tonight too." She doesn't respond. "It's suddenly very quiet in here." I dare to lift the eye mask and find her observing me with a tense expression. "What?"

"You don't seem like a guy in the mood for sex."

"Can't we enjoy the night without complicating it?"

She stares at me for a beat before sliding under the covers. "That's fine. I'm sure it's for the best."

My bubble of confidence bursts. "What makes you say that?"

"Because we're incompatible."

That gets under my skin for reasons I don't fully understand. "How are we incompatible?"

"You're vanilla bean. I'm chocolate chip mint."

My laugh comes out like a chortle. "I'm vanilla?"

"There's nothing wrong with vanilla. It's the most popular flavor for a reason."

I turn toward her and prop myself up by my elbow. "You're calling me bland."

"Not at all."

"People don't have to like the same things to be compatible, you know."

"It isn't about ice cream flavors or movies or anything external. You're conflict avoidant. That's what makes us incompatible."

"I'm a lawyer, Cricket. If I were conflict avoidant, I couldn't do my job."

"You can do it for work because you don't care about it in the same way. No emotional stakes. You avoid hard conversations, like ones with your parents that you know will upset the natural order. I prefer to address things before they have a chance to fester."

"I care about my job."

"I didn't say otherwise. I said you care about it in a different way." She shrugs. "But if you'd rather not get naked again, I'll be disappointed, but I understand."

I'm unsure how to respond, although there are parts of my body that are way ahead of me.

"You said yourself we're incompatible. Sex isn't a good idea if it isn't going to lead to anything more fulfilling." She has no idea how hard it was to drag those words from my mouth.

But I meant them.

"Then why did you kiss me in the lake?"

'Because I couldn't *not* kiss you in that moment' doesn't seem like a solid answer, but if she wants emotional honesty, I'll give it to her. "Because I was exhausted."

She purses her lips, perplexed. "You were so worn out that your lips fell on mine?"

"No. I mean I didn't have the strength to fight my feelings for you anymore. I finally gave in to them."

My answer appears to rock her. "You have feelings for me?"

"I thought that's what we said in the kayak." A thought strikes me. "Wait, are *you* only interested in a fling?"

"No. That isn't my style." She smiles. "I guess we should've been more explicit."

"Doesn't get more explicit than naked kissing." I pause. "Is this what you would consider a hard conversation?"

"Yes," she says in a quiet voice. "And just so it's clear, I have feelings for you too."

I allow myself a satisfied smirk. "Now who's the emotionally unavailable one?"

She flops back onto the bed. "Damn, Charlie. You keep showing me to myself."

"Right back at you." I turn to face her. "You said you didn't want this night to end. Well, I don't want this to end." I motion between us. "Whatever this is, I want to keep it going."

She hooks her finger around the collar of the robe and tugs. "Then climb aboard, sailor. This ship is heading out to sea."

I roll on top of her. "I have no idea how that metaphor works in this scenario, but I get the drift."

She brushes her lips against my jawline, sending a hard shiver through me. "The drift. Even when you're being serious, you manage to be funny."

I don't want her to know the effect those lips are having on me. I dip my mouth to hers. She tastes like mint, not that I'm surprised. Between us, we swished enough mouthwash to destroy bacteria that hadn't even formed yet.

She pulls back, and I see splotches of green on her pale face. I point at her cheek. "You've got a little cucumber."

"I know *you* don't." She smiles. "And now you have pink on your cheeks, too."

I touch the mask that's hardened on my skin. "I should probably wash this off first."

"Do it after," she says, shifting her hips beneath me. "I think we've both waited long enough."

I wake up before dawn to feel the weight of Cricket's arm and leg pressed against me like it's the most natural thing in the world. My whole body stiffens, and I do mean all of it.

She tilts back her head to look at me. "Did my alarm wake you?"

"No. I didn't realize you were up."

"Sunrise yoga, remember?" She smiles. "Last night was pretty great, huh?"

"It was."

Straightening, she twists her torso to regard me. "What is it?"

"What do you mean? I agreed with you."

"Last night you were Mr. Fun. Now you sound like you're at a funeral. What happened?"

What happened is that I had hours in dark solitude to think. I can picture this lifestyle for myself—tranquil, serene, with my favorite person by my side. It's perfection, the kind of life people dream about.

And it's dangerous.

It isn't me. I'm not like Cricket. I wear suits and attend boring cocktail parties. I spend the majority of my days behind a desk at a computer. I'm in a committed relationship with my job. It wouldn't be fair to Cricket, knowing I can never be the man she wants me to be.

"You seem to think I'm not the competitive hard-ass I say I am..."

"That's right. You're not an extrovert either." She pats my leg. "I know you think you're Mr. Mayor, out there shaking hands and memorizing everybody's name, but that's all part of the act."

"Act?" I echo.

"You're not an extrovert, Charlie. You're an introvert forced to walk in the expensive shoes of an extrovert."

I relax slightly. "How does that work?"

"Your social battery runs out by the end of every day. All you want is to be left alone. That's why you like to work late. It isn't because you're a night owl. It's the time of day when you don't have to interact with other people."

It takes me a minute to digest what she's said. "I'm an introvert," I finally repeat.

"It's not an insult. We're all introverts here, for the most part. That's one reason this camp works so well. We understand it isn't personal when somebody wants to go hide in their room for a couple hours to recharge."

Growing up, I wasn't allowed to have 'down time.' If my parents were entertaining, the kids were expected to be charming and engaging until the last guest left for the evening. I took those habits straight to college with me, through law school, and into adulthood, not once questioning whether the behavior aligned with my actual needs.

Maybe Cricket is right. Maybe I don't know myself as well as I think.

She swings her leg over mine and switches to her stomach so that she's facing me. "It's okay to experience joy, Charlie. It isn't a crime."

"It isn't that." I can't explain this to her without revealing more about myself than I'm comfortable with. "If I acknowledge that I'm enjoying myself, that I feel happy, then that increases the odds that something bad will happen to take it all away."

"You're superstitious?"

"Not quite. It's more that if I let myself feel joy, the more it will hurt when it ends. If I don't let myself experience the high..."

"No high means no low. Got it."

"When I was a kid, the second my parents saw that I enjoyed something, it became a skill to master."

"Like baseball?"

I nod. "And if I wasn't deemed good enough, then it was taken away. Doing something simply for the fun of it—that isn't the Thorpe way."

She quirks an eyebrow. "I'm sorry. I'm stuck on the fact that Charlie Thorpe was bad at something. Is that true?"

"Not really," I admit. "I wasn't bad at anything, but that's not the same as being the best. The bar was so high, I'd get neck cramps from always looking up."

She doesn't laugh. Instead, she says, "I'm sorry. That must've been hard for you."

"I liked boats when I was younger. Canoes. Kayaks. Anything on the water."

"You were a different person in the water last night," she agrees, "in the best possible way."

"My parents saw that spark of joy and immediately turned it into a measurable achievement."

"They bought you a yacht?"

I snort-laugh. "Close. They made me join crew. Up at the crack of dawn and out on the water to practice rowing. I avoided boats for years after that."

She threads her fingers through mine. "Couldn't you have said no?"

I try to imagine a scenario where I told my parents no. "My father is a very persuasive man." If bullying can be considered persuasive. And my mother leans toward manipulation to get her desired outcome.

"How did you get out of rowing?"

"Same way I got out of baseball."

"Didn't they hold college tuition over your head?"

"Oh sure. That was definitely a topic of conversation, but I knew they wouldn't let me drop out of college. It would tarnish the family image. Anything to avoid a scandal."

"Was law school your idea or theirs?"

"I thought it was mine for a long time." I pause to reflect. "Lately I'm beginning to see that none of it was about me. Or at least about what I wanted."

"They wanted you to succeed on their terms and you wanted their validation."

"More that I didn't want to lose it." I can't believe I'm sharing all this with her. I don't talk about my family—the real version of it. Everyone thinks the Thorpe family is picture perfect because they've worked hard to cultivate that image. Social media only adds to the pressure to keep up appearances. Each post is carefully curated before it's allowed to see the light of day. I'm fairly certain my brother still sends his posts to my mother for approval before he dares to share them. A world-class surgeon terrified of disappointing his parents by having a hair out of place.

"I hope you don't mind me saying this again, but I don't get the sense you're happy in your other life, Charlie." She rests her head on my shoulder and smiles up at me. "But this one seems to suit you. I wish you'd embrace it."

"I want to." I really, really do. But it's hard to overcome thirty-five years of conditioning in a week or two.

"You may be an introvert, but you have a knack for bringing people together and creating a community, a sense of camaraderie. I admire that about you."

Her cheeks grow flushed. "I'm sure you do the same in the legal community. In case you haven't noticed, you're very likable."

"But mine has a purpose. You... You're just being yourself."

"And what's your purpose in getting everyone at camp to like you?"

Her question brings me crashing back to reality. No matter how I feel about her, she's right—a relationship between us wouldn't work. I'd let myself feel that spark of joy until she digs a little deeper and realizes I'm not good enough for her and cuts me loose.

"That's the thing about this camp," I say. "There is no try, only do."

Laughing, she throws her head back and clips me on the

chin with the hard part of her skull. Realizing what she's done, she jerks forward. "Omigod, Charlie! Are you okay?"

I touch my lip and glimpse a splotch of red on my finger. "Twice in twelve hours. I'm starting to take it personally."

"I forgot how close I am to you. I am so sorry," she says with another snicker.

So am I, I want to tell her, but I love that laugh too much to diminish it.

Chapter Sixteen

Cricket

I don't walk the next day. I glide around the campsite on fumes of pure joy. Charlie returned to his own cabin when I left for sunrise yoga, but not before offering me a departing kiss that turned my organs to jelly.

At breakfast, Angela is the first to identify a change in my demeanor. "I see someone used the self-care package I gave her."

"I most certainly did." I leave out Charlie's involvement. No need to sacrifice myself to the gossip goddess.

Gloria slides onto the bench beside me. "You'd better hide unless you want to crochet penises all day. Esther is wrangling anybody she can. Her deadline is looming and she's still short a couple dozen dicks."

"I mean, who isn't?" Angela quips. "I don't mind handling a few. It'll be the most action I've gotten all week."

I text Charlie a warning to avoid Esther and to let him know I'll be spending the morning at the lake teaching Olivia how to kayak, not that I think he needs to know my every move, of course. It's a small camp; he'll figure it out.

Angela continues to scrutinize my face. "Something else is different about you today."

My stomach churns. She can't possibly tell I've had sex with Charlie by looking at me, can she? Then again, if anyone were to have Sex-Ray vision, my money is on Angela.

She snaps her fingers. "I know what it is."

My mouth opens, ready to play defense.

"You're not wearing your glasses," Angela finishes.

"Oh, right. They're fashion frames. I don't actually need them to see."

Unlike Charlie's reaction to that little nugget, my friends remain unbothered.

"Such a pretty color," Angela remarks. "A little smoky eyeliner would go a long way. We should experiment."

"We should." I down my cup of tea and extricate myself from the table. "I'll see you ladies later. I'm going to change before I meet Olivia and Ben at the lake."

"Don't change that smile," Angela says with a wink. "Your skin is glowing. That cucumber mask does wonders."

I touch my heated cheek. "Sure does."

There is a sway to my hips as I saunter to my cabin and swap my terrycloth shorts and T-shirt for a swimsuit. I slather on sunscreen, still grinning stupidly, which I only notice when I catch my reflection in the bathroom mirror. My hair is tousled, and my eyes are clear and bright. This is who Charlie sees when he looks at me. I wave to the woman in the mirror. To me. She looks happy.

I love that for her.

I hurry to the dock, where Olivia and Ben are waiting.

"I think I'll sit this one out," Ben says. "Mind if I wait at the picnic table, Liv?"

"You don't have to stay," Olivia tells him. "Stefan said

they're painting those figurines for the tabletop game in the craft cabin."

I raise a finger. "Actually, you might want to steer clear of the craft cabin today. Text Gloria. She'll tell you."

I help Olivia into the kayak and settle behind her. My face grows hot as I remember last night. In the harsh glare of daylight, it seems surreal that Charlie and I were alone in the lake, naked and kissing in the moonlight. It felt like we'd teleported to a magical bubble where we were the only two people in the world.

But I wasn't with Charlie now; I was with Olivia, whose enthusiasm for kayaking seems to fade after the first twenty minutes.

"It's hot out here," she moans.

"Did you put on sunscreen?"

"Yes, Mom," she says in a tone that can only be accompanied by an eye roll. Her awkward paddling slows until she reaches a full stop.

"Everything okay?"

She twists to look at me. "I'm bored, and I feel sweaty and gross. Can I swim instead?"

"If you'd rather. Let's get closer to shore first." I paddle us to the dock, and she crawls out of the kayak and onto the wooden planks with movements that would outcreep the girl in *The Ring*.

"This is how I'd scare away a boy who's bothering me," she shares.

As I applaud her acting chops, I catch sight of someone loping toward the shoreline. Mid-thirties with a long, lean build. Light brown hair that's a tad overgrown and swoops over his eye. The clapping comes to an abrupt halt. My heart lodges in my throat as I watch him flip it back in a familiar gesture. I thought I'd never see him again, yet here he is in the flesh.

Patrick.

There's nowhere to hide on top of a kayak. I push the end of the paddle into the water and try to turn the kayak around so that I'm facing away from shore. In my haste, I jerk too fast and end up tipping to the side, hurling myself into the lake. At least the water is warm.

I stay behind the kayak and use it as a shield. The Prick has stopped to talk to Ben, joined by Olivia, who seems to have abandoned her plan to swim. If I can stay here long enough, maybe he won't be there when I come ashore.

A head surfaces beside me, and I release a high-pitched scream.

"Hey, it's me." Charlie peels a wet strand of hair off my face. "Why are you hiding behind an overturned kayak?"

"Because Patrick is here. The Prick." I hear the painful crack in my voice. I'd hoped if this day ever came that I would be A-okay, but I'm not. I'm truly not.

"Here as in the lake? Did you accidentally drown him?" He uses air quotes around 'accidentally.'

"There'd be nothing accidental about it." I peek around the side of the kayak. "He's talking to Ben."

Charlie squints in that direction. "He has a punchable face."

"Agreed."

I'm surprised to see the punchable face chatting so easily to Ben, the older man he once described as "less interesting than a doorknob." That should've been my first clue that he wasn't the man I believed he was. I saw him as Edward Ferrars when he was Willoughby all along.

Charlie's head continues to bob beside mine. "He's shorter than I am."

That elicits a smile from me. "How can you tell from here?"

"He looks about two inches taller than Ben, and I'm three inches taller than Ben." Charlie's brow ripples with concern. "Why would he show up now? Camp is over in a few days."

"I'm sure he has his reasons." Self-serving ones, of course.

"Want to find out what they are?"

"Not really."

Charlie observes me. "What's your plan? Stay here until your skin shrivels?"

That doesn't sound particularly appealing. "Maybe."

"Do you mind if I talk to him?"

"Please don't. He's like a toddler. If we ignore him, maybe he'll go away."

"I don't think that's how toddlers operate."

I steel myself. "I'm going to exit the lake in stealth mode."

"Does that just mean no splashing?"

"And I go alone."

I swim to the shore as far away from the picnic area as I can get, staying underwater like a human submarine until I hit the shallows, where I flee the water and make a beeline for my cabin. I jump straight into the shower and rinse the seaweed from my hair. I may not want him back, but I still don't want Patrick to see me drenched in lake sludge.

As I step out of the shower, I hear a knock on the door. No doubt Charlie followed me. I squeeze the excess water from my hair, then hurriedly wrap a towel around me.

"One second!" I dart to the door and fling it open.

"There she is. My favorite insect." Patrick opens his

arms wide, like he's greeting an old friend. "Been a long time."

The Prick looks more attractive than he has any right to. Why can't people bear external evidence of their assholery? Not a scarlet letter, of course—I wouldn't be in favor of that —but maybe an ugly wart or other mark that denotes a person of poor character or a lack of integrity.

Patrick Faraday would be covered in warts.

My shoulders snap into place. "What are you doing here?"

He leans a casual arm against the doorjamb. "What do you mean? I registered like everybody else."

"You didn't show up, same as last year, so I'm afraid I gave your spot to someone else." I'm so focused on not falling apart at the seams that I forget about the seam of my towel.

Patrick's gaze dips to my chest beneath the paper-thin material as I yank the towel closed. "You look exactly the same as I remember."

If I had a free hand, I'd shove him. Unfortunately, both hands are required to keep my coverage in place. "Why don't I get dressed and then we can discuss your registration in my office?" There. Professional line drawn.

"I don't mind waiting right here."

"Maybe not, but I do."

How dare he show his face here again. I slam the door shut and realize my body is shaking. I take a few deep breaths, my hands continuing to tremble as I put on clothes and whip my wet hair into a ponytail. I hope he's gone by the time I emerge from the cabin. The camp-ground is bad enough; I don't want him in my personal space. I changed cabins after his last summer here so that I wasn't haunted by memories of him in my private quarters. It doesn't help that all the cabins look nearly identical.

I open the door to see Patrick hasn't left. I cradle my arms in front of me to block any attempt at an embrace. I don't want to touch him. I don't even want to breathe the same air as him, but sadly I lack that kind of control over the universe. Otherwise, Patrick would've transformed into a praying mantis that ended up having his head chewed off after sex.

"Camp started over a week ago, Patrick."

"Yeah, sorry. Something came up, but I'm here now."

I'm a deer in headlights. A hand in the cookie jar. I want to make like a tree and leave, but my feet are rooted to the ground. I release a sigh of relief when I see Charlie striding toward us. My phone is also lighting up with text messages. Word must've spread like Patrick's genital warts.

"Hi, Charlie."

The Prick offers his hand to Charlie. "Patrick Faraday. Nice to meet you."

"Charlie Thorpe."

"You must be my replacement."

I don't want the two of them engaged in conversation. "Patrick, I'll be happy to refund your money, minus an administrative fee."

"I don't want a refund. I want to stay for the week. Hook me up with another cabin if mine isn't available. Who's here this year?" He cranes his neck to survey the campground. "What about Stefan? I bet he's not sharing with anybody."

"No, he isn't because he prefers a solo cabin, which he paid for."

Charlie steps an inch closer to Patrick. "It sounds like camp is full, buddy."

Patrick's gaze slides to me, clearly assessing the situation. He may be a cowardly twat, but he isn't stupid. "Why don't I take your cabin, Cricket? It'll be like old times, except you can stay at your house if you'd prefer—or not." His flirtatious smile heats my blood to a boil.

"I stay at camp with everybody else during the season, you know that."

"Then I'll stay at the house. You've got the space, and I don't mind the walk."

"You don't seem to have heard her." Charlie's right; he has a good couple inches on Patrick, in height and other respects that I really don't want to think about right now. "Consider this the little town of Bethlehem," Charlie continues, "and there's no room at the inn."

I feel the churn of testosterone in the ether and realize this could quickly spiral into a physical confrontation if I don't intervene.

"Patrick, if you'd like to discuss this further, you can meet me in my office." I shoot a pleading look at Charlie. "Alone. Take it or leave it."

I sprint to my office ahead of him and slam the door behind me. I'm so deep in my head, I don't register the young girl seated behind my desk.

"What's wrong?" Olivia asks.

I snap back to reality. "What are you doing in here?"

"I got bored." She splays her hands across the desk. "I like pretending I'm a corporate executive."

I laugh. "In this office, you're definitely pretending."

"You have a lot of papers. Can I organize them for you?"

"That's the best offer I've had all day." I feel guilty using a child as a shield, but desperate times...

The door opens, thus concluding my moment to collect myself.

"New assistant?" Patrick asks.

"This is Ben's granddaughter, Olivia."

"Yes, we met by the lake. I didn't know he had a grand-daughter."

Typical Patrick. Too self-absorbed to remember important details about other people.

"My parents are getting divorced," Olivia announces. "That's the reason I'm here this year."

"What a coincidence. Kind of why I'm here too." Patrick shifts his focus to me. "Can we talk in private?"

"This is camp, Patrick. There's not much privacy to be had."

The corners of his mouth hitch up. "I wouldn't say that. You and I managed it."

It takes all my willpower not to haul off and punch him square in his square jaw. "Olivia, would you mind giving us a few minutes?" I grind out.

"Close the door behind you," Patrick calls after her.

"Are your hands broken? Close it yourself," Olivia shoots back as she flees, leaving the door wide open. I don't make a habit of choosing favorite campers, but right now she's definitely mine.

As Patrick shuts the door, I move to stand behind my desk, desperate to put a large, heavy object between us. Then again, this might be the moment I discover my super-human strength and hurl the furniture at him. It's an unlikely outcome to this conversation, but stranger things have happened.

"You look great, Cricket."

"Flattery won't get you a cabin that doesn't exist."

His gaze drops to the desk, as though he's trying to figure out a way to remove the large, heavy obstacle between us. "I had hoped to come last week, but I had things I couldn't get out of."

Bile rises in my throat. "No doubt."

He zeroes in on me. "My relationship is officially over, so one of us had to move. I drew the short straw."

His revelation sends shock waves through me. I try to act unaffected, but my legs betray me and force my butt into the chair. "I'm sorry to hear that."

"Are you?" He looks at me with that expression I know so well. The one that teased me and tempted me with promises he had no intention of keeping.

"It's always sad when a relationship ends."

"Not this one. We weren't right for each other."

"Did you actually tell her that, or did you move all your stuff out when she was at work?"

He huffs, somehow offended that I would suggest such a cowardly move. "I guess I deserve that. We can both agree that communication hasn't been my strong suit, but I'm here now."

"Which begs the question—why?"

"Because I miss you, and I want you back. I waited until I was officially moved out to come here because I knew you wouldn't believe me otherwise."

"You assumed it would be that easy? That I'd be here waiting for you after two years?"

"We can be together now. This is what you wanted, isn't it?" He splays his hands on the desk and leans forward with that penetrating gaze of his. When he looks at me like that, I feel naked and exposed—but not in a good way.

"It was what I wanted two years ago, before I figured out the kind of man you really are."

His eye twitches. "I didn't cheat, Cricket. I know you think I did, but Janessa and I weren't exclusive when you and I hooked up. She and I started seeing each other a couple weeks before I came to camp. I didn't expect—us to happen."

"You could've told me about her instead of pulling a Houdini."

"I was confused. I got home and I didn't know what to do."

"You obviously made your choice."

"For the wrong reasons, I see that now. Janessa lived locally to me. It was easier to maintain a relationship with her."

The easy button pretty much sums up Patrick's entire personality.

"Why did you register last year and not show up?"

"Janessa and I hit a rough patch, but we made up before I was due to leave. I didn't feel right about spending time with you. I was afraid my feelings would resurface." He pushes to an upright position again. "The guy who treated you that way—that isn't who I am anymore. I messed up, Cricket, but I'm in a much better place now."

I fold my arms. "Interesting. All these words coming out of your mouth, yet 'sorry' hasn't been one of them."

"You want me on my knees? Because I'll do that." He moves to my side of the desk and lowers himself to the floor. "I'm sorry, Courtney. I'm sorry for the misery I put you through. It wasn't my intention to hurt you."

It took me a long time to erase his image from my mind, and now his reappearance was dragging that old trauma to the surface. I thought I'd healed it, but maybe I'd simply stored it away in an emotional trunk for later use.

"If I'd told you about Janessa, you would've assumed I was cheating and then you and I wouldn't have happened. Can you blame me for staying quiet about her?"

Laughter rips from my throat. "Yes, Patrick. I absolutely can."

"I felt horrible about ghosting you. If I could take it back, I would. The way I handled the situation was a mistake and I regret it. My therapist said I use women to fill the emptiness inside me. That you were a placeholder for everything missing within myself."

"How long have you been seeing a therapist?"

"Nine months. It's going well. He's helped me understand my behavior. I've already seen a huge difference in how I handle situations."

"But you couldn't save your relationship?"

"It was through therapy that I came to the conclusion I didn't want to. Neither did Janessa, for that matter. We weren't a good fit. In two years, we managed to grow apart instead of together. In hindsight, I should've chosen you, but I was afraid."

"Of me?"

"Of disappointing you. I worried that a relationship with you would require more than I could give and that you'd eventually figure it out and leave me." Then Patrick does something totally unexpected.

He cries.

The next thing I know, I'm comforting him like he's the wronged party. "I never meant to hurt you. You know how screwed up my childhood was. Apparently, I have something called a mother wound."

I remember Patrick's stories of an absentee mom and a workaholic dad. It's difficult not to feel sorry for the boy who had no control over his chaotic upbringing.

He slides his fingers through my hair. "Every bit as soft as I remember," he murmurs. "You have no idea how many times I've dreamed about holding you again."

"Technically I'm holding you." And now I sound like Charlie.

The intrusive thought of Charlie Thorpe shocks me like a live wire. I jolt out of Patrick's reach.

"What is it?" Patrick asks in a soothing tone.

"I think you should leave." I spent a full year carrying around a box of tissues wherever I went, knowing that at some point during my waking hours, a memory would surface that triggered waterworks. It was incredible how quickly the place I'd been born and raised became associated with a man who sought to claim my heart and then proceeded to shatter it into a million pieces.

"I thought we were having a moment."

"And now the moment's over."

He tilts his head, eyeing me in that intimately familiar way of his. "Am I leaving your office or the campground?"

I sense his neediness. The camp is meant to be a welcoming space for everyone; we're the Ellis Island of misfits. As much as it pains me, I hear myself say, "You can stay. I'll speak to Hunter."

"Cool. Glad to hear he's back this year. And what about us?"

"There is no 'us,' Patrick. There never really was."

"That isn't true, and you know it. Remember how good we were together? Our long walks through the woods. Our moonlight swims."

"Of course I remember." And that's why I hate the reminder. The fond memories are the reason it took me so long to get over him. Whenever my anger unfurled, it would be diminished by the happy thoughts I cherished. My brain had a way of blocking out his bad behavior and only focusing on the good.

His fingers brush my cheek. "See? You still have feelings for me. I know you do."

I jerk my face to the side. "No, I have memories, Patrick, and only because I couldn't *Eternal Sunshine of the Spotless Mind* them out of existence." I take a step back and look at him. "Anyway, I'm involved with someone else, and unlike you, I have absolute clarity on the subject."

He does a slow blink. "Huh."

"What?"

"I wasn't expecting that. Well, whoever he is, I hope he likes competition."

"As a matter of fact, he does, but it doesn't matter."

"Why not?"

My insides grow warm at the mere thought of Charlie. "Because he's already won."

With the weight of Patrick's return on my shoulders, I push open the cafeteria doors, feeling like Aragorn entering Helm's Deep. I find Gloria sweeping the floor while Angela sits on the edge of a table, chattering away. Their one-way conversation ceases at the sight of me.

"You look like you crawled through Hell to get here," Angela remarks.

I don't have the energy to refute her claim. "We have a code red."

Angela's delicate eyebrows move as high as they're physically capable of. "Olivia got her period?"

"Different code red."

Gloria stops sweeping and grips the handle of the broom. "The Prick?"

I nod. "He'd like to stay for the remainder of the week since he paid."

Angela remains unnaturally calm. She points to a smattering of debris on the floor. "You missed a spot, Gloria." Once Gloria resumes sweeping, Angela looks at me. "Isn't Charlie staying in the cabin assigned to Patrick?"

"He is."

Angela fans herself with a napkin. "Two hot guys in one cabin? Sign me up."

Gloria whacks Angela in the arm with the broom bristles.

"Charlie isn't going to share with Patrick," I say.

Angela's smile grows to Cheshire cat proportions. "Then he should keep sharing with you and let Patrick move into his cabin."

"What?" I sputter. "Charlie isn't sharing with me."

Angela flashes me a knowing look. "You're not the only one up at sunrise, darling."

Heat spreads from my neck to my face. Of course she knew. "His cabin flooded. I let him stay for a night ... or two."

Now it's my turn to get whacked with the broom by Gloria. "I didn't know that! Why didn't you tell me?"

"Because there's nothing to tell." I'm not sure there's any point in lying, now that I've told Patrick I'm seeing someone, but this thing with Charlie is too new and too delicate to share with the whole camp, which is exactly what would happen if I confessed to these two.

Angela isn't easily dissuaded. "Where did he sleep? Inquiring minds want to know."

"The bathroom."

Angela's smug expression says she isn't buying the wares I'm peddling. "He's six-four and those bathrooms are designed for children."

"He sleeps in the fetal position." I need to cut off the

conversation before my lies get more outrageous. Before you know it, I'll be telling them I shortened his legs with an axe from the barn to make him more comfortable.

"I hope Patrick finds out you've had another man sleeping in your cabin." Gloria's broom strokes have gone from smooth to staccato. "I can't believe he had the nerve to show his face at camp again."

"He has no shame," Angela says. "It's almost admirable."

"Remember those pranks we weren't allowed to do to Charlie?" Gloria asks.

My heart stops. "No. Absolutely not. Do not engage."

"Can we steal his clothes when he's in the shower?" Angela asks.

"You just want him walking around naked."

Angela shrugs. "Honestly, it's a win-win."

"He'd probably enjoy it," Gloria says. "We don't want to do anything that might give him pleasure."

I snort. "In that case, we should call Charlie's brother to surgically remove Patrick's left hand." I glance at the door, as though he might enter the cafeteria at any moment. "Maybe he's telling the truth, and he has changed. He seemed to be wearing his heart on his sleeve."

Angela rolls her eyes. "Honey, that splotch of red isn't his heart. It's a flag."

"When you're wearing rose-tinted glasses, red flags just look like flags," Gloria adds. "But you're not wearing them now, right?" She sounds ready to rip the glasses off my face and crush them beneath her flip-flop.

"Definitely not."

"What about Charlie?" Angela asks. "Any rose-tinted glasses when you look at him?"

"I see Charlie quite clearly, thanks for asking." I wish I

didn't. I wish Charlie Thorpe was nothing more than a barely discernible shadowy figure instead of a man in danger of burning my retinas with the brightness of his presence.

Gloria pins me with her most maternal look. "It's possible to have an incredible connection with someone who isn't right for you, you know."

Her words hit hard.

"Charlie, on the other hand, is a catch," she continues, "which isn't a sports reference, although it sounds like it could be."

I nearly choke on my relief. Patrick. She was talking about the Prick. "I thought you didn't trust Charlie either."

"I didn't at first, but I've changed my mind. Everyone's entitled to grace." She pauses. "Except Patrick. He's already shown us who he is. Now we need to believe him. *Right, Cricket?*"

"Listen, maybe cut him some slack. You don't know all the crap Patrick went through as a kid." I struggle to share without breaking his confidence. "The women in his life ... we were the collateral damage in his war with himself."

Gloria pinches my arm.

"Ouch!"

"Don't you dare do that." Her voice is low and menacing.

"Do what?"

"You have compassion coming out the wazoo and you're using it to justify someone else's shitty treatment of you. You're prioritizing his feelings over your own."

Was I? "Patrick's therapist told him he was using me to fill a void, but he insists it was more than that."

Angela offers an inelegant snort. "More like he was filling your void."

"He's single now. That's why he wasn't here last week. He was moving out of their house."

Gloria's scowl deepens. "I don't care if he was flying the Millennium Falcon. He has no business coming back here after how treated you."

"Are you considering giving him another chance?" Angela asks.

"Definitely not."

"Because of Charlie?"

"No, because of me." Patrick isn't the only one who's changed. I'm not the person I was two years ago either. Present Cricket doesn't try to make a meal out of bread-crumbs. She deserves nourishment for her mind, body, and soul—whether Charlie is the right chef for the job, however, remains to be seen.

Chapter Seventeen

Cricket

With Patrick once again infiltrating my sanctuary, I go out of my way to avoid him. As luck would have it, the only empty cabin outside of the residential cabins is the aptly named Escape Room. I'm thrilled when Charlie offers to join me there.

"Are you sure you wouldn't rather be outside?" I ask. "It's a gorgeous day."

"Consider me your emotional support camper."

I smile. "If only you fit in my pocket, then I could carry you everywhere."

"For what it's worth, Patrick seems like a real jackass, and from the comments I've overheard, it's the camp consensus. I'm surprised he had the nerve to show up."

"He's very good at compartmentalizing."

Charlie scoffs. "That's one way of describing it." He picks up the first card and reads aloud. "You're on a spaceship that's supposed to depart for your favorite interplanetary saloon. Unfortunately, you discover at the last minute that a rebel faction has planted a bomb onboard." He glances at me. "Are we Stormtroopers?"

"Officially no, because that would be intellectual property infringement."

He continues with the card. "If you don't locate the bomb in the next fifty minutes, the ship will explode and kill everyone onboard. A literal ticking time bomb." He chuckles. "No room for subtlety." He spins around, his gaze searching. "Is there a timer somewhere? How do we know when the clock stops?"

"Wait. You haven't done an escape room before?"

He raises his eyebrows. "Why is that so shocking?"

"It was all the rage for a while. Every birthday party seemed to involve a themed escape room."

"Not the kind of parties I went to."

"Ooh la la. Apologies Monsieur Fancy Pantaloons."

"They weren't fancy. They just didn't involve escape rooms."

"Describe a typical party for young Charles Thorpe the Twentieth. I'll determine where it falls on the fancy scale."

"They were mostly at home."

That sounds too wholesome. "In the house where they lived?"

"Or a vacation home, depending on the season."

"Ah, yes. The ubiquitous second home amongst the gentry. I suppose the kitchen staff prepared the food and baked the cake in the butler's pantry."

"Don't be silly. We hired caterers."

I can't tell if he's being serious and part of me doesn't want to know.

He folds his arms. "Courtney Abernathy, are you money shaming me?"

"What? That's not a thing."

"Of course it is. It's basically the same as shaming a

woman who's thin. Just because it's the more desired societal standard doesn't make it right."

I gape at him. "I *am* money shaming you." I clap a hand over my mouth. "I'm so sorry."

Charlie squeezes my shoulder. "It's cool. I'm used to you ribbing me by now."

"No, it's not okay. I won't do it again. I pride myself on creating a safe, nonjudgmental space, yet here I stand in my black robe, smacking you on the head with a gavel."

"Growing up with money has downsides, too," he says.

I look at him, genuinely curious. "Like?"

"Oh, you want evidence, Your Honor?"

"I'm interested."

He wanders over to the painting of an interplanetary saloon. "Pressure to keep up the success of your forebears."

"And poor people have pressure not to live in poverty," I counter. "One is about ego, the other is about survival."

"What if it *feels* like survival though?"

I give him a long, lingering look. "Do you think your father would be less of a dick if he had less money?"

He chuckles. "I don't think he knows how to be anything else at this point."

"Did he grow up with money?"

"No. His father did, but he lost the bulk of his fortune in a bad business deal when my dad was ten. Pretty sure that was the day my father vowed to get it all back. Every penny and then some."

"And he probably worked to make sure his children never found themselves in that predicament either."

Charlie stares at the painting with a faraway expression. "I can see that. It doesn't excuse being a tool though. You can endure hard times and use that experience to become a better version of yourself."

I don't disagree.

Slowly we make our way through the puzzles in the cabin. Morse code. Einstein puzzles. While he's unraveling the mystery of the Escape Room, I feel like I'm making progress with the mystery that is Charlie Thorpe. Every personal comment reveals what seems like pertinent information and solidifies my growing attachment to him.

"How do you do it?" he asks in amazement.

"Do what?"

"Get me to talk about this stuff."

"It's called a conversation, Charlie. Humans have been participating in them for centuries."

"Not this kind of deeply personal conversation. This isn't me." I sense a subtle shift in his demeanor. "How much longer do we have?"

"Not sure." In truth, I stopped paying attention to our surroundings half an hour ago.

"Where are the rules? Aren't they written somewhere?"

"We need to figure them out. Part of the fun is not knowing," I explain.

Charlie shakes his head. "That sounds like hell to me. I would much rather have certainty."

"The only certainty is that you'll enjoy yourself if you go with the flow and stop trying to control the outcome."

He tugs at the collar of his shirt.

"You look pale, Charlie. Are you okay?" I'm genuinely concerned. If his rock-solid body drops in the middle of the cabin, I won't be able to budge him.

"This is your Escape Room," he says. "How do you not know all the answers?"

"Gloria handles this. Feeling trapped fuels her anxiety, so she sets it up and then doesn't participate."

"Can you get us out of here?" he rasps.

His face has gone from pale to downright translucent. Shit. I scan the interior and suddenly remember the magnetic key that opens the emergency exit door.

"I've got you."

We spill into blessed daylight. Charlie slides down the wall into a crouched position and I huddle beside him. "Are you okay? Should I get a paper bag or something?"

He shakes his head. "I'll be fine in a minute."

"Why didn't you tell me you get claustrophobic?"

"Because I don't." His lip curls in annoyance.

I try to make light of it, so he doesn't feel embarrassed. "Hey, there's no blue ribbon for escaping, but I may have a penis plushie to offer you as a consolation prize."

He doesn't respond, which only makes me talk more. The less okay he seems, the more I want to *make* him okay.

"You don't have to be embarrassed," I tell him. "It isn't a sign of weakness or anything."

If looks could kill, I'd be splat on the ground right now. I decide to stop talking before I make things worse.

"I said I'm fine. Let's forget it."

I can tell this is more than the fact that he 'lost' a game. He truly felt unsafe in that room when he was unable to leave. I wonder if it brought up his feelings of helplessness that he endured while trapped in the back seat of his parents' car, suffering through their litany of criticisms.

Then he adds a gut-punching statement. "This was a mistake."

My body tenses like a seventh-grade grammar lesson. "This, meaning the Escape Room?"

He gazes at me with an uncomfortable intensity. The kind that doesn't send a pleasurable zing down my spine.

"I see." My voice is quiet even to my own ears.

"You don't really know me, Cricket," he says.

"I thought we were working on that."

"I'm a guy in an overpriced suit and shoes. I belong in a high-rise making deals, not in the middle of nowhere trying to act like I'm one of you. I have no business being here." He pulls himself upright. "Correction, business is the only reason I'm here, but you already knew that."

"It may be the reason you showed up, but I know it changed for you, Charlie. *You* changed."

"No, that's where you're wrong. I'm incapable of change. They're going to have to pry these Gucci loafers off my cold, dead feet. You and I... We wouldn't work in the real world."

"This *is* the real world, Charlie."

"It might be yours, but it isn't mine."

His words sting. When he makes a break for it, I resist the urge to run after him. The Escape Room clearly dredged up whatever fears he's been harboring. He needs time to recalibrate, that's all, and I vow to give it to him.

As challenging as it is to carry on with my day, I make the rounds, first stopping in the cafeteria to check on meal prep with Bernie, then moving on to the group activities. Fan fiction and DnD are going strong. By the time I see Patrick among the outdoor enthusiasts, it's too late; I've been spotted.

I force myself to continue to the picnic tables. "Hey, everyone. How's it going?"

"Patrick was complaining about Charlie," Angela says. Her lips thin. "Gee, I can't imagine why."

Patrick shades his eyes as though he can see the object of his derision in the distance. "What's he doing at a place like this? He wouldn't know Chewbacca if the Wookie walked up and bit him in the face."

"Which a Wookie wouldn't do," Stefan adds, brows drawn together.

Angela shrugs her delicate shoulders. "Charlie fits in perfectly fine. We're all big fans."

"You, I can understand," Patrick tells her. "Although he seems a little young for you. He'll outlive you."

Stefan winces. "Ouch. A direct hit."

Angela licks her lips, appearing to choose her words carefully. "It might surprise you to learn that I don't wish death on all my husbands, only the ones I dislike."

"Charlie's a lawyer whose client wants to buy the camp," Olivia offers.

"You're kidding." Patrick's gaze swings to me. "How much are they offering?"

"It doesn't matter. This place isn't for sale."

"What's his plan then? Make a nuisance of himself until you cave?"

"Charlie is far from a nuisance." My response is more heated than I intend, which doesn't escape Patrick's notice. He quirks an eyebrow without comment.

"Who's up for LARPing?" Adam interjects.

"It isn't on the schedule until four," Bradley objects.

Adam throws an arm along his shoulders and steers him away from the picnic area. "Be a rebel, Brad."

"Does anybody have spare blue and red tights?" Bradley asks. "Mine have a run in them."

"I have a pair of black fishnets," Angela volunteers.

Bradley clutches his heart. "Spider-Man would never."

"Darling, have you seen Tom Holland's lip sync battle? I beg to differ."

I forgo LARPing in favor of a visit to my preferred thinking spot. Charlie isn't the only one who needs to recalibrate. I change into my swimsuit and let Gloria know where

I'm headed in case anyone needs me. Once in a blue moon, someone gets carried away during LARPing and needs to be ... well, carried away.

The clifftop is adjacent to the forest and somewhat secluded from the campsite. It was my father who first showed it to me and encouraged me to jump. His penchant for taking unnecessary risks wasn't all bad.

It's a beautiful day. I gaze at the crystalline lake below. It feels good to be standing here again, despite the familiar tremor that ripples through me when confronted with my own mortality. *A hero isn't someone without fear,* I remind myself. *A hero is someone who's scared but jumps anyway.*

The sound of rustling leaves jolts me from my inner monologue. My mouth drops open when Charlie steps through the brush.

"Gloria said I could find you here." He glances around. "I didn't know this spot existed."

"Glad to see you're still here."

"I wouldn't ghost you, Cricket. I needed a minute to breathe, that's all."

"I got that."

"Saw you talking to Patrick earlier," he says. "You two seem to be getting along. Is a reconciliation in the offing?"

"I'm working on forgiveness."

"Is that all you're working on?"

The lump in my throat cracks wide open and unleashes a torrent of emotions. When I envision myself in a moonlit kayak gliding across the lake, it isn't Patrick with his legs wrapped around me.

It's Charlie.

"Does it matter? You decided that you and I can't be a thing."

"It doesn't mean I want to see you back with someone

who treated you like the gum under his shoe. Why would you ever consider that to be an option worthy of you?"

"I'm not worthy of you, but he's not worthy of me? Is that how it works?"

He gapes at me like I solved a Rubik's Cube in under a minute. "No, Courtney. That is not at all how it works. Your worthiness was never in question."

"Then what was?"

"Mine."

My hands close into fists and I feel my nails digging into my skin. When did my life get so unbelievably complicated? I miss when the only problem I had to solve at camp was how to clean the axes after Stefan dipped them in glitter. Now I have another man who seemed to have potential playing tug-of-war with my heartstrings.

I'm not one of those women who enjoys the chaos of dramatic romantic entanglements. My ideal partnership involves a porch swing and two single kayaks because my grandmother once told me it's important to maintain a certain amount of independence.

I'm almost afraid to ask a follow-up question. "And now?"

He sidesteps the question. "Gloria said this is your thinking spot. I thought I'd give it a try." He leans over the side and whistles. "You really jump into the water from up here?"

"Every summer. It's exhilarating."

"Have I mentioned I'm not a fan of heights?"

"No escape rooms. No cliff jumping. Noted."

"How about Patrick? Did he like it up here?"

"No, it's too far to see his reflection in the water."

Charlie grunts his amusement. "I am sorry about the escape room. It wasn't my best moment."

I nod. "I accept your apology." I wait for a follow-up, that he was wrong about not wanting a relationship with me.

Instead he says, "Tell me what happened with Patrick. I know he was a prick, but I'd like to know the details."

"Why?"

"Because I've shared a lot about me, and I'd like to know more about you. That's how relationships work, right?"

Relationships. I proceed with caution.

"He failed to tell me he was seeing someone when we got involved and then ghosted me after he left camp. No response to my texts or calls."

"How did you find out if he didn't tell you?"

"Angela. She has a sixth sense when it comes to cheaters. She worked her magic on social media and found evidence of a girlfriend."

"Wow. And yet he had the balls to register again the next year?"

I nod. "I almost had a heart attack when I saw his registration come through. I thought it was a mistake, and then he didn't show up. Of course, he now swears that they only became exclusive after he left camp."

"And you believe him?"

"I don't know what to believe. In the end, it doesn't matter. The damage was done."

"Why ghost you though? Why not tell you he was now in a committed relationship and apologize? It wouldn't have been ideal, but it would've been the more honorable course of action."

"Because he's a coward."

"Do you think less of him for that?"

His question surprises me. "Of course not. His fear isn't the issue. It's how he chose to handle it."

"How do *you* handle it?"

I point to the edge of the cliff. "Leap of faith."

"Sounds like that last jump broke you. I'm surprised you'd be willing to climb back up here."

"It was the right idea. Wrong guy."

Charlie inches closer to the edge and peers over the side again. "Wow. That really is a long way down."

"But the end result is worth it."

"Are you disappointed that I'm afraid?" His voice is steady, but I don't miss the undertone of desperation. He needs me to tell him that it's okay.

"Your feelings are valid, Charlie. I wouldn't want you to commit to anything you aren't ready for."

"If it helps, you make me feel brave."

My chest cracks open, overloaded with the weight of his vulnerability. "Come on then. I'll hold your hand. We'll do this together." I extend mine, willing him to take it.

"You're ahead of me, Cricket."

"Then catch up."

Charlie's swallow is audible. It's a big gulp without the drink. "What if I fail?"

"What if you don't?" I wiggle my fingers, hope flaring in my heart. It's a scary feeling, and I'm terrified to see what he does next, but he has to rise to my level because I refuse to lose the ground I've worked so hard to cover. And if he isn't up to the challenge then he isn't the man for me.

Better to know now, even if it kills me.

Chapter Eighteen

CHARLIE

I know we're talking about more than the cliff right now, but I'm too distracted by the distance to the water to give the subtexts due consideration.

There's no point in telling her I want to be with her if I'm about to die.

On the other hand, she's right—worth it.

As I reach for her hand, a familiar voice calls my name. It has to be a hallucination, except my gut tells me it isn't. The blood in my veins turns ice cold as Matt Lyman clambers up the cliff path.

"Hey, loser." He looks down at his professional attire. "Looks like I wore the wrong kind of suit." He leers at Cricket. "I'm a big fan of yours though."

I move to stand in front of Cricket, effectively blocking his view. "How did you find me here?"

"Easy. I followed the scent of failure, plus some dude named Patrick pointed me in this direction."

"What are you doing here?"

"Came to see what was so amazing about this place that you'd miss a charity auction with your best clients. You

missed an excellent chance to hobnob with the senior partners." He cocks his head, angling for another view of
Cricket. "Now I see why."

The moment with Cricket is ruined, but I'm more
concerned about my whole future being ruined. Matt is a
snake in the grass. If he's here, it's for a shady reason. Best to
ascertain his intentions and fast.

"Aren't you going to introduce me?" Matt asks.

"Matt Lyman, this is Courtney Abernathy. Courtney
owns the camp. Matt is a work colleague."

"Nice to meet you," Cricket says, but there's zero
warmth in her voice. In fact, she sounds ready to toss Matt
off the cliff. I wouldn't stop her.

"I didn't mean to interrupt your private swim lesson,"
Matt says. "I expected to find you tossing dwarves or whatever nerds do at camp."

Cricket bristles. "We wouldn't do that." She swipes a
towel off the ground and wraps it around herself. "It's
inhumane."

As hard as it is to tear myself away from her, I know it's
for the best. I have to put as much distance between them as
possible. Patrick's presence is bad enough for Cricket. Matt
would be worse.

Much worse.

"Why don't we go somewhere less dangerous and talk?"

"That's a good idea," Matt says. "It's unlikely the firm
has liability insurance for this kind of thing."

The moment we're out of Cricket's earshot, I go on the
attack. "What are you really doing here?"

"Like my old man says, when one door closes, kick it
until you break it off the hinges."

Or kick it until it becomes as unhinged as you are.

"This place is ridiculous, dude," he continues. "I saw a

guy dressed like a Viking playing cornhole. So many losers gathered in one spot. It's like the wall of the high school gym all over again."

I escort him to my cabin before one of the campers overhears his insensitive remarks. "They're not losers, Matt. They're actually really great people."

Matt looks me over with a grunt. "Riggieri was right. You don't have the stones for this."

"Wait. Riggieri sent you to check up on me?" I close the cabin door behind us.

"It was my idea, but he ate it up and left no crumbs. Why do you think I drove up so fast? LandStar says jump. I put on my anti-gravity boots and go for launch."

"Well, I'm sorry you drove all the way here for nothing."

"Not for nothing. I figured I'd help you out. We're colleagues, right?" He glances out the window as two campers in costume step into view, engaged in a foam sword fight. "Dude, nerd camp is so lame. She'd be better off running this place as a furry camp. She'd make bank with all those perverts humping each other."

"I'll pass along your idea."

"Don't bother. Between the lake and the acreage, LandStar can develop the hell out of this property." His eyes narrow. "Why do you have a Chucky doll? Is that like your teddy bear?"

Oh shit. I should've known better than to invite him inside.

I hear a thump, and the cabin wall vibrates, shifting my thin mattress. I hurry outside to make sure the LARPers are okay.

A cloaked wizard dusts himself off. "Sorry about that," Ben says. "Dodging a spell."

"Are you hurt?"

"Nothing two ibuprofen and a gallon of water can't fix."

Matt appears beside me. "Where's your magic wand, old-timer?"

Ben limps away without a word.

"I think you've insulted enough people today. You should probably hit the road before rush hour. The highway gets backed up." Not that I mind the image of Matt stuck in a horrific traffic jam, but I am desperate to get him far away from the camp in the shortest time possible.

"Sure thing."

Okay, that was far too easy. I also don't like the smirk on his face, like he's harboring a secret he can't wait to spring on me.

"It's easy to get lost. I'll walk you to the parking lot." Since it's the only way to insure he actually leaves. "Seriously, what did you think you would accomplish by coming here?"

"I originally planned to grab a few soil samples to take back with me, maybe doctor them a smidge, enough to shut down the camp. LandStar can afford amelioration, but the nerds can't. Riggieri scoops up the land for a song."

"So your plan as a lawyer was to lie, cheat, and steal in order to give our extremely important client something he wants but has no business owning?"

"Give me a break, Chuck. Most of our clients have no business owning anything. It's the capitalist way." His smile sets off alarm bells. "But then I discovered something better. Something that doesn't even involve a little well-placed fraud."

My stomach lurches as he dangles a familiar document in front of my face. "Where did you find this?" It's a futile question, given I know exactly where he found it.

"And here I thought we ran a title search," he says.

"We did." I stop walking and snatch the paper from his hand.

"How did we miss a judgment lien? A tax lien I can almost understand—sometimes those can be hard to identify, but this..." He motions to the document. "This is exactly the leverage we wanted, and you've been sitting on it this whole time."

"I haven't. I only found it recently."

"And instead of sending a screenshot directly to Riggieri, you decided to hide it under your mattress? What was your plan, dude?"

I fully intended to chuck the document in a bonfire and not mention it to another living soul, but I haven't had the chance to do it without being seen. Knowing the campers, at least one of them would be curious about my kindling. Not that I can admit any of that to Matt.

A projectile flies toward us and pelts Matt right between the eyes, quickly followed by a second one that hits the breast pocket of his jacket.

Matt eyes them with vengeful fury. "What in the hell was that?"

"Foam-tipped arrows. No harm, no foul."

"This suit is Armani, dude."

I move to dust the dirt from his jacket, but he smacks my hand away.

"I think you've lost your mind since you've been here, you know that? And you're going to lose the partnership too."

Cricket stifles a laugh as she jogs toward us. "I'm so sorry. Are you all right?" Her question seems more directed to me.

"I'm fine." Matt's nose scrunches. "Are you wearing elf ears?"

"No, they're naturally pointy."

Now it's my turn to stifle a laugh. I realize my mistake when I notice Matt's scowl. Cricket and I have just done the worst possible thing to a fragile guy like Matt Lyman—we've bruised his ego. His shoulders square and his jaw tightens.

"You want to know why Chuck is really here? He doesn't care about your nerd shit. He was using you to get dirt for his client. He's been acting as a spy for someone who plans to tear this place down to the studs."

Glaring, Cricket folds her arms. "I already know all that."

"And now that he's delivered that pertinent information, he's leaving," I interrupt.

"Like hell I am." Matt grabs the rolled-up document from my back pocket. "If you two are so tight, then I guess he already told you about this too." He hands the document to Cricket, and I brace myself for impact.

Her expression waffles between rage and agony as she reads. "I'm going to ask you to leave now, Mr. Lyman."

"You shouldn't have come in the first place," I tell him.

"Unlike you, our client's best interest is my top priority," Matt shoots back.

"Leave now before I call Chief Johnson," Cricket says. "His granddaughter will be here in approximately one week, and I know he won't be comfortable with grown men trespassing on camp property."

"Kicking me off your land won't make that lien go away," Matt says. "Hope you have a good lawyer, unless you'd rather save your money and sell to LandStar now."

My teeth clench. "Matt." My warning tone drives him to walk backward, out of reach.

"The countdown is on, Thorpe," he yells from a safe distance. "If you don't take that to LandStar, then I will."

I'm torn between racing after Matt to make sure he doesn't do anything stupid and staying here to convince Cricket I won't do anything stupid. Rock meet hard place.

"What's the lien?" Cricket asks. Her voice is so small, so unlike her, that my throat closes up at the sound.

"It's when another party—"

"No, I know what a lien is. I'm asking what *this* lien is, specifically." She shakes her head. "Why didn't I know about it? No one's ever come to enforce it."

"It appears to have been misfiled. It's rare, but it happens."

"If it was misfiled, where did you find it?"

"This copy was in your office. I found it when I put Chucky in your drawer. I wasn't there to snoop, I swear. The paper was jammed underneath the files. You should really have a better organizational system, by the way. The files aren't even alphabetical."

If looks could kill, I'd be a pillar of salt.

"Strike that last comment from the record, Your Honor," I say, desperate to keep things from spiraling out of control, although I know in my gut that kayak has launched.

She glances at the date. "This is from almost five years ago. Right before my dad died."

"He may not have been aware of it."

"I don't recognize the name of the lien holder."

"It seems to have been an unsecured creditor. Your father owed them money and failed to pay."

"Shocker," she says without a trace of irony. "And they were able to put a lien on the camp?"

I nod. I hate this conversation with every fiber of my being. I'd hoped to avoid it in perpetuity.

"If it happened five years ago and they haven't enforced the lien, what does that mean?"

"In this case, there's a five-year statute of limitations, which runs out in twenty-one days."

"Twenty-one more days and it would've been null and void." Tears cling to her lashes, and I long to kiss each one away. I hate this for her.

"I'm sorry."

"I can't afford to pay it off."

"I know."

"What happens now? You take this to Riggieri, and he assumes the lien and enforces it?"

"Do you think I would do that to you?"

"You were holding on to it for a reason, weren't you? You could've destroyed it when you found it, but you kept it, which means you hadn't decided what to do."

"I was planning to destroy without anyone knowing about it. I had no intention of telling Riggieri."

"But were you tempted?"

I choose my words carefully. "I considered it, but only for a nanosecond. I don't even think it crossed the threshold of a full second."

"Why not? This promotion is important to you. You've made that abundantly clear."

"It's not as important as you."

She bites her bottom lip. "Why didn't you tell me about it?"

"I swear I wasn't keeping it a secret to use against you. I didn't want you to worry. I planned to burn it when no one was around, but someone always was, and then I got distracted by you—"

I realize instinctively it was the wrong thing to say. Her eyes pop.

"You're blaming me? Go on then. You don't want Matt to get the credit for this. Go home and get your trophy or your blue ribbon, or whatever the reward is for screwing me over. I know how important external validation is to you."

Ouch. Bullseye. Her words wound me exactly as she intended.

"I was only trying to help. I didn't mean to hurt you, Cricket."

"I've heard that one before." She plucks off her ear extensions and stuffs them in her pocket. "So all the fun and games, none of that was an excuse to access my files?"

"Not a single one." I make a show of crossing my heart.

"Hope to die?" she asks.

"For the sake of the idiom, yes. If I'd intended to use it against you, I would've left the day I discovered the lien. I stayed because of you."

"Then why were you hiding the document from me? Why not show me?"

"Because I didn't want anyone to know, including you."

"Why? Do you think I'm too stupid to understand the consequences of my dad's actions?"

"Because I didn't want you to worry. I can see the pressure you're under here, trying to keep this camp afloat and the community glued together without losing your own home in the process. You ease other people's burdens." I pause, realizing the truth of my next statement. "I wanted to be the hero who eases yours."

She cocks her head and studies my face. "You have no idea how much I want to believe you."

I grip her shoulder. "Then do it. Don't let Patrick or your father or anybody else convince you that you will always be betrayed by men. That isn't who I am, Cricket. I promise."

"Like you said, Charlie, maybe I don't really know you at all." Storm clouds gather across her face. "I think it's best if you leave now. I'll send you a partial refund for the remaining days."

All the air leaves my lungs. I am absolutely, unequivocally crushed. And yet I know I deserve this. Like she said, if I were firmly on her side, then I should've taken the document to her the moment I found it, instead of trying to handle it behind her back. Cricket doesn't need protection.

As though reading my mind, she adds, "And for the record, I don't need a hero. Women like me rescue themselves."

With those parting words, she swivels on her heel and marches toward her office. It isn't lost on me that she doesn't ask me to return the document. She's literally leaving the final decision in my hands.

As much as it pains me, I drag myself to my cabin to pack my things.

Chapter Nineteen

CHARLIE

I use most of the remaining days I'm meant to be at camp and hole up in my house, trying to find a solution to this Matt-shaped problem. I binge *Star Wars*, *Lord of the Rings*, and *Wonder Woman* (only the first one), and the entire MCU franchise, from *Iron Man* to *Endgame*. I get teary-eyed when Gandalf falls to the Balrog in the first movie and cheer in the second one when he turns up at Helm's Deep to save the day as promised. I would gladly take sitting beside Cricket in the dark for the next six hours even if it means my eyes glaze over during the battle scenes. I know I'm a guy, and I'm supposed to feel some sort of testosterone-fueled excitement about men killing and maiming each other, but I don't.

Gandalf is the coolest though. I can see why people like him. Samwise Gamgee is stronger than all of them, though, because he has to watch in real time as his best friend succumbs to a curse that will eventually kill him. I wish there were more people like him in the world.

Unsurprisingly, I haven't slept well. I toss and turn, and when I fall asleep, I dream of floating lanterns and Cricket with golden hair that glows. I am, of course, the villain in every story I conjure. No matter which way I spin it, the end result is that I let her down.

I've managed to put off a meeting with Riggieri, but only because he's in Texas this week on a business trip and is laser focused on whatever's happening at that particular negotiating table. Thank the gods for small favors.

When I finally return to the office, the building feels stuffy, and my suit feels too thick. I miss the outdoors. I miss lakeside picnics and swapping stories with people who seem genuinely invested in the outcome.

Mostly I miss Cricket.

Jeannie can tell I'm off from the moment she sees me. She looks at me with that face of maternal concern, and it's a painful reminder of the kind of mother I would've liked to have had.

I've also managed to avoid the mother I do have. She and my father have been hounding me to make sure I'll be attending their anniversary party with important news to share. I reassure them via text that I'll be there, but I don't mention any news—good or bad.

I go through the motions of returning phone calls and logging time. My suit is a shell and I'm empty inside it. A hollow man, not to be confused with a Hollow Knight, a video game at which Stefan proved to be remarkably good.

The campers will go home today. Another year in the books. Another group chat filled with in-jokes and core memories. I feel a pang of loss for what could've been if only I hadn't been—me.

Matt's face is the last one I want to see, but I welcome him into my office and ask him to close the door behind him. Jeannie knows to hold my calls and leave us undisturbed. This will be the most important negotiation of my career, and I can't afford to screw it up. There's too much at stake.

"I appreciate you taking time out of your busy schedule," I tell him.

Matt scoffs. "We're old friends, Chuck. Let's not insult each other by bullshitting. I take it you had Jennifer summon me here because you want to know whether I shared the information about the lien with anybody."

"For starters, her name is Jeannie, and yes."

He shoots a Nerf ball, and it swishes into the basket. "Not yet."

I have to admit, I'm both surprised and relieved. Part of me worried that Matt had already gone behind my back and was waiting for the perfect moment to reveal his treachery. "It's been days. Since when are you so patient?"

"It was a long drive home from the Poconos."

"And what? You sat in quiet introspection during rush-hour traffic?"

He snorts. "Not quite." He reaches for another ball, but I shut the drawer before he can touch it.

"I have an offer you won't want to refuse."

"And there it is." Matt grins, white teeth gleaming with arrogance. He reminds me of Iceman from *Top Gun*.

Good grief. Cricket really has infected me with her love of mainstream media.

"There's what?" I ask.

"The reason I didn't rat you out." Matt perches on the corner of my desk, still grinning. "Sometimes the predator has to wait for his prey."

"Am I the prey in this scenario?"

His shoulders lift. "If the glue trap fits. Let's hear your offer, Thorpe."

His response takes me aback. "I don't get it. Why not

swoop in with the smoking gun and present it to Riggieri yourself? You get crowned partner, and I look incompetent. A win-win for you." I have no doubt he took a screenshot of the lien document for safekeeping.

"Maybe I'm curious to see how good of a lawyer you really are."

"I'm not buying it."

He heaves a sigh. "Fine. The truth is that, for reasons I'll never understand, people here like you. They *want* you to succeed."

"If that were true, then they wouldn't have pitted us against each other for partnership. They would've just given it to me."

Matt shakes his head. "This firm doesn't operate on vibes, you know that. The partners in your corner still need to justify their decision."

"If you help LandStar get what they want, I think the partners will feel justified promoting you over me."

"Except if I'm the one who shows them the lien, they'll ask how I found it."

"Telling them you found it under my mattress doesn't exactly make me a shining star."

"You can explain it away. You were getting ready to take a screenshot when one of the campers knocked on your door. Whatever. There's no way I can explain my role without coming off as a dick."

I'm confused. "Since when do you care about that?"

"Like I said, it was a long drive back from the Poconos. I had time to think. Remember Bryan Fitzroy?"

"Of course." Fitzroy was a partner who died a few years ago. Everybody hated him, including the other partners. People would check his calendar with his assistant and then deliberately schedule parties and other special occasions when they knew he'd be unavailable.

"I like parties," Matt says simply.

It hasn't occurred to me that Matt's actions have been a misguided effort to belong, but I see it now. And, more importantly, I get it.

"You know, one surefire way to not look like the bad guy is to stop acting like one."

"Which is why I haven't shared your precious document." He snaps his fingers in my face. "Keep up, Chuck."

"How about that? You're not the Lando I thought you were," I say. Having watched the entire *Star Wars* saga from start to finish as part of my penance, I now understand all Lando references.

Matt draws a blank. "The what?"

"Nothing." With the exception of Jeannie, my corporate soul mate, these are not my people.

They never were.

"Still waiting to hear your offer," Matt says. "I said I'd rather not come off as a dick, but I'm willing to take my chances if it means I make partner."

Instead of anger, I feel only pity for Matt. "I think I can help." I draw a deep breath and make the most important pitch of Cricket's life.

Cricket

The final day of camp is always tinged with sadness, but today is next level. The gloomy stretch of gray across the sky only adds to the malaise. The one upside is that Patrick will be gone along with everybody else. I won't be alone afterward though. The children arrive the day after tomorrow, and Adam will stay behind with Chewy to work as a camp counselor for the remaining weeks. He's great with kids and they all love the dog.

I cancel the morning's outside activities due to the light drizzle that started during my sunless yoga session at dawn. Esther manages to corral a group of us into the arts and crafts cabin for a final push to complete her Etsy order.

"Yours is bent," Esther says. "You need to straighten it."

Angela gives my crooked creation a casual glance. "Some women prefer them like that."

I drop my penis plushie in despair. "I don't have the spoons to start over."

Gloria looks up from her mess of yarn. "Why do I think we're talking about more than crocheted cocks?"

Tears prick my eyes. No, please. No crying in front of everyone.

Gloria reaches over and pats my hand. "The last day is always emotional."

Sniffing, I nod. Wendy presses a tissue into my palm. "Do we have permission to dunk Patrick in the lake before we leave?"

"She isn't crying about Patrick," Laura says.

"I'm not crying at all." I scrape back my chair. "I'm going to start prepping for the closing remarks."

"Good timing," Esther says, "because we're officially done with Project Penis Plushie." She angles her head toward Wendy. "That'll be the last one."

A collective cheer punctuates her statement.

Wendy pats her plushie. "Then I'll make this one extra special. Maybe add a little pink bow."

"Or googly eyes," Angela suggests.

Gloria looks at me. "Want a hand with prep?"

"No, stay and enjoy. This is your last hurrah." Soon Gloria will be back in the tractor beam of her mother's orbit in Harrisburg. I don't envy her.

I relocate the closing remarks indoors to the cafeteria. As I zip back and forth across the campsite, my gaze keeps flitting to the parking lot, half expecting a black douchemobile to screech to a stop. But there's no luxury vehicle in sight, only a sea of moderately priced used cars and trucks.

A sigh punctures my lungs. I miss the douchemobile.

Even worse, I miss the douche who owns it.

Outside my office, fingers snap next to my ear. "Earth to Cricket."

I blink away my visions of Charlie and try to focus. "Sorry, what?"

"I'm taking off," Patrick says. "I wanted to say goodbye."

I'd mostly managed to avoid him the past couple days aside from a few minor interactions. Despite his initial bravado when I told him about Charlie, he seemed to respect my wishes. Maybe therapy was working for him after all.

"Safe travels," I tell him, because I have no idea what else to say to him at this point.

He makes no move to leave. "I know it's entirely my fault, but I will always regret that I was too late."

"Don't sweat it. You didn't miss anything you haven't seen or done before."

"I'm not talking about camp, Cricket."

I push down the knot in my throat. "I'm sorry you wasted your time."

A wistful look passes across his features. "This place

could never be a waste of time, Cricket. You've got something special here. I'm glad you're not selling it."

"Thanks. That means a lot."

"That being said, I won't register next year if you'd rather I not be here. I totally understand."

My chest constricts. I see him now with clear eyes and a cleansed heart. "As far as I'm concerned, you'll always be welcome here, Patrick." Everybody needs a safe space to be their authentic selves, even those struggling to figure out exactly what that entails.

"I hope everything works out for you, Cricket. You deserve it." He slings his bag over his shoulder and lopes away.

I watch him go, waiting for the waterworks or the racing heart or the sweaty palms.

I'm relieved to feel nothing at all.

"Cricket!" Fiona's voice breaks through my breakthrough. "Are you ready? Everyone's waiting for you."

"Right. I'm coming." I follow her to the cafeteria, where a quick count of heads tells me I am the last to arrive. As usual, Bernie has prepared vanilla and chocolate cupcakes with Nerds candy as a decorative topping.

"I'm glad to see the cupcakes," Fiona says. "I was going to riot if Bernie didn't make them this year."

I don't mention that my tight budget almost didn't allow for them, but I sacrificed a few other items during the week to insure the presence of the ceremonial cupcakes.

"Where's Patrick?" Laura asks.

"He left," I say.

Gloria raises her eyebrows. "He actually said goodbye?"

"I guess people can change when they really want to." I will not think about Charlie. Will. Not.

"We should get started," Laura says. "Some of us have longer drives than others and the weather seems iffy."

"Too bad Charlie isn't here for this," Olivia says.

I wince at the mention of his name as Ben quietly shushes her.

"What?" Olivia looks at him, genuinely oblivious. "He should be here. He's one of us."

"I'm not sure that he is, sweetheart." The disappointment in Ben's voice crushes me. Charlie didn't just let me down, he let down everyone at camp.

I gather my resolve. "We should start." I refuse to let Charlie or anybody else ruin this final moment with my friends, not when I have to wait so long for the next one to roll around.

Gloria seems to sense my distress, because she moves to stand next to me in solidarity. "He isn't worth it, Cricket."

"They never are," Angela agrees. "Except when they leave you a small fortune. Then they're financially worth it."

I climb up to stand on a bench and address the group. "It's that time again, friends." An audible groan follows. "I know, I know. Trust me. But short and sweet is what makes these two weeks so special. I'd like to thank you all for choosing to spend your precious time and money at Comic-Camp. It means so much to me to gather like-minded people who love and respect one another." Emotions clog my throat as I force myself to continue. "This world is full of challenges, but at the end of the day I know I have a team supporting me and that makes all the difference."

"I'd carry you that last leg to Mordor," Bradley interjects. "Uphill in bare feet."

"I'd battle a hellmouth for you all," Hunter says.

"It's not a competition," I tell them, and my mind immediately conjures an image of Charlie. I mentally punch through it. "Everybody raise a cupcake. May the Force be with you."

"And also with you," they respond.

I hop down from the bench and bite into the chocolatey goodness. Bernie doesn't disappoint. If I had the money to give her a raise, I'd do it in a heartbeat.

I hug each camper goodbye, except those who like fist bumps. There's a certain comfort in knowing their preferences. I expect Olivia to be too cool for a hug, but she surprises me with a tight embrace. "Thank you." Her voice is muffled against my sleeve.

"You're very welcome."

Ben extracts her from my arms. "Try to offer Charlie a little grace," he says. "Remember, our flaws are what make us human."

"That's why our robot overlords will have the advantage," Hunter adds.

"But if humans program the robots, then the robots won't be perfect either," Bradley counters.

Laura releases an existential sigh. "Not this argument again. Save it for the group chat, guys. Ben is trying to dispense wisdom."

The wise old man gives my shoulder a gentle squeeze. "We're all just trying to make it home in the least painful way possible."

"Home?" Hunter nods in the direction of my house. "She is home."

Bradley elbows him. "He means death, genius."

I fold into Ben's arms. "See you next year?" I can't bring myself to mention that next year might not happen.

Ben gives my back a gentle pat. "Wild penile purple ponies wouldn't keep me away."

Chapter Twenty

CHARLIE

I t doesn't take long for the misery to seep in. None of the usual distractions seem to work. The life I'd built B.C., Before Cricket, now feels hollow and pointless. And it has nothing to do with Matt becoming partner. He's the right choice, if only because he's willing to cross lines I wouldn't. If that's the kind of person the firm wants—the kind of example they want to set for the associates and staff —then I don't belong in that seat.

I don't belong at that firm.

Which is why I tender my resignation.

I'm an idiot for taking so long to figure it out. Cricket got there ahead of me. It should come as no surprise since she was ahead of me from the start.

I gird my loins and avoid all thoughts of Cricket. It isn't easy. The simplest things remind me of her—the ribbons of gold at sunset. The chirping of birds during a hike in Wissahickon Park.

I haven't told my parents because I know how they'll respond, and I'm not interested in their unsolicited opinions. My brother and sister have been too busy with their own lives to check in with me, despite my efforts to reach out. It takes a bit of soul-searching, but I realize that's how it's always been. Their pursuits of excellence leave room for little else. It's surprising to me that they've managed to sustain relationships. I wonder if their respective partners will become resentful of the time devoted to external validation, assuming they haven't already.

My parents host their fortieth anniversary party in the backyard of my childhood home. It's a massive property with all the trappings of a privileged life. One sweeping glance at the glittering guests surrounding the waterfall pool and I long to be somewhere else. A place I feel lighter and more like myself. I know such a place exists because I spent two weeks there and wish like hell I could go back.

I miss camp, and I miss the woman who owns it even more.

"Charlie, I'm so glad you could make it."

"Hi, Mom. Wouldn't miss it." I give her a kiss on the cheek and am engulfed in the scent of Libre.

"Have you seen your father?"

"Not yet."

"The caterer says there's a potential storm coming later, so we may have to relocate inside in a couple hours."

I glance up at the clear blue sky. "I bet we make it through dinner without a problem."

Her eyebrows pinch together as she looks me up and down. "You're not wearing a suit."

"No, I'm not," is all I say. I don't owe her an explanation. I'm a grown man and I'll wear what feels comfortable.

Her gaze drops to my shoes. "At least you had the good sense to wear your loafers."

It's only because I didn't want to spend money on new shoes. Choices don't come without consequences, and my clothing budget is one of them.

"There's Melinda and Barnard. I must say hello." With those words she's gone, fluttering like a butterfly in its natural habitat.

My brother spots me from the veranda. He flashes a smile and gestures to his wife's burgeoning belly, then gives me an enthusiastic thumbs up. I'm glad he's here, playing the role of the doting husband and soon-to-be father. I hope for their sake it's real. The last thing I want is for the world to get another generation of my parents—miserable together but sticking it out for the sake of appearances. Pretending all day, every day, to be someone and something you're not is exhausting.

I'm all through with those games. The ones I played at camp were far more enjoyable.

As I cut across the lawn toward the veranda, my sister Elizabeth swoops in from the side. She hooks her arm through mine and matches my pace. "Hey, big brother. I've been searching everywhere for you."

"You found me."

She casts a sidelong glance, assessing me. "Since when do you arrive fashionably late?"

"Since I decided to march to the beat of my own drum."

She pats my arm. "Good for you."

"Where's Bruno?"

"Not coming. We broke up."

"I'm sorry."

"Don't be. He was an ass. I considered holding on to him until after the party to keep Mom and Dad off my back, but then I won another championship, so I figure that'll be enough to carry me through this event until the next one."

I hate that she has to think strategically like that in order to avoid our parents' displeasure. I hate that I did too.

We reach Michael and Kayla, who are regaling the other guests with tales of their prenatal classes. I recognize one of them—my parents' neighbor, Mr. Klein.

"I bet she didn't realize she was dealing with a world-class surgeon when she said that," I hear Mr. Klein say.

"Not to worry," Kayla replies. "Michael was quick to tell her." Despite her cheerful smile, her words have bite.

Michael gives me a brotherly half hug and musses Elizabeth's hair. She swats his hand away. "Stop! Do you have any idea how long this blowout took?"

"How are you feeling?" I greet Kayla with a kiss on the cheek.

"Like a gorilla in the desert."

I laugh. "That's very specific."

Kayla looks at me, hesitant.

"What's wrong?" I ask.

She smiles. "Nothing. It's just that we've been here an hour, and you're the first person to ask me how I'm feeling."

"You're walking for two. It can't be easy, especially in the summer heat, but you look amazing. Apparently, that whole glowing thing isn't bullshit after all."

Her smile widens. "Thank you, Charlie. I appreciate that."

Michael curls a possessive arm around his wife's shoulders. "Are you flirting with my wife?"

Kayla smacks his chest. "Don't be ridiculous. He's being an absolute gentleman."

"Won't last long," Michael says. "As soon as he makes partner, whoosh! It'll go straight to his head."

"Is that what happened to you?" I ask.

Kayla smothers a laugh. Elizabeth jabs me in the ribs with a bony elbow. "Play nice. People are listening."

Ah yes. The people whose opinions matter more than our actual lives.

Elizabeth coughs twice into her hand. I recognize our childhood Dad Alert.

"Here he is." I hear my father's booming voice before I see him. "Finally, all three of my illustrious children in one place."

I swivel to face him. "Hey, Dad."

"Charles, you remember Judd Pinkerton, don't you?" He steers me away from the group.

"Of course," I lie. "Nice to see you again."

The blush of Judd's cheeks and the empty glass in his hand suggests he's not going to recall this conversation later. "You're the baseball player, right?"

"Not for a long time now."

He pumps my hand like he's trying to reach the bottom of a well. "Well, it's good to see you again, son. What is it you do these days?"

"Charles is about to become the youngest partner in his firm's history," my father replies, the picture of paternal pride.

"Actually, I'm not. They made someone else partner."

My father blinks, taken aback by my admission. "I didn't realize they'd made a decision."

"I also made one," I say. "I resigned."

Judd's gaze dances between us, and I can tell he isn't sure whether to stay for the front seat to the family fireworks or quietly extricate himself from what is sure to be an epic showdown between father and son.

"I should check on my wife," he finally says. "Humidity gives her a migraine."

The second Judd disappears, my father's mouth twists into a sneer. "When did you quit?"

"Maybe a month ago. Not sure."

He stares at me for a beat, as though the cloud of insanity might pass us by. "You're a Thorpe for Pete's sake. We don't *quit*."

"I did."

Splotches of red span his neck and face. "They turned you down for partner, so you took your business elsewhere. Is that it?"

"I'm not working for another firm." I swipe a beer from the tray of a passing server and take a long drink from the Pilsner glass.

The color drains from his face. "Penelope," he croaks.

My mother magically appears by his side, as though waiting in the wings to be summoned. "What is it, Owen?"

He unfastens the top button of his collar. "Tell her, Charles. Tell your mother what you told me."

"I quit my job."

My mother swoons like a nineteenth-century debutante. I resist the urge to call for smelling salts.

"What's gotten into you, Charles?" she asks. "You didn't return the RSVP for the party. You showed up late. You quit your job. I don't even know who you are anymore."

"Bruno and I broke up," Elizabeth blurts. I don't realize she's standing beside me until she speaks.

My parents swing their gazes to her. My baby sister is giving me the chance to escape.

I take it and run.

I don't make it very far. I get stopped every couple feet by guests eager to hear about my partnership. I tell each one the truth. No need for a newsletter.

Elizabeth finds me a few minutes later and corners me by the bar. "Did I hear right? You quit the firm?"

I nod. "Sure did."

"Why?"

"I decided my outside didn't match my inside. I wanted to rectify that before I wasted my whole life being someone I'm not."

I expect her to pepper me with a dozen questions. Instead, she pulls me into a warm embrace. "I'm so proud of you, big brother."

"Thanks." It means a lot to hear that from a member of my family. "Don't tell Mom and Dad, but I did take a handful of clients with me."

She releases her hold on me. "I figured you had a plan."

"It's not set in stone. There's one big piece I haven't managed to lock in yet."

"You're Charlie Thorpe. If anybody can manage, it's my big brother."

Her words give me the strength I've been lacking. "I appreciate the vote of confidence."

Michael's voice cuts through the tender moment. "Why is Dad burning through Manhattans like they're water?"

"Because Charlie quit his job," Elizabeth says, keeping one arm slung proudly across my shoulders.

Michael scrunches his face in confusion. "You didn't make partner?"

"Nope. Hey, we should take off our shoes."

Elizabeth looks down at hers. "Amen to that." She kicks off her heels without hesitation.

Michael continues to stare at me. "Bro, are you high? What's gotten into you?"

"High on life." I remove my socks and shoes and pad around the perfectly manicured lawn. The silky grass feels good on the bottom of my feet. I suddenly remember what it felt like to run around the backyard and play tag with the other kids in the neighborhood. When did that stop and why? I can't remember.

Elizabeth performs a cartwheel, causing her dress to hike up. She shrieks with laughter and pulls it down as she lands.

Michael doesn't crack a smile. "Mom and Dad will flip if they see you two acting like fools."

"So what?" I say. "It's a party. We're supposed to be enjoying ourselves."

"It's possible to enjoy yourselves without making a scene."

Kayla looks at her husband, then at us. "I'd like to take off my shoes, Michael. My feet are swollen."

"Do it," Elizabeth says. "Liberate those puppies." She pauses. "Or is it pigs? Who goes to the market?"

Okay, I may not be high, but I'm fairly certain Elizabeth is.

"Kayla, I don't think that's appropriate..." My brother doesn't finish. Kayla is already out of her shoes and barefoot on the grass.

Michael casts an anxious glance over his shoulder. "You're all being ridiculous. This is an anniversary party, not a child's birthday party."

"Ooh, there should be a bouncy house," Elizabeth says. "God, wouldn't that be so much fun?" She begins to jump up and down and pretends she's bouncing.

"Do you know how many kids end up in the ER because of bounce houses?" Michael asks. "They're a liability."

"Who wants to swim?" Elizabeth asks, jerking her own hand in the air.

"I'll dangle my feet in," Kayla says. "It might keep me from overheating out here."

Michael's nostrils flare. "The pool is for show."

"No, it isn't. We spent hours in that pool every summer." Elizabeth throws her arms around me. "Thanks, Charlie. This mindset change is just what I needed."

I tighten my hold on her. I'm clueless as to what she's going through right now, but it feels good to have helped in some small way. I imagine this is how Cricket feels at camp.

Cricket.

Thunder rumbles in the distance. I release my sister as a drop of rain lands on my nose. Uh-oh.

Despite the warnings, the storm catches us by surprise. I recover my shoes and socks before the downpour. We don't make it to the house. Everyone in our section of the yard huddles under the nearest awning.

"This is awesome," Elizabeth declares to no one in particular. I like this Elizabeth. She's carefree and—dare I say it—happy.

And I know exactly how that feels.

Rain pelts the yard. I'm momentarily dazed by it, transported to that day at camp when my cabin flooded. I'm back in Cricket's single bed, trying not to touch her while desperately wanting to.

"Well, I've cooled down without the pool," Kayla says. "How long is this supposed to last?"

"Hard to know with these storms," Michael replies. "My weather app says this system extends all the way to the Poconos."

My brain sputters to a stop. The Poconos. The place that haunts my dreams. The place I haven't had the courage to revisit, despite the steps I've taken to right my wrongs.

I vacate the awning, prompting my sister to grab my arm. "Stick around, Charlie. This, too, shall pass."

What if it already has? What if, like Patrick, I've waited too long to make amends?

"I need to go."

"Where?"

"Somewhere I should've gone weeks ago."

Chapter Twenty-One

CHARLIE

The drive is horrific, and I question my sanity the entire way there. What if she rejects me? What if she's met someone else, maybe a single dad of one of the kid campers? Cricket would make a great stepmom. Any child would be lucky to have her in their life.

My resolve strengthens. The odds of a blossoming romance are low given her reluctance to get involved in a relationship, and the pain I caused likely pushed her right back into her tortoiseshell glasses.

I hurt her. I betrayed her trust, even knowing what her history was, and I couldn't forgive myself for it.

Cricket didn't deserve that. She deserved a hero, someone who would rise to the occasion. I give a cursory glance to the briefcase I grabbed from my house, now flat on the passenger seat beside me.

I hope this offering is enough.

In the parking lot, I spot Rhonda and maneuver next to the vehicle. By the time I exit the car, the light rain has decreased to a sprinkle. Maybe the storm will bypass the area and spare the camp. I offer a silent prayer to Thor,

Mother Nature, and the Force as I cross the familiar terrain in search of Cricket.

The campground is eerily quiet, and I wonder whether it's movie time. That would explain the silence.

I arrive at her office and knock on the door. Terrific. No answer. "Cricket?"

"She's at her house," a deep, breathy voice says, "although I can't promise she'll be pleased to see you."

"Hey, Adam. Good to see you again."

"It's Original Shadow Daddy to you," the kid beside him says. He's on the small side, wearing thick glasses and a Pikachu T-shirt.

"Right. Hey ... Shadow Man. Where's Chewy?"

"Back in the cabin. He's fine. You know how that diva feels about rain."

"Why is Cricket at her house?"

"We can't find the boxes of mini popsicle sticks to make the Pokémon puppets," the kid informs me. "She thinks they're somewhere in her pantry. I offered to help, but she said no."

A cursory glance at the kid's glue-covered fingertips tells me why. "Thanks for the tip."

"Are you a new counselor?" he asks.

"No," Adam interrupts. "He's just passing through."

The kid looks up at Adam. "Why don't you like him?"

"Because he's a brooding villain," I reply, giving Adam an easy out. "He doesn't like anybody."

"That's not true," the kid objects. "He's my best friend at camp. We're going on a hike later to look for Ewoks."

"Sounds fun." I clap Adam's shoulder. "Good luck."

"For what it's worth, I was rooting for you two," Adam says in a low voice.

Me too, I think. "I appreciate that."

"The path to the house picks up after the cafeteria. It'll take you right to the front door."

"Thanks."

I continue past the cabins and the cafeteria until I locate the stone path. The house is exactly as I imagined it, right down to the white picket fence. It's warm and welcoming, and I immediately want to kick off my shoes and enjoy a tall glass of lemonade on the porch. Given our current status, I'd be lucky if she doesn't toss the lemonade in my face.

I leap over the single porch step, releasing some of my nervous energy, and arrive at the front door. The mat beneath my feet features Darth Vader's head with 'Welcome to the Dark Side' written beside it. I can't help but smile. This house may have been in her family for generations, but Cricket's fingerprints are all over it.

I ring the bell and wait, using the opportunity to wipe the sweat from my palms onto my jeans. As much as I want to share bodily fluids with her, this isn't how I want to start.

The door flies open and Cricket stares back at me. Her hair is in a messy bun, accentuating her elf ears, and she's wearing her Nerdy By Nature T-shirt. Affection floods my system at the sight of it; I'm moved by how much I love the existence of that ridiculous top.

"Mr. Thorpe. I didn't expect to see you again." Her gaze lowers to my attire. "You're wearing jeans. I thought you suffered from a denim allergy."

"Only Monday through Friday."

The corner of her mouth quirks when her gaze reaches my shoes. "Couldn't bring yourself to swap those Gucci loafers for Converse though, huh?"

I wiggle my toes inside the shoes. "I'm comfortable in these."

"And we know how important your comfort is to you."

I let the jab pass uncontested. "May I come in? There's a matter I'd like to discuss with you."

She peers past me. "I don't see any law enforcement. Does that mean you aren't here to seize my land?"

"I am most definitely not here to do that."

She studies me, uncertain. "How do I know that's not a lie so I'll invite you in?"

"I'm not a vampire."

"You may not suck blood, but you do suck."

I fight a sigh of disappointment. I deserve whatever insults she chooses to hurl at me. "I do suck, and I'm here to make it up to you."

Her fingers drum the edge of the door. "Someone's optimistic."

"Hear me out, please. If you don't like what I have to say, feel free to boot me from your house."

"Wearing an actual boot?"

"If you feel so inclined. My ass can take it." Not so sure about my heart though.

To my great relief, she takes a reluctant step back and ushers me inside. "You have five minutes to plead your case, counselor."

"Not a litigator," I remind her, and then immediately shut the hell up before she changes her mind and slams the door in my face. This is my one shot to make things right and I refuse to blow it.

"Step into my office, please."

I follow her through a living room that manages to be both spacious and cozy, to a smaller room with no door. The walls are plastered in framed movie posters, including *Return of the Jedi* and *Lord of the Rings: The Two Towers*. A row of bobbleheads line the edge of a desk. I feel a strange sense of pride when I realize that I recognize most of them. I've come a long way since I first met Cricket.

I point to the Jedi poster. "Did you know the movie was originally called *Revenge of the Jedi*? Lucas changed it late in the game."

"And later used 'Revenge' in *Revenge of the Sith*. I'm aware." Unimpressed, she sits behind a desk in a tall wooden chair that resembles a rustic throne. The design is vaguely familiar, and it takes me a second to realize it was inspired by *The Hobbit*. She motions for me to sit, but the only arguable piece of furniture I see is a Baby Yoda beanbag chair.

It's impossible to appear calm and cool as my butt lands in the soft material and sinks. Cricket bites back a smile.

"What brings you to darken my doorstep now that the twenty-one days left on the lien have come and gone?"

"I'd like to offer you an official update."

Her shoulders tense, but she forces an interested smile. "I'm all ears." She flicks the pointy end of one.

The beanbag chair starts to lean to the right, and I shift left to counteract the move. "It took a bit of brainstorming, but I came up with an idea that would satisfy LandStar without hurting you or the camp."

Her jaw sets. "You're a lawyer, not a magician, Mr. Thorpe."

"Please don't call me Mr. Thorpe or I'll think my father is in the room with us."

"Your father is always in the room with you, whether he's physically present or not."

I can see I have my work cut out for me, but I antici-pated this. I don't blame her for any hostility. I showed up at her camp under false pretenses and took time to come clean. I hid an important document that I found in her office and my decision nearly lost her the camp. I'd have to earn back her trust, which I am more than willing to do. Whatever it takes. I hope my next statement helps to bridge that gap.

"LandStar has been set on your land because it seemed like the right spot to implement his vision."

"And?"

I feel my excitement rise, as high as when I first developed the plan. "So I found another plot of land that's more in alignment with that vision."

"Then you got your big promotion. Congrats." Her smile doesn't reach her eyes. "I know how important that was to you."

"Not nearly as important as you."

"Be real, Charlie."

"I didn't finish." I topple to the side and abandon Baby Yoda. Popping to my feet, I tell her the news. "I didn't get the promotion. Matt did."

"Why would they make that slimeball partner instead of you?"

"Because I gave that slimeball the information I found on the new plot of land and let him take all the credit."

"Why on earth would you do that?"

"So he could look like a solution-focused hero. It was part of the deal I made with him. He agreed to let me sit on the lien and let the statute of limitations pass in exchange for an uncontested partnership. His deal fell through, so I gave him mine." I clear my throat, wary of uttering my next sentence. "And then I quit the firm."

Her head snaps up. "Excuse me?"

"I left the firm."

Her eyes search mine. "But partnership was your dream."

"No. As you rightly pointed out, it was my parents' dream. I had no idea what I wanted. I was only following the path they laid out for me, trying to earn their approval." I force down the lump in my throat. "Until I met you."

She leans back. "You can't give up your career because of me."

"I haven't given up my career. I'm still a lawyer. As a matter of fact, I took a couple of clients with me, much to Joel's dismay, and I'd love to take you on as well."

Cricket releases that gangster's moll laugh that I've craved to hear again. "Charlie, this camp is teetering on the edge of bankruptcy as it is. You'd be hitching your wagon to a falling star."

"What if I help you turn it around?" And then I see it, that flare of hope. I plunge ahead. "What if I was the camp's business manager? We could work as a team. It wouldn't be a stretch. We already know we work well together."

"Your office is hours away in Philly."

"My office can be wherever I want it to be."

"As nice as that sounds, I can't afford to pay you, and you need health insurance. Benefits. A 401(k). All the grown-up stuff that I can't provide."

"Pfft. Adulthood is overrated."

"You don't mean that. You know I wish I had more of those things. If I can't give them to myself, I certainly can't give them to you."

"Did I mention I have more than one client? There's a real estate investment firm owned by a woman named Mandy Lowenstein. She's good people. You'd like her."

"Would I?"

"You don't have to take my word for it. You can meet her yourself."

Her smile is faint, but it's there. "I'm not talking about Mandy. I don't know if I'm ready to let you back in the circle of trust."

"I understand that, which is why I came prepared." I open my briefcase and retrieve my laptop. "Would you mind if I set this on your desk?"

"Did you prepare a presentation for me?"

"Will your eyes glaze over?"

"That depends on how many numbers it features. If there's even a whiff of widgets, I'm out."

"No widgets." I tap the keyboard, and a slide deck appears on the screen. I gauge her reaction to the first slide.

A smile ghosts her lips. "This is not at all what I expected."

The slides follow the story of Princess Leia and Han Solo, except I've pasted our faces over theirs. In a series of images, I show her how Han Solo dreamed of piloting the Death Star until he meets Leia and realizes that his true desire lies elsewhere.

"You know that's not remotely accurate, right?" she asks, once the final slide appears.

"I took a few creative liberties." I pause. "And I may have had a little help from the fan fiction group."

This gets her attention. "They spoke to you?"

"We had a video call. I explained the message I was trying to convey, and they offered a few pointers."

"Traitors," she mutters under her breath.

"To be fair, they were resistant to helping me, but I was very persuasive." I don't want her to be mad at her friends. They definitely had her back, especially Gloria, who threatened to send a colony of sugar gliders to rain shit on my car if I let Cricket down again.

Which I absolutely won't. I'd sooner fight a Balrog.

"What about the lienholder?"

I shrug. "I have no obligation to them; they're not my client. They didn't handle their paperwork properly, nor did they follow up in the five years they were legally given. As far as I'm concerned, that's on them."

Cricket slots her fingers together and contemplates the presentation. "I appreciate you coming all this way to update me." When she rises to her feet, my heart feels ready to split in two. Somehow, I keep it together. As much as I want her forgiveness, it has to be on her timeline, not mine. I also recognize the possibility that it might not happen at all.

"So, you'll be in touch?" I ask.

"Maybe." Her tone is every bit as cryptic as the word.

I place the laptop in the briefcase, snap it closed, and show myself out. She doesn't follow.

The rain worsens on the drive home. Gray clouds grow darker and more ominous, and I catch a lightning strike in the rearview mirror.

I worry about Cricket. I worry about Adam and the kid in the Pikachu top, and the children I haven't even met.

The rain is torrential to the point where visibility is almost nonexistent. I check my sideview mirror and cross to the left lane, then I swing across the median in a U-turn that would've made Former Charlie turn himself into the nearest police station for dangerous traffic violations.

But Present Charlie doesn't give a shit about rules. There are no other cars in sight. Nobody else to injure.

I press my foot on the gas. "I feel the need for speed," I tell Hugo. The car wastes no time in complying.

My mind races faster than the Audi as I drive back. What if the camp is completely flooded and they can't get out?

What if I delayed Cricket leaving her house and she's cut off from the campers?

Why did I give up so easily?

I should've stayed. Fought harder.

The windshield wipers can't keep up with the intensity of the rain. The wind is howling, and I keep both hands tightly on the wheel to keep the nose of the car from jerking to the side. Apart from a couple semitrailers, I'm the only imbecile on the road.

The car skids through a puddle and nearly hydroplanes. My heartbeat revs up as I near the exit. I try to drum up a clever line, one that will win her over, but all I can think of is the part in *Star Wars* where Princess Leia tells Han Solo she loves him and he replies, "I know." Leia is stronger than I am. If that happens to me...

No. If that happens to me, it would still be worth saying. I should've said it during the slide deck, but I lost my nerve. Cricket deserves to know how I really feel, even if she doesn't feel the same. Low risk with a potentially high reward. The cliff jump I'd intended to make before Matt showed up and ruined everything.

I laugh at the idea that this is low risk as I swerve around a fallen tree. Six weeks ago, I would've flagged this as high risk, low reward. That was B.C. Now I see myself clearly, like I'm gazing at my reflection in the lake, which I would never do because I'm not Narcissus, a god I didn't even know existed until Bradley told me.

I chuckle to myself as I squint past the deluge. I feel like a lunatic, but it feels euphoric rather than scary. Like my sister, I'm high, except my condition is due to naturally occurring adrenaline and dopamine. The closer I get to the campground, the more elated I am. Cricket is only ten miles away.

Five miles.

I hope she's safe.

My heart thrums as I make the final turn that will lead me to the parking lot where we first met. I hope I'm being overly dramatic and that the camp is muddy but otherwise fine.

Water rushes over the road. I slow to a stop; there's a solid chance it's too deep to drive through. I reverse the car and drive until I spot a possible entry point. If I recall correctly, there's a dirt path that will take me to the campsite closer to the lake.

I park between two mighty oaks and pat the dashboard. "Sit tight, Hugo. I'll be back for you. I promise."

I don't have an umbrella in the car, not that it would've done any good in this storm. More than likely it would've blown right out of my hands or taken me with it, Mary Poppins-style.

Raindrops pummel my face as I fight to see ahead of me. Vines and sticker bushes drag against my jeans and I'm grateful to be wearing long pants.

The ground is soggy, and I suspect the local creek has become a raging river. As the cabins come into view to my right, a flash of yellow draws my eye to the left.

It's the Pikachu kid. He's drenched and clinging to a post on the bridge. Even in the gloaming, Adam is easy to recognize in his costume. He's standing at the opposite foot of the bridge trying to coax the kid across to safety as the wind whips past them.

"Nooooo!" the kid wails, clinging more tightly to the post.

Adam's voice is muffled by the mask as he says something I can't hear.

"You're not my father," the kid shouts.

Lightning crackles in the air, splitting a nearby tree branch in half. The heavy segment falls between them, forcing them both backward and splintering the wood planks in the middle of the bridge.

Water rushes in to fill the gap.

"Stay there!" I shout. I rush toward them before the whole thing collapses. Water spills over the bridge and swirls around the boy's calves.

"Kid, let go of the post and jump!"

The boy shakes his head adamantly and hugs the post.

"He has sensory issues," Adam explains. "He wouldn't let me pick him up."

"I get respecting the kid's boundaries, but these are exigent circumstances."

Adam groans. "Yes, I should've told him that in those words. I'm sure he would've understood and not freaked out and drowned us both."

I see his point. A freaked-out kid could result in one or both of them falling in and getting swept away by the rapidly rising current.

The water splashes against the boy's legs, and I hear him whimper. An idea begins to take shape. "Hold on."

As I start forward, Adam grips my arm. "What are you doing?"

"I'm going to jump in that gap."

"Are you nuts? You'll get swept away."

"I can manage it. Trust me."

319

"Let me guess. You were captain of the men's swim team in law school."

"Something like that." I jump into the empty space and steel myself against the cold as water engulfs my lower half. "What's your name?"

"Nathan."

"Nathan, I'm Charlie. I'm going to help you across, okay?"

Nathan shakes his head like a wet dog. "Don't pick me up."

"I won't, I promise."

Gripping the plank near Nathan, I lower my chest to the water and kick out my legs, resting my shins on the separated half to form a human bridge. Water rushes over me and fills my nostrils.

Adam claps his hands. "Come on, Nathan. You can do it, buddy."

I feel his small feet pound along my spine and then a relieved whoop from Adam. I roll to the side and tuck in my knees, switching to a seated position on their side of the broken bridge. Careful to maintain my balance, I pull myself to my feet.

"Charlie!"

I whip toward the frantic sound of Cricket's voice. Her hair is matted to her head, and her clothes are soaked to the point of sticking to her skin.

She has never looked more beautiful.

I'm neither a rock nor an island. I'm flesh and bone with a heart that beats for her. God, that sounds so romantic. I wish I'd said it out loud, so she could've heard it. Maybe if I'd put that in the slide deck, she would've said yes to me right then and there.

When she rushes into my arms, I forget all about how I want to present myself and instead I'm just present.

"You came back," she half whispers.

I tuck wet strands of hair behind her elf ears. "I never really left."

Cricket

I couldn't believe my eyes when I spotted Charles Owen Frederick Thorpe IV, Esquire, soaked to the skin, rescuing Nathan. He didn't even hesitate. He dropped those Gucci loafers straight into the water like he was barefoot. The Charles Thorpe who I first met wouldn't have dared to risk damage to his designer shoes.

I pluck wet strands of hair from my face to see him better. "Why are you here?"

"Adam and Nathan needed help."

"I don't mean the bridge. I mean camp. I thought you left."

"The storm... It was bad and I wanted to..." He trails off.

"You wanted to what?"

"To make sure you're safe." His voice cracks with emotion.

"We're fine," I tell him. "Everyone's fine." I don't mean to, but I start to cry. "You came back for nothing."

"No, I didn't. I came back for everything. I came back for you."

Next thing I know his hands are cupping my face and he's kissing me. I thought our Skinny-Dipping Kiss in the lake was the best kiss, but this one blows Skinny-Dipping Kiss out of the water, pun fully intended. This kiss is a Princess Buttercup and Westley reunion level of epicness. There are no bad guys to defeat, no villains to vanquish, just two people who needed to get out of their own way.

"Ew, gross."

My lips detach from Charlie's long enough to give Nathan a firm look. "This man saved your life. He deserves to be rewarded."

"Then give him a twenty and call it a day, because whatever this is, it's disgusting." He walks away, shaking his head and muttering to himself.

"Let's get you indoors to dry off," Adam says, ushering him toward the cabins.

"Give him a couple years," Charlie says and slides his arms around my waist. "Then we'll see how he feels about this." He leans down and presses his forehead against mine. "I'm sorry, Cricket. You have no idea how much."

"I have a bit of an idea. You made a slide deck with doctored images without using AI *and* you drove all the way back here in a storm."

He could've been swept off the road. He could've died trying to get to us.

To me.

"I'm sorry too," I tell him. "I could've handled things better. The fact that you didn't send that lien straight to LandStar showed me that I could trust you. Between Patrick and Matt showing up and the ghost of my father's bad choices, I guess I fumbled the pitch."

"Those are two different ... never mind." He hooks an arm around my waist and pulls me close, drawing me taut against his torso. "I love this camp, Courtney Abernathy, but more importantly, I love you, and I want to do whatever I can to contribute to your happiness."

I feel the pounding of my heart as he holds me close. "You can start by getting us somewhere dry."

He leads me to a canopy of trees. "Better?"

I nod. The storm seems to be fading as we speak. I spy a sliver of blue sky in the distance.

"I'm ready to give us a chance if you are," he says.

"You'd have to travel back and forth to the Poconos."

"I like to drive." He holds my gaze, and I am in danger of being swept away by those Caribbean eyes.

"It might make sense to spend weekends at my house," I say.

"Or maybe even half the week," he says. "And if things don't work out, I can leave you in peace, no mess."

I narrow my eyes. "Why wouldn't things work out between us?"

He drops another kiss on my eager lips. "A contingency plan. Any decent lawyer has one. If you'd rather I sell my house to convince you that I'm serious about you..."

"Don't be silly. I think it's a good plan."

"Mark this day down, folks. Cricket Abernathy gave me a compliment."

"Oh please. I've been complimenting you since the day we met. Don't you remember how I mentioned your nice car?"

"You called it a douchemobile."

"Okay, then what about your suit?"

"You shit all over it."

"I believe that was Buffy."

"Yours was metaphorical."

I tilt my head back to look up at him. "Are you sure this

isn't a last-ditch effort to get your grubby hands on my property?"

"I'd rather put my grubby hands elsewhere." He slides them down to covet my backside.

"All right, counselor. Then I accept your generous offer."

When he kisses me again, my mind goes blank. I forget all about the storm and Nathan, about Patrick the Prick and Matt Lyman, LandStar, and the money that would've changed my life.

After all, I don't need money to change my life when Charlie Thorpe already has.

Epilogue

Cricket

Laura fusses over my hair. "They're a little too low. We need to raise them or you'll look like one of the Spaniels." She is determined to honor Carrie Fisher in her iconic Princess Leia role and get the buns exactly right while I fidget in my white dress. It's a simple sleeveless shift with a lace overlay on the bodice.

"These flowers are going to die before you finish," Angela says, holding the floral crown intended for my head.

"They'll be fine. This is a no-negativity zone." Gloria holds my bouquet, a riot of color thanks to the choice of local wildflowers. Her smile is as bright as the golden daffodils in her hand. It feels good to see that smile again. Her mother died right after Christmas, and she's finally getting into a groove of her own. I know it's been hard for her to mourn the same woman twice—first the mother she didn't get in the early years and later the one she did. She deserves all the happiness I feel today and then some.

We chose May 4th for our big day, and the invitations read 'May the Fourth Be With You.' Ben wanted us to get married on Pi Day and serve pie instead of cake, but we decided to leave that date for the math lovers, which we all know I am not. Naturally the wedding takes place at the campground.

"Who's looking after Buffy while you're here?" Laura asks.

"My new neighbor, Ellie. She's great with animals." There's that sparkle in her eye that I've noticed every time she mentions Ellie's name. I decide to leave my prying until after the honeymoon.

Charlie's sister pokes her head into the cabin. "Tee time, ladies."

Butterflies swarm my stomach. Not the ones that spread anxiety, but the good kind that herald joyous excitement.

The sun is shining as I vacate the cabin. The temperature is a perfect seventy degrees. No wind to mess with the carefully crafted donuts on either side of my head.

It's already a perfect day and I'm not even married to him yet.

The music begins. In lieu of more traditional songs, I chose a violin version of "In Dreams" from *Lord of the Rings*. This ceremony is for the bride and groom, after all, and we want it to reflect us rather than society at large.

Olivia is our flower girl. I thought she might object because flower girls are supposed to be much younger, but she actually cried tears of joy when I asked her. Her parents have been ensconced in new relationships and she's not a huge fan of either new partner, so the wedding gave her something positive to focus on. She also asked to work as a junior counselor at camp this summer to "beef up her resume," and Charlie and I were more than happy to agree.

Elizabeth walks behind Olivia. According to Charlie's reports, I half expect her to perform acrobatic feats, but she places one foot in front of the other just like the rest of us.

Chewy is the ring bearer. "The Imperial March" plays as the Yorkie trots down the aisle. He was meant to be first, but his nervous jitters relegated him to the back of the line. We're nothing if not flexible in our approach to tradition.

The music changes to signal my turn. My heart swells as "Across the Stars" begins to play.

All heads swivel to face me. I don't love the spotlight, but I know Charlie is waiting for me at the end of this path and that thought sustains me.

I walk slowly past the rows of chairs, in time to the music, letting my gaze wander. I feel a surge of emotions as I spot a group of campers on my side of the aisle. Charlie worried the song might be too melancholy for a joyous occasion, but there's so much excited chatter, I'm not certain anyone else is even aware of the music.

I focus on the archway that Gloria and some of the others crafted for us to stand under for the ceremony. In lieu of flowers, they used balloons of Yoda's head. Charlie's brother stands beside him. He wears a traditional tuxedo and a solemn expression. I noticed Kayla seated on the groom's side, holding their squirming toddler on her lap.

Charlie stands at the end of the aisle watching me like I'm the only other person on the planet. I bask in the glow of his adoration as I approach the arbor where the OG Shadow Daddy waits to join us in intergalactic matrimony.

I glide down the aisle with my back to the past, ready to meet my future.

Charlie's handsomeness has exceeded all expectations. He wears a traditional tuxedo and bowtie, save for the elven leaf brooch pinned to his suit jacket. Grinning from ear to ear, he taps my foot with his own, prompting me to look down at a pair of brand-new special edition *Star Wars* Converse. His, not mine. I can't remember the last time he wore Gucci or any other dress shoes. For better or worse, he's one of us now.

Our wedding bands are simple gold rings, modeled after —you guessed it—the One Ring. I have no plans to throw mine into the belly of Mount Doom though.

One of the balloons pops when I say "I do," and everybody laughs when the Dark Warlord is the first to hit the ground, covering Chewy in a protective embrace.

"I now pronounce you husband and wife. You may kiss or dance a jig or however the spirit moves you."

Cue the Marvel opening theme song. Everybody cheers. I'm not sure whether it's for the recognizable tune or the conclusion of the ceremony, but it doesn't matter.

Charlie takes my hand and together we walk down the aisle, our first official act as a married couple.

The reception immediately follows the ceremony. I change out of my dress into white satin shorts and a Princess Leia racerback tank top that features her famous quote: I Love You. It seemed apt when I bought it. Melody serves as the wedding deejay, although she was disappointed when we opted for the non-karaoke package. The playlist is perfect, spanning several decades of pop music and Peter Quill's awesome mix tape from *Guardians of the Galaxy*.

Jeannie is the first to congratulate us. She left the law firm a month after Charlie and now works as our company's administrative professional. Without her, we'd be a mess. She keeps the files organized and the schedule running smoothly, dotting all the i's that we—and by 'we' I mean 'I'— miss. She and Ben seem to have hit it off, which I try not to get overly excited about so I don't scare them off.

"Make sure you open my gift before you leave for the honeymoon," she tells us for the third time this week.

"It will be the very first gift we open tonight," Charlie promises.

"You'll need it for the plane," she adds, and I can tell she's desperate to reveal the present before we even open it. Two more drinks and she probably will.

My guess is some sort of matching husband and wife neck pillows. Our honeymoon will be a long flight, but it'll be worth it to see Hobbiton in person, and the rest of New Zealand, of course. My pointy ears are packed. I can't wait to walk those hills and pretend I'm in Middle Earth with my very own Aragorn or Legolas, depending on my mood. I tried to persuade Charlie to grow out his hair a bit, but he nixed that one right away. Even without the hair, he's my hero.

Elizabeth is the life of the party. I'm pretty sure she'll have managed to dance with every single guest at the reception by the end of the night, which is no small feat. There's no denying the lightness in her step ever since she quit the pro golf circuit.

"I hope I find myself like you did, Charlie," she says, shimmying beside us while "Funkytown" plays in the background.

"Keep looking and you will."

Elizabeth presses her pink-glossed lips to my cheek. "Don't tell Kayla, but you're my new favorite sister-in-law."

"Not everything has to be a competition," I remind her.

Her blue eyes widen as she pivots to her brother. "See how ingrained it is?"

"Oh, I know." He envelops her in a hug. "You'll get there, Lizzie. It takes willingness and work, and you've got both in spades."

Nobody bats an eye when Stefan sets a canoe on fire and sends it across the lake like it's a Viking funeral. No one has a clue which ritual this is supposed to be, but we honor the moment with solemn silence. Stefan's plus-one is Lawrence, a guy he met at Comic-Con in New York in the fall. Stefan is waiting until camp begins to ask him to move in, and watching Lawrence as he intertwines himself with Stefan in order to drink from the horn currently hanging around Stefan's neck, I feel confident Lawrence will say yes.

I notice Charlie's parents slip out early on, but he doesn't mind. He's having too much fun to care. His brother and sister-in-law last until ten, when Michael pulls a reluctant Kayla from the dance floor with a reminder that they have a toddler with a strict bedtime routine.

"But we should get together soon," he tells us, "once you're back from New Zealand. We'll hire a babysitter."

"Sounds like a plan," Charlie says, giving his brother a warm hug. Kayla wipes away a happy tear.

Baby steps, literally.

Gloria is next to depart. She has her own trip planned, which is music to my ears.

"See you in June," she says, wrapping me in a maternal embrace.

"Looking forward to it."

I clasp Charlie's hand. "Who's that man dancing with Angela?"

He follows my gaze. "My cousin Kevin."

"Is he single?"

"As a matter of fact, he is. His wife Devon left him for their tennis instructor last year."

"Ouch."

"It's actually okay. Nobody ever liked the fact their names rhyme. Kevin and Angela would be a vast improvement."

Melody packs up her equipment and leaves after Elizabeth. "I'm sorry to go when you could clearly dance all night, but I've got another gig tomorrow and I need my beauty rest."

"Don't apologize," I say. "You were awesome."

She blows me a kiss. "See you when you get back from your trip."

Charlie pulls his phone from his pocket. "One more song?"

I fall into his arms. "Why not?"

He switches on "Let's Stay Together" by Al Green and we sway together, completely out of step with the beat, but we don't care. Fireflies wink at us from the tree line. I wink back in a conspiratorial fashion, recalling what the fireflies witnessed two years ago in June. Two nerds, neither as self-aware as they believed, falling in love.

"I don't want this night to end," I tell Charlie.

He brushes his lips against mine, soft and tender. "If it doesn't end, then we don't make it to the honeymoon."

"Hmm. Good point, counselor. Motion to strike from the record."

He cracks a smile. "Not a litigator."

I thread my fingers through the soft hair at the nape of his neck. "Maybe not, but you sure can be persuasive."

We dance by the lake until the wee hours of the morning. It's a long flight to New Zealand; I figure I'll have plenty of time to sleep on the plane.

Charlie holds me close, and I breathe in the scent of evergreen and musk. My two favorite smells in the world.

He strokes my back. "There's a question I've been wanting to ask you all night."

"You already asked me, Charlie. That's how we ended up with a wedding."

"Not that." He nuzzles my neck. "What are you wearing underneath this ensemble?" he murmurs in my ear. "Is it a gold bikini?"

I look up at him with as much innocence as I can muster. "You can't skinny-dip in a gold bikini now, can you?"

Today has been miraculous for so many reasons and I can barely take it all in, but I try to commit each and every moment to memory. One day, if I'm very lucky, I'll be an elderly woman in a high-end massage chair with time to reminisce, and this will be one of the days I conjure in great and loving detail. Whatever gaps exist in my recollection, Charlie will be there to fill them in with his usual wit and good humor, and possibly a few lawyerly embellishments.

I rest my cheek on his shoulder and release an almost imperceptible sigh, prompting him to drop a kiss on the top of my head.

"Long day, right?"

"The best kind of long day."

I'd been content with my life before Charlie. *This*, however... This is so much better than anything I would've dared to imagine for myself. Truth isn't stranger than fiction.

It's so much better.

* * *

Also by Annabel Chase

Thank you to everyone for taking a chance on a romcom from a fantasy author! If you like my storytelling style, don't be afraid to delve into a new genre. You can check out my other books on my website at www.annabelchase.com, as well as sign up for my VIP List to learn about new releases and sales, and receive FREE bonus content from *Nerdplay*, which may or may not be a proposal scene. You'll have to sign up to find out!